EMMA

Watson

JOAN AIKEN   JANE
AIKEN & AUSTEN

PAN BOOKS

First published in Great Britain 1996 by Victor Gollancz

This edition first published 2022 by Pan Books
an imprint of Pan Macmillan
The Smithson, 6 Briset Street, London EC1M 5NR
EU representative: Macmillan Publishers Ireland Ltd, 1st Floor,
The Liffey Trust Centre, 117–126 Sheriff Street Upper,
Dublin 1, D01 YC43
Associated companies throughout the world
www.panmacmillan.com

ISBN 978-1-5290-9303-2

1 3 5 7 9 8 6 4 2

A CIP catalogue record for this book is available from the British Library.
Typeset by Palimpsest Book Production Ltd, Falkirk, Stirlingshire
Printed and bound by CPI Group (UK) Ltd, Croydon, CR0 4YY

MIX
Paper | Supporting
responsible forestry
FSC® C116313

Visit www.panmacmillan.com to read more about all our books and to buy them.
You will also find features, author interviews and news of any author events, and you can
sign up for e-newsletters so that you're always first to hear about our new releases.

EMMA
Watson

Joan Aiken was born in Rye, Sussex, in 1924, daughter of the American poet Conrad Aiken, and started writing herself at the age of five. From the 1960s she wrote full-time and published over a hundred books.

Best known for her children's books such as *The Wolves of Willoughby Chase* and *Midnight is a Place*, she also wrote extensively for adults and published many contemporary and historical novels, including sequels to novels by Jane Austen. In 1968 she won the *Guardian* Children's Fiction Prize for *Whispering Mountain*, followed by an Edgar Allan Poe Award for *Night Fall* in 1972, and she was awarded an MBE for her services to children's literature in 1999.

Joan Aiken died in 2004.

The Silence of Herondale
Trouble with Product X
Hate Begins at Home
The Ribs of Death
The Windscreen Weepers
The Embroidered Sunset
The Butterfly Picnic
Died on a Rainy Sunday
Voices in an Empty House
Castle Barebane
The Five-Minute Marriage
The Smile of the Stranger
The Weeping Ash
The Girl from Paris
Foul Matter
Mansfield Revisited
Deception
Blackground
Jane Fairfax
Morningquest
Eliza's Daughter
The Youngest Miss Ward

EMMA
Watson

1

'What a very fortunate circumstance it was that Robert and Jane chose this day to visit their friends at Alford,' said Emma Watson, walking into the wash-house with a large bundle of table-linen in her arms.

'Indeed yes!' agreed her sister Elizabeth, briskly giving a stir to various tubs of laundry soaking in solutions of household soda and unslaked lime. 'Those cloths you have there, Emma, can go straight into the copper, unless any of them is badly stained.'

'Only this handkerchief of my father's, which has ink on it.'

'Spread it out in a pan of oxalic acid. Or spirits of sorrel. You will find the bottles next door, on the shelf.'

The wash-house at Stanton Parsonage was a large, draughty room with a York stone floor, a copper, and a range of wooden tubs. The bleaching-room, next to it, was used for ironing, mangling, and drying. These two rooms were, of course, on the ground floor, with doors and windows giving on to the stable-yard; all the windows were wide open at the moment to let out the steam.

Both sisters wore pattens, and had tied voluminous linen aprons over their cambric gowns.

'I do think that Margaret, at least, might have stayed behind and helped us, since she knew poor old Nanny was laid up with her bad foot,' observed Emma dispassionately, spreading out the stained kerchief in a pan of bleaching solution.

'Hah! Margaret would be of no more use than a child of three. Less! She would grumble and stand about and argue and complain that the soda spoilt her white hands. No; we go on very well as we are, Emma! I am infinitely obliged to you for your good nature in sharing the work with me, and only thankful that it is such a capital drying-day; if we can get the bed-linen out into the orchard by nine o'clock, everything may well be put away before our guests return for dinner. For once it is an advantage that they like to keep late, fashionable hours.'

'I am only sorry that you could not go with them, Elizabeth; you never seem to get a day's holiday.'

'Oh, it pleases me much better to get this great wash done,' said Elizabeth simply. 'Besides I would not, no, I would not *at all* have wished to go along with Robert and Jane today – not for the universe, indeed! The visit would only arouse the most painful recollections; in fact –' Her voice was choked, she stood silently over the boiling copper, biting her lips in an effort to control a rising sob, as she stirred the white and steamy brew with a wooden batten.

Emma threw a quick, unhappy glance at her elder sister.

Elizabeth Watson was now twenty-nine, long past all hope of matrimonial prospects. The sisters had been parted for fourteen years, and Emma's last recollections of Elizabeth were from when the latter was fifteen, a tall, lively, handsome girl, with a fresh complexion and a wonderful head of thick, pale-gold hair, like that of a Nordic princess; now her face was thin, careworn, and at the moment flushed and greasy with steam; the hair, lank and flat, long since concealed under an old-maid's cap.

It is so unfair, thought Emma helplessly; Eliza was far prettier than either Margaret or Penelope; why should she have been obliged to waste her youth and good looks in this kind of task while they may go away visiting and enjoying themselves?

In a wish to distract her sister's sad thoughts, she asked a question:

'Who is this friend of our brother's that they are to visit at Alford?'

The question was not a lucky one. Elizabeth's mouth quivered again, but she regained hold of herself and replied:

'His name is Purvis – I think you have heard me speak of Purvis?'

'Yes, now I remember, you mentioned him the other evening when you were driving me to the Assembly in Dorking.'

But, recalling the context, Emma's heart sank, for she could see this was the very last topic to allay her sister's sad recollections. But the latter went on, as if talking eased her:

'Purvis was my first, my only love. At the time, he was a curate, over in Abinger. He used to come and relieve my father sometimes on Sundays. And he – I – we liked each other very well. Everybody thought it would have been a match between us. But I am sorry to say that our sister Penelope set him against me. She told him untrue tales about me, that I had a flirtatious disposition and had formerly been plighted to Jeffrey Fortescue – which was wholly untrue – and so – and so – that was the ruin of my happiness.'

'But why, *why*, should Penelope play you such a terrible trick?'

'Because, my dear, she wanted him for herself. She thinks any trick fair for a husband – I only wish she may gain one for herself!'

'She failed, then, in her plan to ensnare Purvis?'

'Yes, she failed; he did not like her ways. The end of it was, he discontinued his visits here. And, very shortly afterwards, he removed to a greater distance and married a young lady of some fortune who lived in Leith Hill. And,' said Elizabeth sighing, 'I hope he has been happy. But I have never, never since seen another man whom I could love as I loved Purvis. Indeed, I have not seen many at all.'

'How *could* one sister so betray another?' demanded Emma hotly, wringing out a couple of napkins with great force and flinging them into the rinse water. 'It is the most shocking story I ever heard! I do not like the sound of Penelope. I shall be afraid of her. I hope she does not return home for a long time.'

'Well, my dear, I daresay she will continue to stay with the Shaws in Chichester as long as she is able to stretch out the visit. She has an eye on a gentleman there, you see, a rich Dr Harding, the uncle of her friend Miss Shaw. He is a great deal older; but she is twenty-five now, so she has not much time left to be looking about her. We cannot afford to pick and choose, you know, there is no provision for us. We must all marry if we can. Still, Penelope cannot prolong her stay for ever, so, sooner or later, you will be obliged to meet her again. Do not trust her, though! Penelope has no scruples, none, if she sees a chance to promote her own advantage. But still, I think she will have a considerable respect for you, although you *are* the youngest.'

'For me? I see no reason for that, since I have been returned home like a parcel of unwanted goods,' said Emma drily.

'But, Emma, you have such an air of refinement and fashion! That is bound to impress Penelope very much. Those fourteen years you spent with Aunt Turner have turned you into a person of quality, my dear!'

'And much good may it do me,' returned Emma with a sigh, 'since she, or rather her new husband, has cast me off.'

'It was infamous – considering your expectations – you are greatly to be pitied, I am sure. But still, you need by no means despair of forming an eligible connection – considering your looks, and fashionable appearance, and well-bred way of speaking. Only think what an impression you have already made on Tom Musgrave and Lord Osborne! Just from their setting eyes on you at the Dorking Assembly! I was never so surprised as when they came here to the house!'

'And what use is that, pray, when they are such worthless beings?'

'How *can* you be so proud and fastidious?' cried Elizabeth in amazement. 'Why, all other girls I know would give their eye-teeth to be honoured, as you were, by both gentlemen coming to call, and giving you such admiring looks. And then Tom Musgrave coming *again*, the other evening, and staying to play cards! It was beyond anything, indeed.'

'Yes, but he soon sheered off and never appeared again when he found that our sister Margaret was come home.'

'Poor thing,' said Elizabeth, '*she* is under the delusion of Tom Musgrave's being more seriously in love with her than he ever was with anybody else. She has been expecting him to come to the point since January. But, of course, he never will. *I* think (quite between ourselves) that he will never marry unless he can marry somebody very great; Miss Osborne, from the castle, perhaps; or at least some young lady of fortune.'

'Well, whomever he chooses is quite welcome to him. *I* think him no better than a rattle,' said Emma, picking up a basket of damp cloths and walking away into the orchard, which lay beyond the stable-yard, past a duck-pond.

It was a dry, blowy day in October, entirely suitable for the sisters' great wash. The last of the leaves had fallen from the trees, and been burned, but a few late apples scattered the grass. Emma bit into one, and found it still sweet and firm. As she pegged out the cloths on the line, her spirits could not help insensibly rising. The morning was so fine, and, at the age of nineteen, nothing seems impossible; even if you *have* been sent home like a parcel of unwanted goods. She looked with pleasure at the prospect around her. It was handsomer and far more spacious than that commanded by her former home, which had been with her Aunt Turner in Shrewsbury town.

Stanton Parsonage lay in a snug hollow of the North Downs, with a wide view opening over the small village of Stanton and on towards Dorking. The parsonage house was old, but respectable and commodious, the gardens pleasing and well-kept, bordered by a line of spruce firs. Up at the top of the hill lay the small ancient church in its cluster of yews.

I am sure I can be happy here! thought Emma, by no means for the first time. Elizabeth and my father are so sweet-tempered and full of candour. If only my sister Margaret had not come home! For I am not sure that I will be able to make friends with her.

The Margaret in question, Emma's immediate elder, aged twenty-two years, had returned to Stanton several days earlier, accompanied by their eldest brother Robert and his wife Jane, whom she had been visiting at their home in Croydon. Robert, an attorney, was the most prosperous of the family, having been so fortunate as to marry the daughter of the man whose clerk he had been. Jane had a fortune of six thousand pounds and they occupied a very smart house in Croydon, where they gave genteel parties.

Emma was now joined by Elizabeth, carrying a great basket of sheets, which the two sisters, working together, folded, spread, and hung on the clothes-lines.

'It is a lucky thing Jane does not see us at such work,' said Elizabeth cheerfully, draping towels over the hedge. 'She would never be able to lift up her head in Croydon again if it were known that her sisters-in-law did their own wash.'

'When do you think she and Robert will return home?' asked Emma, who had taken a strong dislike to her sister-in-law. 'And do you think Margaret will return again with them?'

'I think they had rather take *you*, my dear,' Elizabeth answered, laughing. 'Jane, I can see, has been much impressed by your looks and style; she will be proud to show you off to her fine friends in Croydon.'

'Yes! And tell them how I have been ill-used and thrown off. I do not require her triumphant compassion. I have no wish at all to appear in Croydon as a kind of Cinderella.'

'It was very unkind of our Aunt Turner to use you so,' observed Elizabeth, reverting to a well-used and familiar theme. 'How *could* she throw herself away on an Irish captain, and that only two years after Mr Turner died? And after she had brought you up in expectation of becoming her heir? It was very bad – very bad indeed. And then to leave you behind when they went to Ireland –'

'There, I believe she acted not from her own wish but on the persuasions of Captain O'Brien,' said Emma. 'But – to tell truth – I did not greatly care for him and should not have wished to travel to Ireland with them, even if I had been invited. I will not assert that he was not to be trusted – but a friend of mine, Miss Squires, considered him quite a profligate and told shocking tales of his flirtations with other ladies; and once or twice he has given me such a pinch, or such a look, that I would by no means venture myself alone with him in a strange country.'

'And this is the person that our aunt has thought fit to marry!'

'Yes,' sighed Emma, 'he is certainly a sad contrast to our uncle – who was always like a kind father to me, so thoughtful, so sweet-natured; but Captain O'Brien *is* very diverting, and our aunt was quite captivated by him, anybody could see that. I hope she may not live to rue the day she married him.'

'Ireland is such a long way off, should any ill befall her.'

'I know it. I must acknowledge I miss her sadly, and am often anxious about her – how will she go on without me, who know all her ways and her likings – but, Eliza, who is *this*, coming up the hill in a carriage? It is not our brother back so soon, surely?'

'Mercy on us!' cried Elizabeth. 'Who can it be? And the wash-house still all in puddles, and old Betsey King but just now arrived to help – surely it cannot be Tom Musgrave and his friend the lord, yet again?'

'No,' said Emma, shading her eyes against the sun, 'for Tom Musgrave drives a curricle and this is a gig.'

'A gig? Who can it possibly be? And they must be coming here – the road leads on no farther than our house. Good heavens! I must warn my father!'

Elizabeth fled indoors, casting off her apron, and Emma soon followed her, pausing only to pick up a few scattered clothes-pegs.

The front hall of Stanton Parsonage was small and dark, with doors opening on to the parlour and dining-room. When Emma arrived there, she found the hall apparently swarming with people, but most of them seemed to be very small; opening the parlour door to throw light on the scene she discovered that the morning visitors consisted of a lady and four children.

'Mrs Blake!' Elizabeth was saying in nervous, hasty tones that only imperfectly concealed her astonishment. 'How very–! I am so–! But I must run upstairs to my father's study and inform him. He will be so very – he is a trifle hard of hearing and most probably was not aware of your arrival. We are in a little disorder today as our old Nanny is ill – and I am only sorry that my brother and sisters are from home, which is such a pity, for it is probably they whom – but now you will pray excuse me if I go to inform my father – ah, there you are, Emma, why do you not take Mrs Blake into the parlour? There is sweet cake on the beaufet – perhaps the children – or they may like to try our baked apples, which are particularly good this year . . .'

'Please do not put yourself out, dear Miss Watson,' said Mrs Blake kindly. But Elizabeth, who dreaded and detested morning visits, had already fled upstairs.

It was left to Emma, more collected and more at ease in company, to usher the unexpected guests into the parlour and offer them refreshments.

Mrs Blake was a lively, pleasant-looking little woman of five- or six-and-thirty. Her dress was plain to a degree, but in admirable taste. Her children, three handsome little boys and a baby girl, resembled her to a marked extent, and all appeared very tidy and well-behaved. The boys clustered around their mother, the baby lay in her arms and gazed about her with silent interest.

'I would have waited on you sooner, my dear Miss Emma,' Mrs Blake was saying, with a very pleasant, unaffected earnestness, 'but two days ago I received a lightning visit from my husband. We naval wives, you know, cannot command our time, we are always liable to be swept from one side of the country to the other, or dropped in upon with no notice at all. And so it was in this instance – my husband wished to bring me news of his promotion in person – though he had but thirty-six hours in which to ride from Southampton and return there again.'

'Papa is promoted captain,' one of the smaller boys told Emma solemnly.

'Is he indeed, my dear? That is very grand! I am so happy for you all.'

Now Elizabeth returned, breathless and apologetic.

'My father hopes that you will excuse him, Mrs Blake – but, you know, he is a sad invalid—'

'Oh, my dear Miss Watson, I would not disturb him for the world. Besides – to tell truth, it was really your sister Miss Emma whom I am come to see – to thank her again for her unexampled kindness to my little Charles here.'

'Oh?' said Elizabeth, surprised, amid her hospitalities with the sweet cake and the baked apples. 'I did not know. That is – what, when was this?'

'Did Miss Emma not tell you about it? Fie, for shame! You hide your light under a bushel, my dear!'

'It was so very trifling a matter,' said Emma, smiling and blushing. 'Anybody – anybody without a heart of stone would have done likewise.'

'It was at the Assembly the other evening – when my poor boy here was disappointed of the two dances he had been promised by Miss Osborne – she choosing at the very last minute to renege on her engagement and dance with Colonel Beresford—'

'—which, my mamma says, no true gentleman or lady would *ever* do,' interposed little Charles, looking up at Elizabeth with serious grey eyes.

'So, without an instant's hesitation, Miss Emma steps

forward. "I shall be very happy to dance with you, sir, if you like it," says your sister – so sweetly – and restores all my poor boy's happiness in a twinkling – did she not, Charles?'

'Ay, indeed! We had a famous dance of it – did we not, Miss Emma? And, you know, you have promised, as well, to come and see the pony from the castle stable that I sometimes ride, and play at bilbo-catch, and walk out to look at the ice-house in Osborne Park, and see George's and my great collection of horse-chestnuts.'

'Indeed I have,' said Emma, laughing. 'And *I* will not go back on my promise, I assure you. I can take my after-noon walk in your direction on any fine day that you care to designate.'

'Ay, it is not above a mile from here,' agreed Elizabeth. 'Mrs Blake's is the small white house, Wickstead Cottage, not far inside Osborne Park gates – you may see it from the road.'

'Or Charles and the children and I will be happy to come and fetch you,' said Mrs Blake. 'Shall we not, chil-dren?'

'Yes, Mamma!' they all chorused. 'And now may we go and look at Miss Watson's ducks on the pond?'

'Another time, my dears,' said their mother, rising to her feet. 'For now I suspect that Miss Watson, on a busy Monday morning, is wishing us all at the other ends of the earth. Come, Charles – come, George, come, Frank – say your goodbye and we must be off.'

Mrs Blake was as brisk as her words. In a moment she had her children marshalled and out of the house. But, climbing actively into the gig, she turned to say, 'Oh, by the bye, Miss Emma, my brother asks to be remembered to you most kindly. The two dances he enjoyed with you are, he avers, by far the pleasantest recollections he has of the ball. And he was sorry not to be able to accompany me this morning, but had to ride out with Lord Osborne on an errand of Lady Osborne's.'

'It is of no consequence – I mean – I am greatly obliged to Mr Howard,' said Emma, colouring deeply.

'Now we must be off. Come up, pony!' And the gig dashed smartly away.

'*Well!*' said Elizabeth, turning back into the house. 'What a thing! But how was it that you never told me about your dance with the little boy?'

'I thought I had done so – that was how I came to dance with his uncle, Mr Howard, and I am sure I told you about *that* . . .'

'Indeed you did, and I was very much astonished, for he is quite one of the great and grand ones. But his sister, I must say, seems to be very affable and unassuming, and I shall be glad of her further acquaintance.'

'Only just now you wish her at the devil,' said Emma laughing, 'because she comes to the house on a Monday morning. Now – shall I take up our father's egg-nog, or do you prefer to do that while I make a start on the ironing – I believe the cloths will now be full dry enough in this fine breeze.'

'*You* take up his egg-nog, Emma, a pleasant chat with you is just what does him good at this time of day. And then you can come and get up the frills on the pillowcases and tuckers with the tongs, for that is what you excel at.'

Elizabeth hurried back into the wash-house.

Mr Watson was a small elderly clergyman who had once been robust, but was now very frail. He suffered severely from asthma, and had been obliged to relinquish many of his parish duties to others, but still conducted a service whenever he could. In appearance he strongly resembled his youngest daughter Emma, having her bright dark eyes, nut-shaped head, small stature, and clear brown complexion. But his scanty hair was now snow-white, soft as thistledown, and he bore a settled air of ill-health, though he was seldom heard to complain. He spent most of his days in a small, snug upstairs study on the sunny side of the house. His window commanded a pleasant prospect of the walled garden, the row of spruce firs, and the home meadow beyond, overhung by tall elm trees.

'Thank you, my dear,' he said, receiving the egg-nog from his youngest daughter. 'It is very pleasant to hear voices of children again from downstairs. I only wish I were well enough to take more part in entertaining guests. But I find that to have Robert and his wife with us in the house is tiring enough, quite tiring enough, I cannot undertake more. Jane's voice is so very loud and quick! It was civil, though, of Mrs Blake to call – very civil. Her brother, Mr Howard, is a man for whom I have a true respect, he is a scholar and a gentleman; I recall what a very pleasant, kindly attention he paid me only last week when, on the day of the Visitation, he helped me up the steep stair – it struck me as highly becoming in so young a man. By the bye, he made an inquiry, then, after one of my daughters – did I remember to tell you of that? I am not sure which one of you he had in mind, but I suppose you will know among yourselves . . .'

'That was most obliging of Mr Howard,' said Emma warmly. 'And I like his sister extremely. Now I must leave you, Papa – if you have all that you require? – for it is not fair that poor Elizabeth should bear all the burden of the great wash on her shoulders.'

'Thank you, my dear, yes indeed, I am well placed, and have all I need.'

But, as Emma ran down the stairs, she was aghast to catch the sound of yet another set of carriage wheels on the gravel sweep outside the front door.

Poor, *poor* Elizabeth! she thought. Who in the world can it be this time? On a Monday morning?

Without pause or hesitation she ran to the front door and threw it wide. Perhaps whoever it was could be sent swiftly on their way . . .

Outside, a barouche-landau was drawing to a halt, and a smartly uniformed groom had sprung down to open the carriage door.

Out from the carriage emerged a couple who, at first sight, were utter strangers to Emma: a portly, red-faced elderly gentleman who walked slowly with a cane, and a very dashingly dressed lady with a great many feathers on her bonnet.

The lady started violently at sight of Emma, and then exclaimed, in a shrill, affected voice: 'Why, heavens above! Can this indeed be Emma – my little sister, Emma? Dear, sweet reminder of days long ago and our departed mother! What a charming surprise – what a gratifying encounter!'

Emma stared, coloured, hesitated, and doubted.

'Are you,' she then ventured, 'can you be my sister Penelope?'

'Why yes, indeed, who else? Certainly I am she!'

Emma's last recollection of Penelope was as a rather plump, fair, ill-tempered girl of eleven, who ordered her younger sisters about a great deal, but was often in trouble herself for not completing her tasks. Could she have been transformed into this dazzlingly dressed fashionable stranger? But yes, the look of slight permanent ill-temper was still there, in the frown marks etched between her brows and the deep-cut lines at the corners of her mouth. At this moment, however, she was all smiles.

'Ah, the dear old home,' she sighed. 'Humble, but so charming.'

For once, Emma was quite as lacking in composure as her sister Elizabeth. 'I – you – I did not – I think you were not expected?' she stammered. 'Will you – will you please to come in?' Surely there had not been the least intimation that this arrival was impending? 'I will summon Elizabeth directly – but I fear that Robert, Jane, and my sister Margaret are from home – have gone out for the day, paying calls on old friends – they will be back this evening, but . . .'

But her heart sank at the thought of how all these people were to be accommodated. And *who* was the elderly gentleman? So far he had not spoken a word. But he was looking alertly about him.

'So Robert and Jane are here as well? Why, that is capital – most advantageous – we can impart our joyful news to one and all at the same time!' declared Penelope with a series of arch nods, a triumphant smile, and an expressive flutter of the eyelids. She bore, Emma now realized, quite a strong resemblance to Elizabeth in her colouring and shape of face, though she was a great deal plumper. Her lips were thinner, and her blue eyes smaller.

Elizabeth, who had evidently been apprised of the new arrivals from her post in the back regions of the house, now made her appearance, looking flushed and harassed.

'Good gracious! Penelope! This is wholly unexpected. Indeed we had not the least idea that you were about to return to us. Why—'

'And nor did I myself! And neither *am* I returning!' declared Penelope exultantly. 'For – only fancy! – this is my husband, Eliza! This is Dr Harding!' With a radiant smile. 'And we are on our wedding journey, just passing by! But of course we felt that we *must* pause here in our itinerary so as to impart our festive tidings. Pray, where is my father?'

'He is up in his book room,' said Elizabeth, looking moithered, as if she had hardly yet taken in her sister's words. 'He spends most of his time there these days – of course I must summon him – dear me – the chaise had better go in the yard – had it not? Oh gracious me – your men? You must know that our poor old Nanny is laid up at present with a bad foot – I do not quite know . . . were you proposing to pass the night here? There is, of course, the *attic* – but I fear it may be sadly damp – my own room I already share with Emma, so – but of course we must turn out for you—'

'Pray don't put yourself in a pucker, my dear creature!' cried Penelope gaily. 'Our men may procure themselves a nuncheon at the Bird in Hand without giving the least trouble to anybody – and if you can find *us* the merest morsel of cold meat and a drop or two of Madeira . . .'

'I will go to my father directly. Emma, pray do take them into the parlour.'

Elizabeth disappeared up the stairs, plainly in need of a moment or so to collect her wits. Emma civilly ushered the new arrivals into the parlour, heartily wishing that she had thought to remove traces of the Blake children's invasion before taking her father his egg-nog. There were cake-crumbs scattered on the floor, and three small dishes with spoons and traces of baked apple on the pembroke table.

'Ah, this dear old parlour!' cried Penelope, quite in a rapture. 'Scene of so many happy childhood hours. Quite half my life has been passed in this room, imagine it, Dr Harding!'

Emma, reflecting that this could hardly be the case, since the family had moved to Stanton when she herself was four and Penelope ten, and she knew that Penelope and Elizabeth had been sent to boarding school in Epsom when they were eleven and fifteen respectively, invited the new-married pair to be seated.

Dr Harding still seemed somewhat confused. He spoke at last.

'Eh? Eh? Ahem? And – and who would you be then, young lady? One of Penelope's sisters – eh? Is that it? I know that she has a deal of sisters?'

He spoke with something of a north-country accent – Emma, wholly unfamiliar with those parts of the kingdom, knew not whether it might be Yorkshire, Cumbria or Scots. He seemed a kindly, unassuming, well-meaning person, a little dazed, perhaps, by the rapidity of the change that had overtaken him.

'Yes – I am the youngest sister, Emma. And, later, you will meet Margaret, and our brother Robert, and Robert's wife.'

Her heart much misgiving her at the thought of such a gathering, Emma whisked away the apple saucers, and returned with the Madeira decanter, some biscuits, and a tray of glasses. By now she could hear her father's slow footsteps on the stairs.

'So you intend travelling still farther today?' she inquired, breaking in on Penelope's guided tour of the family miniatures round the parlour walls – but the Hardings' destination that night seemed to her a point of high importance, essential to have established without loss of time. 'May I ask whither you are bound?'

'Why, my dear,' cried Penelope, 'you see, my husband's daughter Martha, by his first marriage, is herself getting married – in Northampton, next week – and he, naturally, wishes to solemnize the occasion with his presence – and, believe it or not, Martha and I have not yet met.'

'Surely you cannot expect to reach Northampton today?'

'No, no, no, my dear creature, of course not. The very idea!' said Penelope, rippling with laughter. 'No, no, we propose going no farther than the Pulteney Hotel in Piccadilly today. There we shall pass a night or two, and buy a few trifles, before travelling on to Northampton.'

Emma and Elizabeth exchanged brief glances of profound relief.

Mr Watson, making his slow way into the room, now required to have everything explained again to him, clearly and simply.

'Penelope and Dr Harding are *married*, Papa. And here,

to make our acquaintance, is Penelope's husband. This is
Dr Harding.'

'Married? They wish to be married? Then we must
have the banns called – somebody will have to go down
the road and fetch Mr Nicholls the curate – but, dear me,
where will the gentleman be able to stay for three weeks?'

'No, no, Papa dear; they are married *already* – they
were married in Chichester, in the church of St John. See,
Penelope shows you her wedding ring!'

Penelope did so, most exultingly. And along with the
gold ring was another, with a large and remarkably handsome stone.

'But, harken to me, we mean to be with you again very
soon,' she was informing Elizabeth, in what Emma could
not help considering a tone with a wholly uncalled-for
degree of patronage in it. 'No, no, not in *this* house, my
dear girl. That would hardly suffice. Or be fitting. But,
guess what! Only guess what we have done, this very
morning!'

'I cannot possibly guess, Penelope,' said Elizabeth
faintly. Emma divined that she was trying to estimate
whether there would be sufficient pease soup in the larder
to offer to the unexpected guests, along with the remainder
of the pigeon pie, before they proceeded on their journey.

'We have been to view Clissocks! We have purchased
Clissocks!'

'Clissocks,' murmured Mr Watson, who was still only
half abreast of the conversation. 'Now, there was an
example of a fine old Saxon settlement, and a house waste-
fully fallen to rack and ruin. And not so very long since!
A sad business; a very sad, shocking business, that was.'

'I had written and asked my friend Tillie Sawyer – you remember her, Tillie Partridge that used to be, who married and moved to Guildford – and she replied and told me, yes, Clissocks still stood empty. And so, I made the suggestion to *monsieur mon mari* – why do we not take it in on our way, inspect the property, as we shall be passing close by, and, of course, bring along with us *monsieur mon mari's* man of business, our esteemed, invaluable Mr Thickstaffe – and, upon my word, *never* was a purchase so swiftly transacted! Poor old Sir Meldred, you know, living on bread and cheese in the lodge, was happy to accept our very first offer. But he looks not long for this world–'

'Clissocks?' Mr Watson was still bewildered. 'You are thinking of purchasing Clissocks? But it has stood empty these ten years. Nobody would buy it – it was in such a shocking state of disrepair, even before Lady Torridge died. No, no, you would be well advised to put *that* notion quite out of your heads.'

'But it is done, Papa. The thing is accomplished.'

'But – Dr Harding – do you not own a house in Chichester?' Elizabeth ventured to ask.

'Ay, to be sure, he does, a little hencoop, a little doll's house of a place, with a garden the size of that table. But now we shall come and be neighbours to you all. Dr Harding, you see, is just retired from medical practice; and I tell him we shall require a great deal more room to stretch out in.'

Penelope gazed about her, effulgent, smiling with happiness and triumph. She had, Emma thought, very much the same air as Mrs Blake's baby girl earlier, surveying the scene around her, confident in her total power over it.

Now the sound of horses' hoofs could be heard outside.

'Oh no!' cried Elizabeth, almost in despair. 'Not *more* visitors?'

'Can it be our brother Robert, returning?' suggested Penelope hopefully. 'I vow I quite long to see Jane again. And Margaret. The dear creatures!'

'No, it cannot be Robert,' said Emma. 'For I do not hear carriage wheels. Whoever comes is on horseback.'

Her heart sank, as she thought of one possible explanation; and, sure enough, glancing through the casement, she saw the figures of Tom Musgrave and his friend Lord Osborne, and a third horseman in the distance, who appeared to be riding off in the opposite direction.

'I fear it is Tom Musgrave,' Emma murmured to Elizabeth, whose expression revealed only too plainly how little she relished the news.

'Tom Musgrave?' cried out Penelope. 'Well – I protest! I am amazingly surprised! To think that *he* – of all persons – should come by, just at this juncture. Tom Musgrave, I must inform you, my dear sir,' she told her husband, 'is a young fellow who used to dangle after me, oh, most pertinaciously. But, I am glad to say, I pretty soon despatched him about his business! I wanted no dealings with such an empty-headed, self-satisfied puppy. Oh, he was a fop! No, no, I *very* quickly sent him to the right-about! Did I not, Eliza! And then – after that' (without waiting for Elizabeth's response) 'I believe he started a flirtation with Margaret; he is one of that sort, you know, who will trifle with any young lady that may catch his eye. And I suppose' (laughing affectedly) 'he has now turned his attention to *you*, little Emma, has he?'

Emma was spared the need for reply by a rat-tat at the front door.

There was nothing for it but to admit Tom Musgrave and Lord Osborne, though they were the very last people Emma would have wished to see.

'Hollo, there, Miss Emma!' said Tom, very jovially, stepping into the hall – and Emma, recalling her aunt O'Brien's new husband, became instantly aware that he and his companion must have dropped in at the Bird in Hand, or some other hostelry, before making their call, since a strong aroma of sherry emanated from one or both. They were, as well, mud-stained, scratched, dishevelled, and wind-blown. 'Hollo, there! We have had such a cursed piece of bad luck – lost the fox, a cunning old rascal who got clean away from hounds at High Down Gorse! Up to that point we had a capital run of it, both of us well in the lead – and then the shrewd old brute whisked away to the side of us and into Fotherby Wood – so there was an end of our sport, hounds quite at a stay – for, you know, Sir Giles won't permit hounds on his demesne – it was the most vexatious thing – was it not, Osborne? – so, to cut a long tale short, as we were within half a mile of you on our way home, we thought we might just as well cast round this way and pass the time of day – ran into Howard, too, but he sheered off . . .'

Tom Musgrave was running on in this manner, very freely and convivially, without taking particular note of his surroundings. He stood in the hall, smiling, flushed, and quite at ease, with his thumbs tucked into his waistcoat pockets and his whip under his arm. He was a well-set-up, goodlooking young man with dark hair and a somewhat florid complexion. He had a confident, cheerful air, as if he expected the world in general to treat him well, and had hitherto been justified in such expectations. His friend Lord Osborne, somewhat younger, was fair-haired and had narrow, patrician features; his manner varied between callow, unsure, awkward, and then suddenly supercilious – as if he thought himself above his society, yet was not certain of his welcome. Now, perhaps because he was more sensitively aware, or possibly because he had imbibed a little less freely at the Bird in Hand, he jogged his friend by the elbow and murmured, 'Hey-day, Musgrave, here's company in the house – company, you know. Here's folk, other folk, in the parlour over and beyond the family.'

'Why, the more the merrier,' declared Tom happily, rolling into the parlour. 'But, I say, you know, Miss Emma, what it was, we were disappointed not to see *you* at the meet. Did I not tell you expressly that we were to throw off at Stanton Wood at nine o'clock? We looked to see you there, we were sadly put-about at your absence, I can tell you.'

'Thank you, sir,' replied Emma, very coldly indeed, 'but, first, it was quite out of my power to be at such a place at such a time; and, secondly, I understood from you that the meet was to be on Wednesday, not on Monday.'

'Oh, well, ay, that's so, certainly, I found when I got home that it was at Larchbrook Spinneys this day, not Stanton Wood the day after tomorrow – but, nonetheless, we were deuced sorry not to see you there. Were we not, Osborne? By the bye, where is Howard? He was with us but now.'

'He rid off,' said Osborne. 'He would not stay. He said

my mother was expecting him. And that it was not a suitable time for a call at the parsonage.'

'Ay, did he? Ay, that's right; he suddenly fetched up some pettifogging reason why it would be best not to enter the parsonage—'

By this time Emma was heartily annoyed with herself that she had ever let the gentlemen into the house, and wondered how in the world to get them out again, when suddenly Penelope stepped forward.

'Why – I do verily believe that it is Thomas Musgrave!' Her voice was shrill and unfriendly, the smile she launched at Tom was like a javelin. 'What a very singular coincidence – that you should choose to step into this house, just as I am come by on my wedding journey. Is not that laughably bizarre! But – dear me – how you have changed, Mr Musgrave! How you have – well, I can hardly say *gone off*, can I? That would not be civil! But you seem so much older than when I saw you last – indeed and truly had I met you in the street I would hardly have known you – nor here, indeed, had not my sister spoke your name. I would have thought that you were your own father – indeed I would! But now you must let me make my husband known to you – for I am no longer Miss Penelope Watson, I will have you know – my name is now Mrs Joseph Harding. And we shall soon be your neighbours, my husband and I – for we have bought Clissocks, and plan to settle there as soon as may be!'

Tom Musgrave seemed quite bemused by all this information, which was delivered in a high, breathless tone without any pauses. He stood rocking slightly back and forth, his countenance flushed and puzzled.

Dr Harding, almost equally at a loss, stood up, bowed, said, 'Your servant, sir,' and sat down again.

Mr Watson, exhausted, it was plain, by all this unexpected company, observed faintly to his daughter Elizabeth, 'Eliza my dear, I think I must retire again to my chamber. All these strange voices fall too harshly on my ears. I believe I was informed just now that somebody had been married? Now who was that again? I would not wish to seem uncivil, but, indeed, I fear I must return to my chamber.'

He rose up and began to move with faltering steps towards the door.

Tom Musgrave, meanwhile, was gazing at Penelope in stupefaction.

'Miss Penelope? *Married*, you say? Good God!'

Lord Osborne now acted with more propriety and good sense than he had shown hitherto.

'Allow me to give you joy, ma'am! Come, Musgrave, we are in the way here, I believe. We had better follow Howard. You may recall, also, that Mr Watson likes to take his dinner at this hour.'

And he plucked at Tom's arm, almost pulling him from the room. Tom at last allowed himself to be led out, muttering to himself, 'Penelope Watson married? *Married? Can I credit my ears?* Did she really say that?'

'Ay, old fellow, but come along; Rajah and Bendigo will take cold if we do not get them back to the stable within the next half-hour.'

'And did I hear her say that they had bought Clissocks?'

Tom's voice now came from outside the front door.

Lord Osborne's reply was lost in the clatter of hoofs as

the two gentlemen mounted their muddied steeds and rode away.

Penelope, pale with fury, was heard declaring to the world at large: '*Well!* Upon my word! Is *this* what country manners are coming to? I was never so shocked! I could hardly believe my eyes! Or my ears! If it were not for our strong wish to see my dear brother and sister later today—'

Emma, seizing a chance to slip away from this not unnatural indignation, assisted her father back up the stairs and hurriedly set and carried him a tray with some cold meat and a glass of negus to consume in peace at his own hearthside.

When she returned to the parlour she found that Elizabeth was endeavouring to placate her sister with the remains of the pigeon pie and some damson tartlets which had been intended for the company at dinner that evening.

Dr Harding still seemed a trifle confused, as if the recent inundatory flow of events had left him solitary and stranded in its aftermath. Emma sat by him and did her best to put him more at his ease by asking civil questions about the wedding.

'Oh, ay, it was a very pretty ceremony; very pretty. Special licence, you know; no guests, except for my niece Miss Shaw, and my man of business, Percy Thickstaffe; and after the wedding breakfast we were soon on our way . . . And, do you know, my dear Penelope, I believe we must be running along, now,' he added, with more of a collected manner than he had displayed hitherto. 'If we are to reach the Pulteney before dusk, I reckon we should be taking our leave.'

Penelope was not pleased. She still, evidently, hoped to show off her rings to Jane and Margaret.

'But our men have gone down to the inn,' she objected.

'I can soon send the garden boy for them,' said Elizabeth, immensely relieved at the prospect of at least a short intermission between batches of guests.

And, when the Hardings had been seen off, with flutterings of handkerchiefs, and many promises from Penelope for a speedy reunion, 'As soon as there is a bedroom at Clissocks fit to be slept in!'

Elizabeth heaved a huge sigh of deliverance, and said, 'Do you know, Emma, I believe that still, with a little good luck and contrivance, we may be finished with our laundry before the others are returned from their round of visits. And old Nanny says she is well enough to get up and help us this evening, and Betsey King has promised to remain and wash the plates.'

2

Mr Watson was not to be prevailed upon to join the party at dinner that evening – a fortunate circumstance, perhaps, since Robert, Jane, and Margaret were sufficiently late back from paying their round of calls on friends to make their dressing for dinner a somewhat scrambled affair, and the meal greatly delayed. Robert, as on the previous days of the visit, received a scolding from his wife for the insufficiency of the powder on his hair.

'There is quite enough powder for my wife and sisters,' said he, shortly. 'Do be satisfied, Jane, with having put on a very smart gown yourself.'

Emma, seeing her sister-in-law's expression, hastily began to praise the gown.

'Do you really think so, my love?' cried Jane, instantly all amiability. 'You do not consider it over-trimmed? I had some thoughts of putting this gold lace on my drab-coloured satin that I wore yesterday – what do you think? Would that enhance it? La! I vow it is useless to ask your sister Margaret – for she is such a flatterer! She praises all my gowns with equal fervour.'

'But perhaps they all deserve it?' suggested Emma.

'Oh, my dear child! Pray do not be satirical! I shall think you as shocking a quiz as Miss Margaret there,' said Mrs Robert, with a complacent look.

Robert's wife was dressed very fine, and did her hair very skilfully, despite the lack of her maid, a deficiency which she continually lamented; she was decidedly short in stature, and had a broad nose and a wide mouth, but the vivacity of her countenance made ample atonement for these fallings-off from complete beauty; her face, indeed, was hardly ever at rest, for she was in a perpetual flow of spirits and repartee, abusing her husband for his silence, and teasing Margaret about her suitors at Croydon, especially a particular one, a Mr Hobhouse. When at rest it could be seen that the skin of her face, though soft, was marred by a thousand tiny wrinkles like the glaze on a piece of china-ware that has been left too close to the fire.

Margaret Watson, the next sister above Emma in age, was not without beauty; she had a slight, pretty figure, and rather wanted countenance than good features, but the generally sharp and anxious expression of her face made her beauty a secondary consideration. She was so intent upon marriage as a goal that the need for some grace in the preliminaries to this state had quite escaped her.

When she learned that Tom Musgrave and his friend had made a brief visit to the parsonage during her absence from it that morning she made no attempt to conceal her vexation.

'He *and* Lord Osborne, both? What did they *say*? How long did they stay? Did they make any inquiry after me? Did they disclose any plan – announce any intention of returning here?'

Emma could not put forward much hope of such a possibility in the immediate future. Margaret's displeasure at this news, however, was quite swamped and overborne by the unbridled and clamorous astonishment displayed by both Robert and his wife over the unexpected matrimonial triumph of their sister Penelope.

Robert Watson was a slight, dark-haired man, superficially resembling his father in build and figure, but so dissimilar in character that the mark of it appeared on his countenance: not handsome, though gentlemanlike, he had a careful, nervous, calculating expression which at all times detracted from the joviality and animation that he affected when in company.

'Penelope married?' said he. 'Are you in good earnest, Elizabeth? This is not some Banbury tale that you and Emma have concocted to divert us?'

'*Married?*' cried Jane Watson shrilly. 'In what church, pray? Are you certain about this? Did she have wedding clothes? Did she have a ring?'

'Indeed she did, and, besides that, a great big diamond, the size of a pea,' said Emma, who found her sister-in-law's vulgarity, and habit of begrudging anybody else's good fortune, even when it did not detract from her own, almost insupportable.

'Well! I never was so astonished in my whole life. For it must be five years at least since Pen lost any reasonable expectation of attaching a husband; let alone a wealthy one. What is his income? What is he like?'

'He seemed a respectable, estimable man,' replied Elizabeth calmly.

'And *very* proud of his wife,' added Emma. 'He looked at her most fondly.'

Jane darted an irritable glance at her, but Robert said in a considering manner:

'This astonishing news does, I must confess, greatly augment my esteem for my sister Penelope. Indeed I never could have imagined that she would bring off such a consummation. And I will not deny that it is no small weight off my *own* mind. For I had every reason to fear that she might have been a considerable charge upon us in years to come – when the inevitable melancholy event befalls us –' with a glance at the ceiling in the general direction of his father's bedchamber. 'Now that at least *one* of my four sisters is respectably and satisfactorily disposed of, we may perhaps have better hopes of further good fortune –' nodding in a kindly, patronizing manner towards Margaret and Emma. 'For our poor Eliza here, I am afraid we cannot entertain any such expectations; but pewter can breed gold (as they say), and since Penelope has established herself so creditably, she may, not unreasonably, be depended on to find husbands for her younger sisters. Clissocks, indeed! Well, well, well! Dr Harding must be a warm man, indeed, if he can afford to put *that* place in order. It has been on the market for I do not know how many years. I myself would never in the world undertake such a costly piece of renovation – no, not if I had all the wealth of Dives – but it may do excellently for Dr Harding. Yes, indeed! And I do not deny that it will sound well – "My brother-in-law, Dr Harding, of Clissocks!" Yes, indeed, yes, indeed!' rubbing his thin hands together. 'This has been a most favourable day for the family. And Tom Musgrave came calling, with his friend Lord Osborne, you say, as well?'

'I would place no dependence on the favour of either

of *those* gentlemen,' said Margaret spitefully, and Emma was obliged to agree.

'It was a mere whim, because they had been disappointed of their day's hunting.'

'But Mrs Blake called, also! We have not yet told you about Mrs Blake!' put in Elizabeth eagerly.

'And who, pray, is Mrs Blake?' inquired Jane in a light, scoffing manner. 'Mrs Blake! That hardly sounds a name to raise one's hopes high. A decidedly flat, commonplace designation. Mrs Blake! Humph! She sounds like a good, tedious body of the village.'

'There, my dear sister, you are wholly mistaken!' cried Elizabeth warmly. 'Mrs Blake is both delightful and very well-bred; she is the sister of Mr Howard the Chaplain at Osborne Castle, and I believe her connections are quite as high up and grand as those of Lady Osborne; and her husband has just been made a captain. In the navy.'

'Oh! Well! I am very glad to hear it. The navy must always be unexceptionable,' said Jane graciously, perhaps recollecting that Blake was no more commonplace a name than Watson. 'It is true, I have heard talk in Croydon that Lady Osborne is to marry Mr Howard.'

'Why,' cried Margaret in disgust, 'how *can* that be? A baron's widow to stoop so? And sure, she must be ten years older than he is – twenty, even!'

'Yes, my dear creature; but in those high circles so many years' difference is considered of small consequence. Besides, to look at Lady Osborne, one would never guess that she is such an age. From her appearance, one would suppose her no more than thirty years at most – she is so delicately fair, with such fine grey eyes and dark lashes, and she carries herself with such an air, speaks with so much brilliancy and grace. Not at all like that red-headed daughter of hers! I have seen Lady Osborne, many times, from a distance, at Assemblies in Croydon, sometimes with Mr Howard; it is true, doubtless, that she *could* do vastly better for herself, but it is also plain that she has set her heart on the gentleman, and it can't be denied that he is personable enough. A fine figure of a man. Also I have heard tell that her former husband, old Lord Osborne, was a regular bear, and she was persuaded, even coerced, into that match by her parents, the Bungays. No doubt, this time, she feels herself entitled to please her own fancy. She has provided an heir; she has done her duty.'

Emma felt impelled to put a question: 'And is Mr Howard equally devoted to her ladyship? Is it known that he, too, wishes for the match?'

'Lord, child, she has ten thousand a year of her own! He would be a great fool if he did not fall in with her wishes. But I have also heard it said that he is perfectly complaisant. These great ladies, you know, are accustomed to their own way. They carry all before them. And Mr Howard himself, for all his cleverness and handsome looks, is not a wealthy man.'

Emma sighed. She could not help feeling it a great pity that a man of such apparent good taste, insight, intelligence, and compassion should permit himself to be manoeuvred into such an ill-balanced match. If, indeed, that was the case. Yet, she thought, what do *I* know of his inner wishes and intentions? I danced two dances with him at that Assembly, nothing more than that. Besides, where does prudence end and calculation begin? Very likely he may be able to put ten thousand a year to better use than the lady would do if she were alone, or married elsewhere. And it is sheer presumption on my part to make any judgement in the matter when I have so little acquaintance with the gentleman, and none at all with the lady. She may be all that is benevolent, and wholly deserving of his affections.

Endeavouring to withdraw her thoughts from a subject which could have no comfort or relevance to herself, she listened to the others.

They were now giving Elizabeth an account of their day's encounters with old friends and former acquaintance.

'How poor old Mrs Selbourne has aged! I should scarcely have known her!' – and, 'Lord! What a shocking change in Frederick Winston! He was used to be so smart, quite a beau, but now he looks no more than a middle-aged yokel farmer!' was the general tenor of Robert's and Margaret's narrative, and the latter might have been absent from Stanton for three years, rather than three months, to judge by her descriptions of amazing general deterioration and decline in the district. Jane confined herself to comments on wardrobes, and a pervasive astonishment that, only twelve miles from Croydon – that seat of modishness and brilliant taste – fashions should lag so far behind what was permissible.

'Even ladies of the better class wearing *pattens*! I hardly knew where to look! I was not aware that such a practice still prevailed, even among the lower orders.' Guiltily, Emma managed to withdraw her eyes from those of Elizabeth. 'And, my dears, in *one* house, a lady – for such I suppose she must be termed – received us wearing what

I believe used to be called a Caraco jacket – I was obliged to keep my gaze on the mat – three petticoats – when nobody now wears more than one – stays, my dear, when every person of fashion has left off even corsets – *shift-sleeves* – when even a chemise is now unheard-of. Truly, in these country districts, one might be in the Middle Ages.'

'And – and did you call, as you said you meant to, on Mr and Mrs Purvis?' inquired Elizabeth in a faltering voice.

('It was old Mrs Fitzsimmons, wearing the Caraco jacket,' put in Margaret. 'Even when I was a child she was a frumpy old quiz.')

'Oh, the Purvises, yes,' Robert answered his sister carelessly. 'My word, though, *she* has gone off, poor thing! So frail and sickly as she looks, I shall be exceedingly surprised if Purvis does not repent of that alliance. And but one little puny daughter to show for the marriage – ay, he would have done better to stay by you, Eliza, though at the time it did not seem so. Did he not cast an eye in your direction, some ten years ago? Still, I do not say but what events have turned out for the best; my father needs your services now, it is plain; and though, as it came to pass, my sister Emma could have filled that office, it was not *then* to be anticipated that Aunt Turner should throw her bonnet over the windmill, behave with such arrant folly. No, no, matters are best as they are. I suppose you do not receive any word from your aunt, Mrs O'Brien as she now is?' he asked Emma.

During Robert's speech Emma had felt most acutely for Elizabeth who, it was plain, could only just contain her tears; but, by good fortune, at this moment, their father rang his bell upstairs, and, with a muttered excuse, Elizabeth hurried from the room.

Emma told her brother that she had received a few letters from her aunt, none of very recent date. He nodded, and said, 'It was a bad business. A shocking bad business. I daresay she has by now greatly regretted her rash act. But no remedy can be found now. Only you are cut out of a fortune, Emma. Poor Eliza,' he went on, '*she* has gone off quite amazingly, too. I wonder at her loss of looks. I do indeed.'

'Indeed, *yes!*' agreed his wife with great composure. 'One can say so, now she is out of the room. Dear me! It seems quite hard to imagine that she can ever have had a serious suitor – so coarse her complexion has grown, and her hair so thin and pitiful. It makes me quite sorry that my maid Hargreaves is not here, to try what effect bandoline might have to improve it—'

'Oh, fiddlesticks, Jane,' said her husband impatiently. 'What in the world, pray, do you imagine would be the use of such trickery? (And where, in any event, could you put your maid in this house? In the stable-loft?) Besides, where would be the sense – Eliza has long since—'

He was obliged to cut short the rest of his argument, for Elizabeth now returned to the dining-room. The brief interlude upstairs had been enough to render her once more quite in control of her features. She said calmly, 'Emma, my dear, our father has expressed a wish for your company. He asks if you will go and read aloud to him. So – if you do not object to forgoing dessert—'

'Not in the very least!' cried Emma with great eagerness,

pushing back her chair. 'I shall be very happy to go and keep him company. Pray excuse me,' she added to the company in general, and almost ran from the room. As she mounted the stair she heard Jane's high, assertive voice commenting:

'Little Emma would not be quite so much amiss if she had rather more stature and a *deal* more countenance. But that pert, self-assured manner of hers! It is of all things unfortunate – quite the outside of enough – I do not know how we could introduce her to our friends –'

Odious, *odious* woman, thought Emma, continuing to climb the stair. But I am very glad if she has taken a dislike to me, for then perhaps she will cease urging me to come back and stay with them at Croydon, which is the very last thing I would ever wish to do. Her friends! I can imagine what they are like! Sharp young lawyers and rich, patronizing tradesmen.

She tapped at her father's door and entered. The silence and peace of his chamber came as a deep refreshment in itself, after the loud self-satisfied voices and commonplace pronouncements to be heard downstairs; and when he said, 'Ah, Emma, my dear child; I should be glad if you would sit for a while and read to me,' she was wholly happy to be of service to him. He had been seated by the fire in an easy chair, but she persuaded him that his bed would be more comfortable, and assisted him to make the transfer.

He then expressed a wish to be read to out of his own sermons, of which he had a tolerably large collection, going back many years, preserved and transcribed from the days when he had been able to be more active in parish affairs.

'I had thoughts of offering them for publication,' he

told Emma. 'Mr Howard informs me that volumes of sermons, such as that of the Reverend Fordyce, command substantial sales these days – when, alas, young clerics are not so industrious in preparing their own texts as they should be; Mr Howard kindly undertook to advise me regarding the preparation of a selection from my works. So I should be obliged, my dear, if you would assist me by reading them aloud, in order to refresh my memory.'

'There is nothing I should like better, Papa.'

Indeed, this was no more than the truth. The discourses were sober, well-argued, and sometimes intensely moving homilies, as, for example, the one Mr Watson had preached after his own wife's death; throughout the ensuing weeks Emma, daily reading through the greater portion of them to her father, received the benefit of their quiet wisdom.

On this first occasion he halted her after twenty minutes.

'Thank you, my child. That has calmed and made me drowsy. I think that now I shall sleep peacefully. It has proved a somewhat trying day. Did not some person inform me that Penelope was *married*? But never mind that at present. Goodnight, my dear; you have a gentle voice – "an excellent thing in woman", as the bard puts it. I am reminded by it of your dear mother.'

Emma felt very well rewarded, as she lowered the flame of the lamp and tiptoed away; this brief, peaceful interlude contained, for her, greater value than all the rest of the strangely variegated day.

Four days later Robert and Jane returned to Croydon, taking Margaret with them again. There had been a half-hearted invitation to Emma to accompany the party, for Jane's dislike of her was in some degree overmastered by the undoubted fact that Emma's wardrobe, formerly furnished and governed by the comfortable means and superior taste of Aunt Turner, would be matter for much interest and discussion among Jane's circle of friends in Croydon. The offer, accordingly, was made, but in so languid and insincere a manner that Emma had no difficulty in parrying it.

'Thank you, but my father has asked me to read aloud all his sermons to him – it is a task which will take a number of weeks, and my sister Elizabeth is by far too busy – besides, she does not like reading –'

'Oh la, my dear Emma, I am afraid you are quite a Bluestocking!' cried Jane archly. 'Poor Mag here and I will never be able to keep up with you, so learned as you will be when you have perused them all – am I not right, Mag, my love? *We* must confine our poor selves to discussions of figured cambric and pearl-edged ribbon. Well, dear Emma, you must come to Croydon another time – must she not, Robert, Maggie? In the spring we shall renew our entreaties – in the meantime we must content ourselves with returning our charming Mag to the disconsolate Mr Hobhouse – if he has not pined away from melancholy in the meantime . . .'

Robert adjured her to finish off her goodbyes, for heaven's sake, and get into the carriage, or they would never be home in time for dinner.

The departure of Margaret came, to Emma, as a considerable relief. She scolded herself for lack of affection to a sister, but was honest enough to admit that it was almost impossible to like her immediate elder who, although not lacking in shrewdness and intelligence, took no pains to study the needs of others, and cared for nobody but herself. Upon her first return to the parsonage Margaret, evidently wishful to impress Emma with her gentility, had assumed a soft, cajoling manner, had spoken with almost languishing slowness and restraint, had expressed nothing but the most laudably charitable and unexceptionable sentiments, and found not a single object about her that did not deserve praise. But, by degrees, either deciding that Emma's opinion was of small consequence, or that such a demeanour was too difficult to maintain over a long period of time, she had reverted to what was evidently her normal mode: a whining, fretful, continual displeasure with the amenities of the parsonage, and repeated querulous attacks upon Elizabeth, who bore them with the indifferent calm of long usage.

Invited to return to Croydon with the married pair, and having apparently given up hope of Tom Musgrave, she made no secret of her eagerness to quit Stanton once again.

Kind-hearted Elizabeth was a little distressed by this.

'You return to our home for so *very* short a visit? You do not wish to spend more time with Papa? Or with our sister Emma?'

'Oh,' cried Margaret carelessly, 'there will be time enough for that when Penelope has come back with her doctor and set up house at Clissocks. Then, indeed, there will be something worth – I mean, there will be more society in the neighbourhood.'

'The fact of the matter is,' explained Jane in a loud confidential whisper to Elizabeth, 'that young Mr Hobhouse, my husband's junior associate, you know, has been paying Miss Margaret such decidedly marked attentions, that – oh, I quiz her about him amazingly, do I not, Robert?'

Margaret was ready with a simper, but Robert, busy anticipating a dirty road and a slow journey, had no time for such social niceties.

'No doubt we shall find Mr Hobhouse waiting at home with the liveliest anxiety to see if Margaret has continued to honour us with her company on the return journey to Croydon!' ran on Jane. 'He had heard such tales of the beaux at Stanton – especially one Tom Musgrave!'

Just at this moment Tom Musgrave and a friend cantered past in the adjoining meadow, adding weight to Margaret's decision by failing to make any effort to pause or engage in conversation, merely waving hats and whips as they rode by.

'I declare that Mr Musgrave is a very disagreeable young gentleman and quite eaten up with pride,' snapped Jane Watson. 'You are far better off, my dear Mag, in the city of Croydon where one can, at least, walk the streets in one's nankeen half-boots without sinking into the mud, and where you will have Mr Hobhouse to escort you.'

So the trio took their departure, and a quiet daily routine was re-established at the parsonage.

But one observation made by Mrs Robert Watson had remained to tease Emma's mind.

The next monthly Assembly in Dorking was now a month away. This time, Emma had self-sacrificingly resolved that she herself would remain at home to keep their father company, while Elizabeth, who so dearly enjoyed any form of sociability, should not be deprived of the pleasure of dancing.

'And, my dear sister, do pray permit me to try the effect of bandoline on your hair. My aunt Turner has always been used to apply it, with the most improving results, and I am persuaded that it would do wonders for your appearance.'

Elizabeth was doubtful, hesitant, hard to convince, either that she should go to the ball in place of her sister, or as to the efficacy of the bandoline.

'Besides, we have none,' she added as a clincher.

'No, but I wrote down the receipt for it, which my aunt's maid Trotter gave me, in my journal, and here it is. All we need is some gum tragacanth, some essence of almonds, olive oil, spirit of rosemary, and a little old rum. All these ingredients are here in the house, with the exception of the gum, and I am sure that can easily be procured. Do, do, my dear sister, at least let me make the attempt.'

'I do not think Papa would approve of attempting to better one's appearance.'

'Nonsense! He likes us to look neat and proper, and this is but a step forward from that. Besides, it is all Lombard Street to a china orange that he will never notice the difference. If only you could have a new gown,' sighed Emma regretfully. 'It is a thousand pities that you are so much taller than I, or you could wear one of mine. But I plan to re-line your velvet pelisse, so as to give it a more elegant drape; and I am going to make you a black lace cap to replace the one which you have been wearing ever since the death of Lord Nelson.'

'Oh, Emma! You should not exert yourself to such a degree – just for me! Where is the use of it? *You* should be going to the ball in my stead – young, pretty, stylishly dressed as you are, you should be making the most of your chances.'

'My dear goose, I shall have chances enough by and by. Only imagine, as my sister Margaret evidently does, the dramatic enlargement of our neighbourhood when Penelope and her doctor return to occupy Clissocks. I am content to wait for that happy epoch. In the meantime it is entirely unfair that you should be immured here always, for you have, I daresay, a whole host of acquaintances who will be pleased to see you at the Assembly, whereas I have no friends at all, and am bashful at being confronted by so many strangers.'

'And is not a ballroom the very place where introductions can be made? However, this time I will not try to thwart your kind intentions. When the following Assembly falls due, though, you must take your turn and go to it; I will brook no denial. But in the meantime, my dear sister, you do have one friend who should be called on; her civility in visiting us last week should certainly be requited without more delay.'

'Mrs Blake. You are very right. I will go to her this morning.'

'And I wish that I could accompany you, but while old Nanny is still so lame I do not care to venture so far from the house in case our father requires assistance . . .'

'No, it is not to be thought of. And I well remember her house; is it not the one where old Mrs Henshawe used to live, who often gave me gingerbread men?'

'Yes; not far inside the park gates. I would suggest that old Peasmarsh drive you in the chair, but he is hard at work just now, building the new henhouse – but if you like to drive the mare yourself, you are very welcome – it would present a better appearance—'

'My dear sister, no! I need no chair and can walk a mile without the slightest exertion. I shall enjoy it, indeed.'

'Only the lane is probably very muddy,' said Elizabeth doubtfully. 'You had better pin up your petticoats.'

'Don't trouble yourself. I shall wear pattens – now that the arbiter of fashion from Croydon has left us,' said Emma with a wicked smile.

Thus accoutred, she set off, intending to enjoy the pleasant downhill walk on a chalky farm track where a tracery of ice crisped over the puddles. It was a dry, windy winter morning and large clouds sailed overhead. Emma, who took pleasure in her own company, hoped this was not one of the days when the local hounds met at Osborne Castle, and that she ran no risk of encountering Tom Musgrave and his friend.

There was a great deal to occupy her thoughts. Firstly, she could not conceal from herself a deep disappointment in her brother Robert and his wife. Robert, whom she remembered from childhood as a kindly, obliging elder brother, had become, perhaps under the influence of Jane, a mean, dull, calculating man. As head of the family, which he would become at their father's demise, he could be of little support or comfort to his sisters – and that demise, Emma knew from Elizabeth, could not, in the natural course of things, be long delayed. 'Our brother Sam has told me so,' Elizabeth confided to Emma with tears in her eyes. 'Sam knows Papa's constitution so well – and Sam is a very clever surgeon, whatever the Edwards family may think of him. Sam believes that our father never fully recovered from the grief of Mamma's long illness and death – and that grief has just worn him out.' Emma had not seen her brother Sam since he was ten, but she was inclined to put faith in his opinion; she felt that her father was voluntarily saying goodbye to life, and peacefully looking forward to another existence. This grieved her very much, for she had, in the months since she returned home, become deeply attached to the gentle old man; nor could she imagine how they would go on without him. Retired though his way of life must necessarily be, yet his calm steadfast spirit permeated the household. When he had passed away, the sisters would be obliged to leave the parsonage, which would pass to the next incumbent, and where could they go? It seemed dismally probable that Robert and Jane would be obliged to receive them into the household at Croydon: a prospect to appal the stoutest heart. Emma was almost tempted to write an appeal to her aunt in Ireland; but, considering the very strong mutual antagonism between herself and her aunt's new husband, this must be a last resort.

Perhaps brother Sam may achieve some improvement in fortune, she thought hopefully, and set up a household in which he can accommodate Elizabeth and me. Though as Sam was at present no more than a struggling young surgeon in Guildford, this did not seem too probable. Of course Penelope, once established at Clissocks with Dr Harding, might offer asylum to her sisters, but this possibility still seemed remote. And far from enticing, Emma ruefully admitted to herself. How strange it is, she thought, that my father, such a lovable man, can have engendered three such thoroughly unattractive children as Robert, Penelope, and Margaret! How can it have come about?

Then, scolding herself for uncharitable thoughts – what would Papa think of me? – Emma turned in at the open gate of Osborne Park. No lodge guarded this entrance, which was but rarely used; the main entry to the park lay on the farther boundary, five miles to the south. The road on this side ran between a stretch of oak and hazel coppice and a thorn hedge, liberally laced with brambles. Emma could recall coming here as a little girl with her elder sisters, to pick blackberries, and going on afterwards for milk and gingerbread to the house of kind old Mrs Henshawe who had a spinning-wheel and spun yarn from sheep's wool gathered by children from thorns and thickets.

How long ago that seems, she thought wistfully, walking along the puddled driveway, which curved in its course between two gentle swells of grassy land, grazed by sheep. How happy we were then!

Ahead of her lay another gate, and a pair of small houses just large enough to avoid the term cottages; they were square and plain, with pillared porches, and stood in modest gardens against a purplish grove of holly and oak trees. One was occupied now by Mrs Blake and her children, the other by Mr Nigh, the steward of Lord Osborne.

As Emma approached the houses, she heard the sound of hoofs thudding over the grass behind her, and turned to see Mr Howard riding towards her on a fleabitten grey cob.

His face seemed to light up at the sight of her. He raised his hat, then dismounted.

'Miss Watson, good day! Are we bound for the same destination?'

'Certainly, sir, that is, if you are visiting your sister?' she said smiling.

At this moment the door of the nearest house burst open, and a cascade of children emerged from it, which then resolved into Mrs Blake's three little boys followed by their nurse bearing the baby.

'Uncle Adam! Uncle Adam! Are you come to walk with us? Or to play bilbo-catch?'

'Whichever you prefer! But where is your mother? And where are your manners? Here is Miss Watson, come to visit you – let me hear your greetings.'

'Good day, Miss Watson!' they all chorused, and Charles came shyly to take Emma's hand.

'Have you come to walk with us, Miss Watson? And may we show you the ice-house?'

'If there is time,' she said laughing, 'I shall be happy to see it.'

'I understand that you have already met George and Frank and my little niece?' inquired Mr Howard.

'Yes, I have had that pleasure. And now I am come hoping to meet the pet hare and see the collection of horse-chestnuts.'

'You can walk round outside the house to see Harriet Hare,' said Charles, tugging her towards the garden, which was a pleasing mixture of rose-bushes and cabbages, sweet-briars and vegetable beds.

'I think I should first make my salutations to your mother,' objected Emma.

Luckily at this moment Mrs Blake herself appeared in the doorway wearing a sturdy warm pelisse.

'My dear Miss Emma! Forgive this unceremonious

greeting! We are delighted to see you here – are we not, children?'

'Yes, Mamma!' they all clamoured.

'Now, are you so tired from your walk as to wish to come into the house at once and take some refreshment? Or shall we first take our promenade in the park, which had been our intention?'

'Oh, the park, by all means! I have a great curiosity to see this ice-house.'

'That is capital. Harriet Hare and the chestnuts can be displayed on our return,' Mrs Blake soothed Charles, whose face had fallen. 'When we hope that Miss Emma will step in and take her cold meat with us. Our usual procedure on these walks, Miss Emma,' she added, 'is for my brother to lead Dapple while the boys take turns riding him. That way, nobody becomes too tired.'

'But *you* may take a turn too, Miss Emma, if you grow tired,' Little George offered kindly.

'Thank you, my love, but I think I might fall off. I am not accustomed to riding on a man's saddle,' she told him.

Little Sophie and her nurse being left behind in the garden, the party set off across the grass. It was plain that this inner section of Osborne Park had been improved with care and taste, perhaps about ten years previously; artful vistas between young clumps of trees directed the eye towards a curving man-made lake, the narrowest part of which water was spanned by a graceful high-arched bridge. And beyond, on rising ground, at the farthest extremity of the park, stood Osborne Castle itself, which Emma recalled only very indistinctly from fourteen years ago, for she had not seen it more than once or twice. She studied it now with interest and realized that what she had taken, in the innocence of childhood, for towers and battlements dating from some distant period of history were, in fact, fairly recent additions.

'Gracious me! I had forgotten how very big it was.'

'And how very Gothick?' said Mr Howard, smiling. 'The greater portion of what you see, and the castellations, were added on by the present Lord Osborne's grandfather about forty years ago, and his son, Lord Osborne's father, built the two tall turrets; perhaps luckily, the present baron has no architectural aspirations. In fact I have heard him describe his home as a "hummocky old pile" and he much prefers the shooting box at Melton.'

'You taught Lord Osborne for a period, I believe?' said Emma.

'Yes, I tutored him and his younger brother Chilton until last year, when Chilton went up to Cambridge. Now I have transferred my attentions to my nephews,' Mr Howard said, removing Frank from the saddle and replacing him by George. 'And I find them very rewarding scholars, do I not, boys?' His tone conveyed that they far outshone his former pupils, but Emma was too tactful to ask for a comparison of abilities. She could imagine that Lord Osborne had not proved a shining student; there was something slow and lackadaisical about his way of utterance which suggested that, if he had been born into a less privileged walk of life, he might have been dubbed shallow-pated, if not positively wanting in wit.

Still, as a lord he does well enough, thought Emma charitably.

While the party walked along, at an easy pace adapted

to that of Little Frank, the children bombarded Emma with pieces of information about their surroundings. 'This is where we saw hares dancing.' 'That piece of wood is said to be haunted by the ghost of a gamekeeper who was accidentally shot by old Lord Osborne.' 'In that copse you may find Butcher's Broom growing, with red berries, very fine.' 'Over there Uncle Adam saw a heron nearly choke on a fish.' 'Our papa is made captain of the *Antwerp* now, and she is gone to the Mediterranean.' 'Lord Osborne has promised to take Charles out hunting next season.'

In between this artless wealth of information the adults exchanged remarks in a friendly, random manner on topics as they were suggested by the children's chatter: plants, the countryside, politics, books, art – Mrs Blake liked to paint landscapes, she disclosed – but without endeavouring to go deep or pursue any subject in a serious manner. It was like a pleasant game, Emma thought, in which the players tossed the ball without troubling as to who caught it, and there were no rules . . . I have not felt such a sense of easy and comfortable companionship since those walks I used to take in the meadows around Shrewsbury with my aunt and uncle, when we would talk about music and history and poetry and the news of the day. Emma was obliged to admit to herself that Elizabeth, though an affectionate sister and a sweet-tempered companion in the house, was in general so beset with domestic cares that she never opened a book from one month to the next, seldom troubled to glance at a newspaper, and confined her talk to household and neighbourhood topics. Despite this, Elizabeth was by no means a dull house-mate, for she had shrewd good sense and was keenly observant of other people; but it made a delightful change to be with minds commanding wider interests who could provide new ideas on all the topics of the day, and converse with knowledge, spirit, and flow.

They were all exchanging views on 'The Lay of the Last Minstrel' which Mrs Blake said she had been reading aloud to her boys, when the sound of hoofs and carriage wheels made them turn, and Charles exclaimed, 'Why! It is Lady Osborne in her phaeton coming this way across the grass.'

Lady Osborne (as Jane Watson had said) was so extremely elegant, fair, and charming in appearance that no one who did not know her could possibly have supposed her to be much more than thirty years of age. Her daughter, Miss Osborne, did not by any means equal her mother's standard of beauty; she was thin and lacking in colour, and the brilliant russet hue of her hair served only to emphasize the pallor of her complexion; today, moreover, she looked gloomy and out of temper, in marked contrast to her manner at the ball when, Emma recalled, she had appeared lively and vivacious enough as she excused herself from the dance with little Charles. She did not speak.

Lady Osborne, casting a perfunctory half-smile and inclination of her head towards the two females, reserved her attention for Mr Howard.

'Why, my dear sir!' she accosted him, with an air that balanced finely between arch, caressing, and crisp, 'why, my dear Mr Howard, had you forgot that you were to confer with me this noon regarding the plans and funding for the new alms-houses?'

'No, Lady Osborne, I had not forgotten,' he replied

courteously, pulling out his hunter watch and consulting it, 'I had by no means forgotten, but it still wants an hour and a half to the time of our appointment. My sister and I have been combining exercise with natural history for the boys and the pleasure of Miss Emma Watson's company on our walk – ah – may I be permitted to introduce –'

'However I believe I must rob the ladies of your company,' Lady Osborne swept on briskly, with another smile which made no attempt to extend from her lips to her eyes. 'A number of other subjects have come to mind which I wish to discuss with you – if you will now be so obliging as to follow me back to the castle.' And, without more ado, she had the carriage turned round and set off at a rapid pace in the direction from which she had come.

Mr Howard, with a decidedly rueful air, sighed, apologized briefly to his companions, removed little George from the saddle, and mounted himself.

'I hope that we may resume this very agreeable conversation another time, Miss Watson,' he said. 'Goodbye, dear Anna, for the present. Goodbye, boys.'

And he cantered away after the phaeton.

'Oh, *botheration*!' said Charles. 'That means that we cannot walk as far as the ice-house – does it not, Mamma? Since it is much too far for Frank to walk both ways.'

'I am afraid that is so,' agreed his mother. '(Do not let me hear you say *botheration*, my love. It is an ugly word.) I believe the ice-house must be a treat we shall have to reserve for another day, when Uncle Adam can give us more of his time. Never mind! You have plenty of treasures at home to show Miss Emma. I think, my dear, if you do not object, we would do best to turn back now,' she added to Emma. 'Frank is a doughty walker, but this is about the limit of his capacity.'

A slight cloud had overspread her countenance. Emma did not greatly wonder at it. Lady Osborne's dismissal of Mr Howard's pair of female companions had verged on ill manners; and her single glance at Emma had, surprisingly, been chilled by pure cold dislike. As a powerful neighbour, just across the park, Lady Osborne must, Emma thought, present something of a liability to Mrs Blake. And if, as Jane Watson had hinted, the lady really did entertain matrimonial intentions towards Mr Howard, this might, for his sister, constitute an anxious and not particularly agreeable prospect, and one likely to put an end to many pleasant family habits.

Of course Emma did not give voice to any of these thoughts. Instead she said, 'Does Lady Osborne engage in a great variety of charitable work?'

'Oh – yes indeed – she has many benevolent interests,' Mrs Blake answered rather vaguely. 'She and my brother – he is chaplain to the castle, you know, as well as vicar of this parish – they work together a great deal on such affairs. She is very clever and able – besides, of course, being so elegant and charming.' She sighed.

George and little Frank had got ahead of the others, running races across the grass towards their home. Charles, however, walked by his mother, holding tightly on to her hand. Looking up, he said, 'Will Uncle Adam marry Lady Osborne, Mamma?'

'Good gracious, my dear boy! What put such an idea as that into your head?'

'Jem said so to Mrs Fisher. He said everybody in the village thinks it will happen.'

'Charles, I do not like you listening to the gossip of maids and garden-boys. Still less do I like your repeating it. What Uncle Adam and Lady Osborne decide is none of our affair.'

'Yes, Mamma,' he said in a subdued tone, but added, after a moment or two, 'Still, I very much hope that he will *not* marry her. For if he did so I suppose he would have to go to live at the castle, and we should not be able to run in every day to ask him questions as we do at the vicarage. Then it *would* be our affair, don't you think, Mamma?'

'Hush, child! What will Miss Watson think of us? She will conclude that we do nothing but tattle about our neighbours.'

3

On the following day, a Sunday, Emma and Elizabeth were returning together from the service in Stanton Church, which had been conducted by the curate, young Mr Marshall (fortunately by this time old Nanny had recovered sufficiently from her indisposition to be left in charge of Mr Watson), when they were once more surprised by the sound of horse's hoofs in Parsonage Lane.

'Not Tom Musgrave *again* so soon?' cried Elizabeth piteously. 'No, no, it cannot be that! Not on a Sunday, surely?'

Emma had her own instantaneous flash of recollection and vain hope, thinking of Mr Howard as he came riding across Osborne Park, and the glow on his countenance as he caught sight of her; but such a notion she knew to be nonsense, for would not Mr Howard at this very moment be concluding his own church service in Wickstead Church, and, furthermore, very likely be on the point of returning to Osborne Castle to take his Sunday roast beef in the company of Lady Osborne and her family? No, no, however often it might recur to plague her, she must endeavour to banish the intrusive image of Mr Howard from her mind.

But now Elizabeth was calling out joyfully: '*Sam!* Dearest Sam! What a charming surprise! We had not at

all looked to see you. Not but what,' checking a little
ruefully, 'our father will be sadly grieved at you for riding
this distance on a Sunday – oh me, I fear he will be shocked
and sorry that you have done such a thing—'

'Phoo, phoo, Liza, I daresay he will never regard it,'
replied her brother Sam, throwing his leg forward over
the pommel of his saddle and dismounting to give his
sister a hearty hug. 'Chamber-fast as he mostly is, these
days, it is odds that my father hardly tells one day from
another.'

'No, there you are quite out, brother, he keeps a strict
count of the calendar, and reads the office for each day
most steadfastly. Still I am sure he will be very happy to
see you, nonetheless. But here you have been ignoring
sister Emma, who is, I suppose, the principal reason for
your visit.'

'Emmie? Is *this* our little Emmie?' exclaimed Sam,
turning to view her. 'I had taken you for some grand lady
from the neighbourhood, you are grown so fashionable
and handsome!' And he swept her a deep bow.

'Oh, come, Sam!' said Elizabeth, laughing. 'She is not
grown so grand but that you can give her a kiss.'

'Indeed I do now begin to recognize the countenance
of our little Em,' said Sam, and followed Elizabeth's instructions with an affectionate smile and squeeze of Emma's
hand. She, too, began to retrace in him the features of her
old playmate. Sam, the younger of her brothers, was the
one of whom she had always been particularly fond. Only
four years older than she, he had frequently entered into
her childish games, carved her spinning-tops, taken her
for rambles, and told her stories. When she left the family

home to be adopted by her uncle and aunt Turner, she had been especially grieved to part from Sam. He had promised to write to her, and had kept the promise for a considerable number of years very faithfully; but, latterly, as the demands of his medical training and practice made more inroads on his time, the correspondence had dwindled and become less regular.

Now she studied Sam with unaffected pleasure and interest.

He had grown into a personable young man; not handsome, no, but decidedly personable. His hair, medium-fair, was cut quite short in the new fashion. Like his brother Robert and their father, he was of slight build, but a little taller than Robert, compact and muscular, and somewhat tanned as a consequence of many hours spent in the saddle. The features of his face were not striking, but a pair of intelligent lively grey eyes redeemed them, and his expressive countenance was so merry, forthright, and sympathetic that no stranger could help but take a liking to him on the spot. At the moment, however, the merriment was in abeyance. After his fond greeting of both sisters, Sam's smile began to waver, and he said:

'I am come to you also for condolences, Liza; the Edwardses won't allow my suit.'

'Oh, my dear Sam! I am so very sorry! But,' said Elizabeth, rather shocked, 'sure you have not been calling at the Edwardses on such an errand today? On a Sunday? That, of a certainty, won't have advanced you in their favour.'

'But what could I do, Liza? I am tied up all the week

– out on my rounds fifteen hours a day. It's as much as I can do to snatch a meal here and there. See how thin I have grown.' He thumped his chest. 'Old Master Curtis is failing fast; all the work falls on my shoulders. I thought that fact would have recommended me to Mr Edwards – he can't say I do not work hard – but it's of no avail. The Edwardses intend something grander for their Mary than a scrubby surgeon.'

'Oh, my poor Sam, I feel for you – indeed I do. But I am afraid that is true. Did you see Mary Edwards herself?'

'No,' he said bitterly, 'they would not even let me see her to plead my own case. Do you know, Eliza, does she take an interest in any other man?'

Elizabeth looked doubtfully at Emma.

'My sister saw her last – three weeks ago, at the Dorking Assembly –'

'It is true,' Emma said with reluctance, 'Miss Edwards danced a great deal on that occasion with a Captain Hunter – she had at least four dances with him – but her parents were not at all pleased with her about this, afterwards. Her mother gave her a great scold for letting herself be surrounded by Red Coats.'

'Well,' said Elizabeth hopefully, 'that means very little. Any young lady's head may be turned by a red coat. Such a fancy often leads to nothing of lasting importance.'

'But I did hear two ladies at the ball,' Emma went on with even more hesitation, 'who asserted that Mrs Edwards hoped for a match between her daughter and Lord Osborne. It seems the Edwardses are in expectation of an inheritance from some great-uncle which would make their daughter into a very desirable match.'

'Great heaven!' cried Elizabeth, aghast. 'Mary Edwards! An heiress! Emma, you never told me of that.'

'No, it went clean out of my head until this moment – it meant nothing to me as I was so little acquainted with the persons concerned. And the Edwardses did not tell me themselves.'

'I suppose that would be Mrs Edwards' uncle in Plymouth, the merchant; I have heard it said that he is very well-to-do,' Elizabeth said doubtfully. 'Oh, my poor Sam! If this is true, I fear that it does put Miss Edwards entirely out of your reach.'

'But why does *Lord Osborne* require an heiress?' asked Emma with great indignation. 'Surely he has enough money of his own?'

'Oh, but they say his father, the old lord, was a great waster, and the estates are sadly encumbered,' Elizabeth told her.

'But Lady Osborne has ten thousand a year! Jane said so.'

'Ah, but that is her own money left her by her grand-mother – she does not choose to spend it on paying her husband's debts.'

No, but on attracting the favour of Mr Howard, thought Emma.

'Such grand gentry are not always what they seem.'

'Well, I think it is very unfair!'

'But, Sam, you have not heard our news!' cried Elizabeth, recollecting, as they walked towards the stable-yard. 'Our sister Penelope has just been here, and, what do you think? She is married!'

This piece of intelligence, which came as a complete

surprise to Sam, had precisely the effect Elizabeth had hoped, of distracting him from his own melancholy situation and giving a new turn to his thoughts.

'*What?*' he exclaimed. 'Our sister Penny actually married? She must have been working like a coal-heaver to bring it off, for I saw Robert ten days ago when he came to Guildford on legal business, and he spoke no word of it. Well! I was never so astonished! Are you sure that it is true? It is the most amazing thing!'

'Yes, perfectly sure, for she was here with her husband. Now they are gone into Northamptonshire, but when they come back they are going to take up residence in this neighbourhood, for they have bought Clissocks.'

This staggered Sam even more.

'Her husband must be mad! Or else he is as rich as Croesus. Who is he?'

'A Dr Harding from Chichester.'

'Why, I know him! He was one of my tutors when I was at medical school. He is as decent an old fellow as ever stepped, and used to be very kindly disposed towards me. This is famous good news. I wonder if he plans to set up a practice in this neighbourhood?'

'I do not think so,' said Emma. 'I am fairly sure that Penelope said he plans to retire from professional work and live as a gentleman of leisure. She said something about investments.'

'Penny would certainly prefer that. She would not wish a trail of patients to be coming to the house at all hours.'

Mr Watson was delighted to see his younger son, and though he did, as Elizabeth had predicted, gently reprove Sam for making a twenty-mile journey on a Sunday, the pleasure of his son's company outweighed the disapproval, and the long, hard-working week was accepted as sufficient excuse.

Sam at once entered with great enthusiasm into his father's scheme for publication of some of his sermons, and said that he considered it an excellent notion.

'For I am sure, sir, yours are fully as erudite and well constructed as many of these volumes that appear – *Cambridge Sermons* and *Foundations of Old Testament Criticism* and the like – and written in far better English too, I'll be bound.'

Mr Watson even prepared to make one of his rare trips downstairs to eat his cold meat in the dining room with the rest of the family, and they had a pleasant time together exchanging memories of occasions long gone by, in Emma's early childhood, when they had lived in Hampshire and Mrs Watson had still been alive. Emma, though she had spent happy years with Mr and Mrs Turner, felt all the blessing of being with her true family again (forgetting that three members of it were missing).

After Mr Watson had retired once more to his chamber, Sam said, 'This is really a capital scheme about the sermons, Lizzie, and I am as grateful as can be to Howard for putting it into my father's head. For Papa talked to me upstairs, expressing a great deal of anxiety as to what will become of you girls when he is carried off – which, I won't attempt to conceal from you, may occur at any time. He plans, Emma, to leave you in his Will such moneys as may accrue from the publication of the sermons, since, he says, you have been of such signal help to him –'

'Oh, Sam!' cried Elizabeth, turning very pale. 'Is the end really so certain? So near?'

'No use trying to wrap things up, sister. My father is very frail, and his heart is in a shocking state. And serious worry about what will happen to his daughters after he is gone don't help. But this scheme will keep him engaged and in tolerable spirits – it was a rare notion of Howard's. He said it arose from some suggestion made by Purvis.'

'Purvis?'

Sam threw a quick but penetrating look at his sister and remarked, 'That surprises you, but Purvis has always looked up to my father and, I believe, entertained a high regard for several other members of our family. Small wonder if he should have given some consideration to the future of you and your sisters when Papa is gone. And Purvis, I understand, has a cousin who is a bookseller and publisher in Maiden Lane.'

'I suppose our father's death is a matter of speculation all over the countryside,' observed Elizabeth in a choked tone.

'Ay, indeed; Robert and I were putting our heads together about the future, too, when I saw him last week; Rob could take in two of you, he said, when you are obliged to quit this house – in fact I am quite surprised to find Emmie still here; I had thought Jane proposed to invite her to Croydon . . .'

'She may have planned to do so,' said Emma in a dry tone, 'before she met me, but once having seen me she very quickly changed her mind.'

Sam raised his brows but forbore to comment. 'Well,' he said, 'then it seems my father's anxieties are well founded. But he hopes – he very strongly hopes – that if his sermons can find a publisher, the moneys arising from that may help to support you two after he is gone.'

Emma and Elizabeth exchanged glances. In this swift eye contact their entire lack of faith in such a providential outcome was expressed.

'But still,' said Elizabeth, 'anything that gives such hope and comfort to our father in his last months must be accounted a blessing.'

'I only wish,' fretted Sam, 'that *I* could provide an establishment for you girls later on. If I had married Mary – but – two ill-furnished rooms over a funeral parlour in Guildford High Street! It is not to be thought of.'

'Never mind it, dear Sam! One day you will be Lord Watson of Guildford, Surgeon in Ordinary, or Extraordinary, to His Majesty. Then both Liza and I will keep house for you, and usher in your patients, and make your tea, wearing aprons of silk.'

Shortly after this conversation Sam took his departure, for he had a two-hour ride back to Guildford. He bade an affectionate farewell to both sisters and his father, and urged Elizabeth to send for him at any time without the slightest hesitation if she had any anxiety about Mr Watson.

'And, Sam,' said Elizabeth with a quivering lip, 'try – *try* not to repine. Try to put Miss Edwards completely out of your thoughts. It is by far the best – the *only* – way, I *assure* you.'

'And you should know all about that – hmn?' He gave her a rueful, kindly smile, and swung himself into the saddle.

'Sam is by far the best of the whole family,' sighed Elizabeth, as the sisters stood watching him ride down the hill. 'And he has the hardest lot of all, I sometimes think.'

Emma was not entirely inclined to agree with the latter sentiment.

'He works very hard, true; but, at least, he is following his chosen profession. He must have that thought to console him, if he is treated in a slighting way by those who should esteem him. And matters will not always be so. He is able to use his talents. He is so clever, and applies himself to his career with so much energy, that I am *sure* he will rise high in it.'

'Dear, dear Sam! Indeed I hope so!'

'Here is a letter to you from Ireland, Emma!' cried Elizabeth a few days later, after the post boy had splashed up the lane on his muddy pony. 'Perhaps Aunt O'Brien has changed her mind, and now wishes to request your company after all.'

For one of the things that Sam had said, privily, to Elizabeth during his visit, while Emma sat upstairs with her father, had been, 'In my opinion, Eliza, by far the best thing for Emma, after my father's death, would be for Aunt Maria to invite her back again, even if there are to be no expectations of an inheritance in that quarter. With our aunt, Emma must surely stand a better chance of making a respectable match. For Aunt O'Brien is – or was – known as a lady of fortune and intelligence, such as will always gather round her a superior set of friends. Whereas I won't deny to you, Eliza, that Robert and Jane appear to have conceived quite a strong dislike to poor Emma. Why this should be I won't pretend to understand; to me she appears a most amiable, taking little thing, good-natured, and not at all lacking in sense and wit. But it seems unlikely that they will make any push to help her. Robert told me that Jane found her overweening and rude and much too set up in her own esteem.'

'What nonsense!' cried Elizabeth indignantly. 'Why, she is the dearest girl in the world, and was *perfectly* civil to them, particularly to Jane, when they were here, I am positive. But the truth is, Sam, she is far too well-bred for Jane, whose own manners do not stand the comparison. And Robert, of course, never does anything but echo Jane's opinion.'

'Well,' said Sam, 'all I can say is I do not think she would have a happy time of it if she were obliged to live with Robert and Jane in Croydon. And I cannot like their friends . . . Perhaps Emma might do better with Penelope and her old doctor? By the bye, I shall certainly go to see him as soon as they are returned into this country; I am wondering if he might be able to put me in the way of some better connections.'

'Oh, Sam, yes indeed, what an excellent notion! Yes, yes, you must certainly do that. Penelope also would be glad, no doubt, to see her brother more advanced in his profession. But, as regards Emma, do you think that she and Penelope would really settle well together? I very much doubt it. They are so different: Emma perfectly candid and forthright in her dealings, while Penelope is so devious – I hesitate to use the word treacherous – but I must confess to you, Sam, I am not thoroughly easy in my mind about her return to this neighbourhood . . .'

'I wish with all my heart,' cried Sam, 'that I could provide a home for you and Emma. Poor Eliza! You make no claim for yourself, but I know how you must feel at the prospect of soon being obliged to quit this home which by your hard work and devotion you have made into such a pleasant haven – and I cannot imagine that *you* look forward with pleasure to life either with Jane or Penelope.'

Elizabeth's silent shake of the head and swimming eyes told him only too plainly how little she relished either alternative.

He clasped her hand with a strong, affectionate pressure, and said no more.

So it was with the most eager interest and concern that, some days afterward, Elizabeth handed her sister the letter from Ireland, and waited to hear its contents, which Emma proceeded to read aloud, making her way with some trouble through the cramped and crossed lines.

My dearest Neice,

I have but just received yr letter written in October. Alas! I have all too much reason to believe that Missives directed to me frequently go astray or fail of delivery. Those who should be solicitous for my Comfort are not within the house, or do not care, and oh! how many times, how many many times do I lament the loss of my kind, sweet-tempered, thoughtful, obliging little Neice and her ever-welcome attentions and ever-loving ways! Here I am surrounded by gross and ignorant Rustics, who do

not care whether I live or die, and often leave me for
Hours at a time unattended and solitary.

My husband Capt O'Brien has not yet fulfilled his
promise of taking me to his own house, Carahoy in
County Cork; indeed at times I begin to wonder
whether such a house really exists. When I
mentioned it to my brother-in-law, Mr Fergus
O'Brien, he burst into a loud, rude laugh and told
me 'the place was little better than a ruin, I was far
better off where I am' – which filled me, as you may
imagine, with the liveliest Apprehensions. At present
we still reside with Mr Fergus in his house, Castle
Knocka. Castle! *It is liker to a Tenement than a
castle.* Heaven only knows how many indigent
families scramble about in its basement quarters,
and my brother-in-law's household is most
indifferently governed by a stout Slut named Mrs
Hegarty whose manifold functions I dare only guess
at. She slops about Barefoot with a great hank of
black hair hanging down her back and behaves to me
with the greatest Incivility.

Oh, my dear Emma, how often, how very often,
do I long to be back with you in our snug quarters
in the Foregate! How safe, how happy and content
we were, visiting the Circulating Library, taking
coffee at Oates's, meeting our acquaintance in the
Abbey precincts. I have no acquaintance or callers
here, save Father Maloney, who goes a-hunting with
my husband and brother-in-law five days a week –
and, to be sure, some very unruly hogs who invade
the lower floors at the slightest opportunity.

*I do not know how long my Health will survive
this existence of incessant rain, cold rooms, vile food
served in Squalid conditions, and Boorish neglect.
And my husband less charming than he was used to
be, not so kind as he was – but on that score I must
not let my pen run away with me. My Lips are
sealed.*

*Do not write to me at this address, however,
dearest Emma, for Captain O'Brien proposes next
week to remove to the City of Dublin, where we are
to attend the races. My hopes of more comfortable
circumstances there are counterbalanced by an acute
dread that my husband will gamble away immense
sums on betting and Hazard, as he did when we
passed through that City on our way hither.*

*I will write again when I can give you some
reliable Direction in Dublin –*

> *Your afflicted Aunt*

The two sisters stared at each other in consternation
when Emma had finished reading.

'Oh, *poor* Aunt Maria!' whispered Elizabeth. 'I recall
you had said, from the tone of her earlier communications,
that you feared she was beginning to repent of her rashness, that she was not as happy as she expected to be
– but I had not thought – never anticipated – anything so
bad as this . . .'

'I feel so helpless – so wholly unable to do anything.'

Emma stared at the blotted black scrawl of her aunt's
writing as if it might yield some clue to her whereabouts.
'By this time she will doubtless be in Dublin – but who

69

knows at what address? And I have no money – I could not travel to Ireland – and if I could, where should I look for her? And if I found her, what assistance could I render? What could I do? She is married to this wretched man. Oh, if only we had some sensible male person to help and counsel us – if only Robert were other than what he is . . .'

'Or if we could tell my father – but we must not do that,' agreed Elizabeth. 'For it would distress him so terribly in his enfeebled state – his only sister – she that was used to be so comfortable and lively – reduced to such a sad and anxious pass – oh, what a dreadful alteration in her life.'

The two sisters were silent, thinking of their poor aunt with dismay and deep anxiety.

'I do not know how you can be so convinced, Elizabeth,' burst out Emma presently, 'that marriage is a woman's best hope. When its chances are so hazardous! I had far rather be an old maid than make such a terrible error as that of my aunt.'

'But,' said Elizabeth, 'that is because you have not yet been in love, Emma. When love enters, judgement flies out of the window. And, after all, poor Aunt Maria has made only *one* such mistake; her first choice was both prudent and well rewarded.'

'But I am better informed than you,' said Emma, 'and I can tell you, for my aunt told me, that Uncle Turner was not her first choice. She had been courted by a young naval lieutenant, with whom she was very much in love, but her parents would not permit the match until he was more advanced in his profession. And that was never to be, poor dear, for he met his death in the battle of Sangre

Grande, and so she was persuaded by Grandfather and Grandmamma to accept Uncle Turner. Who, it must be said, made her a most kindly and solicitous husband, and left her a large fortune.'

'Which she is now in process of losing to this wretch,' sighed Elizabeth. 'Well, her story appears to show that such decisions are best left to parents.'

'What if there are no parents to consult?'

'Some older friend . . .' said Elizabeth hesitantly. 'Some person of judgement and repute – a clergyman, perhaps, one such as Mr Howard. I would certainly be prepared to take *his* advice on such a question . . .'

Would you, Elizabeth? Even though he appears to be on the point of making a somewhat ill-advised step himself? Emma was on the point of asking this question, but just then James led round the pony and chair, for Elizabeth had been persuaded to take one of her rare excursions into Dorking to visit the milliner for new laces and ribbons, to buy an ounce of gum tragacanth from the pharmacy, and to pay a call on her friend Mary Edwards. The unstated object of the last visit being to discover, if possible, the true situation regarding the legacy from the rich uncle in Plymouth, Lord Osborne's intentions, Miss Edwards's wishes, and poor Sam's chances.

'Do not concern yourself about our father,' Emma said, kissing her sister goodbye. 'I will put my head around his door every fifteen minutes. And will remain in the room with him if he desires company. Go! Take a holiday, you deserve one. Pass a pleasant hour with Miss Edwards, and say everything that is proper from me to her and her parents. Do not scold her if she truly prefers Lord Osborne to Sam; between ourselves I thought Mary Edwards a dull girl and I suspect, as regards intellect, that she and Lord Osborne are more of a match than she would be with our dear clever brother.'

'Oh, Emma!' expostulated her sister, half sighing, half laughing, as she seated herself in the ancient pony-chair and picked up the reins, 'you have such a clear-headed way of putting things.'

'Do not forget the gum tragacanth!' Emma called after her, as she set out down the lane.

Across the lane from the parsonage at Stanton was a tolerably large duck-pond set about with willows and alder-bushes. Elizabeth maintained a flock of ducks on this pond, and it was her agreeable custom, as the afternoon closed in, to regale these birds with a basket of crusts and potato-peelings from the kitchen.

Emma, having first ascertained that her father had fallen into a gentle doze, as was his habit, these days, more and more often, strolled across to the pond with the basket of scraps and watched in amused pleasure as the ducks, recognizing the basket if not the benefactor, came coursing over the water like so many brown-and-white arrow-heads, quacking and gobbling as they came, leaving a trail of intersecting ripples across the surface of the pond behind them. She flung them their food in handfuls; then, as the evening was a mild one, more like spring than winter, she sat on a bench at the top of the bank to enjoy the spectacle of their feast, as well as the sunset, which, that day, was a particularly fine one, overspreading half the sky with pure golden light.

But soon, eclipsing Emma's peaceful mood as swiftly

as a thunderstorm, came the thought of her aunt Maria, forlorn and wretched among uncaring strangers in a comfortless place – that kind companion, infallible source of solace and sympathy, who had taken the part of her lost mother and grown, by stages, to be mentor, confidante, social example, and friendly comrade. It had been Aunt Maria, for instance, who condoled with Emma over the sudden defection of Mr Windrush. This young man, having commenced what appeared to be a sincere and serious courtship, had completely changed his manner after the announcement of Mrs Turner's approaching nuptials to Captain O'Brien, had vanished clean away and never called again at the little house in the Foregate.

'My love,' cried Mrs Turner, 'if his object had been only the fortune he hoped would pass from me to you, he is not worth a moment's heartache, and you must endeavour to forget him as quickly as you possibly can. Indeed, my dearest Emma, I am very sorry that your prospects may seem in some eyes to be diminished by my marriage to Captain O'Brien, but I hope still to be able to leave you a competence, in the course of time. And I know – for there is such confidence between us – that you will understand the necessity for a husband's interests to come first.'

'Of course, my dearest aunt! I never for one moment imagined that it would be otherwise!' Emma had assured Mrs Turner, and with complete sincerity. Her nature was calm and prudent, and after her uncle's death she had looked ahead with practical realism, and felt it highly probable that her aunt, still handsome, lively, fond of society, kind-hearted, and, above all, possessed of a more than passable fortune, would be provided with plenty of opportunities to remarry. And so, indeed, it had proved.

'If only she had not chosen Captain O'Brien!'

Although smiling, agreeable, and filled with Irish charm, the captain had entirely failed to beguile the observant, unimpressible niece of the lady he was pursuing so whole-heartedly. And, for his part, Captain O'Brien soon developed quite a strong antipathy to Emma Watson, and made it plain from the start that her presence would not be acceptable to him in his married ménage. Aunt Maria was grieved at this, but compliant. 'My dear, we must learn to submit to the wishes of our husbands and masters. I always did so with your dear uncle, and in consequence was granted twenty-two years of perfect married happiness and security. And I sincerely hope it may some day be the same for you, my dearest Emma.'

And for you also, my dearest aunt, Emma had thought; but her doubts, her apprehensions had, nevertheless, been deep, and now, it seemed, well founded. Too late, she berated herself bitterly for not having made more effort to hint or suggest a warning; to urge delay, at least, until Captain O'Brien's nature had more fully revealed itself. Yet, how could I, indeed? she thought. It was not my part to do so. Young, subordinate, lacking in worldly experience, and having been the recipient of so many benefits and favours, I was in no position to urge greater caution; it would have seemed officious, intrusive, impertinent. And highly self-interested, also.

None of which reasoning helped to allay the misery that Emma now felt at her complete inability to be of any assistance. Or even to send off a letter of loving solicitude to her aunt.

Even Elizabeth, sympathetic and dismayed as she had been, could not enter fully into her sister's deep distress; Elizabeth had not lived with Aunt Maria for fourteen years, had not been her daily associate, participated in all her activities, shared her sincere mourning at the death of Mr Turner.

Oh, Emma thought, if only there were somebody to whom I could turn for advice! Even Sam – honest, sweet-tempered fellow as he is – would probably be of the opinion that Aunt Maria has made her bed and must lie on it, that she has only herself to thank—

Mr Howard, riding up the lane on his grey cob, had his first view of Emma in profile, as she sat in seeming idleness on the bench near the water, with her hands clasped in her lap, the empty basket at her feet.

Only when he came closer did he observe the tears coursing continuously down her cheeks. *She* did not observe him at all, had not heard his approach, for the clamour of the ducks, fighting over crusts, had drowned the thud of his horse's hoofs on the grassy track.

He hesitated, hardly knowing whether to intrude on her trouble, or to leave her undisturbed. But the evening, now that the sun had set, was growing chilly . . .

His problem was solved by the grey horse, which snorted at the squabbling brood. Emma turned and for the first time became aware of the visitor.

'Oh – Mr Howard – I never heard you – you must forgive me . . .'

She gave him a small half-smile, making no attempt to conceal the tears which glazed her cheeks. She looked,

Howard thought, like the mask of Tragedy, with wet cheeks, parted lips, and eyes that looked past him into some far-off unhappy distance.

Deeply disturbed, he left his horse and came to her side.

'Miss Emma! Is it – can it be – your father? May I help – do anything?'

She shook her head and, pulling out a handkerchief, unaffectedly wiped her cheeks.

'Thank you – no – no. My father is no worse, thank heaven. He is asleep.'

'Then what – ? I do not wish to intrude, if it is a private matter – but to find you in such distress . . .'

'Oh – thank you. You are very kind.'

There were long pauses between her words, as she struggled to achieve command of her voice. But on the next sentence it quivered and broke again. 'It is my unfortunate aunt – Aunt Maria – I have had such a wretched, wretched letter from her.'

Here Emma gave way altogether and for a few minutes covered her face with her hands, crying uncontrollably. 'My poor aunt –' she gasped again. 'It is the feeling – the knowledge – that there is nothing – *nothing* – I can do for her – not even knowing where she *is* – and I dare not inform my father – he would be so horrified – so utterly cast down . . .'

'Dear Miss Emma, let me lead you into the house. A glass of wine – ? Perhaps your sister –'

'No – no – Elizabeth is gone into town. And I am better here, in the fresh air.'

'But it grows cold.'

'I shall be quite well in a moment. I am – I am very

much obliged to you for your sympathy, sir.' And she added, in a forlorn attempt to restore matters to a normal basis: 'Will you not walk into the house yourself, and see my father? You are too old a friend to need announcing . . .'

'In a moment,' he said. 'Indeed it was Mr Watson I came to see. Purvis and I have been putting our heads together – as a matter of fact I expect Purvis here presently. But, Miss Emma, I cannot leave you by yourself in such trouble. It is my duty as a clergyman – and, of course, my sincere wish – to help you. Advise you. Can you not tell me what troubles you so? What has happened to your aunt?'

And he sat down beside her on the bench.

Emma frowned, shifting away from him slightly.

Her first feeling, at the sound of his voice, had been simple relief and joy. Here was, of all others, the person she would have chosen to confide in. But as a friend, not as a priest. And, as a friend, it seemed, he was debarred from approaching her. Lady Osborne's proprietorial jealousy would soon poison any such relationship. Friendship was not offered. 'It is my *duty* to help you,' he had said.

I don't want your duty, Emma thought. Your duty is no use to me.

She could not deny, however, that his mere presence beside her on the bench was some comfort, some distraction.

And presently, telling herself that it would be foolish to refuse help and counsel when it was offered, she took out Mrs O'Brien's letter and showed it to Mr Howard.

He read it slowly, in silence, compressing his lips. Then he handed it back to her.

'My poor child,' he said. 'I do feel for you most sincerely.

The fact that your aunt has only herself to blame for her predicament can be no alleviation to *your* distress about her. But it must be borne in mind. Also, ladies often take these matters too seriously. She may exaggerate. Let us hope that matters are not as bad as she describes.'

Why should we hope so? thought Emma. I see no justification for such an optimistic outlook.

She said coldly, 'My aunt is not given to exaggeration. Over and over again, I have known her to make light of difficulties and remain cheerful through troubles.'

'Well! Well! Such new relationships often settle down very happily after a period. The pair have not, after all, been married very long. Adjustments may need to be made. And doubtless will be made.'

On whose side? thought Emma. I know more about married relationships than you do, my good sir. I have lived with a married pair for fourteen years. You have not.

'I *never* liked that man!' she burst out. 'I always thought him insincere – distrusted his grand tales of high living in Ireland. If only I could have found some means to undeceive my aunt – caution her – prevent her taking such a step—'

He was shocked. 'My dear Miss Emma! It was by no means your place to do such a thing. A young person! And your aunt's protegee. Putting yourself forward – no, no. That would have been most improper.'

'But if only I could have persuaded some older person to give her a word of warning . . .'

Somebody such as yourself, she was on the point of saying, but then doubted if he would have accepted the commission. His next words seemed to prove this.

'Such warnings are seldom heeded,' he said. 'Younger folk, of course, are obliged to take the advice of their older friends, but a woman of your aunt's age and experience must be assumed to know her own mind, permitted to commit her own follies. Perhaps as an example to the rest of us! So, people learn life's harsh lessons. All we can do is pray for her; and that I will most certainly do.'

'Thank you,' said Emma in a choked voice.

As a comforter, he was falling far short of her ideal. All that he had said so far seemed to her mechanical, delivered by rote, shaped on a formal, accustomed pattern. It had no value for her. But talking to him for this length of time had at least eased her heart of its load of uncommunicated woe; she felt a little calmer and more in control of herself. She stood up, putting away Aunt Maria's letter.

'One practical measure I can take, however,' said Mr Howard, standing up likewise, 'is to write to a friend of mine, Charles Montagu, who is rector of a Protestant church in Dublin. We clergy, as you know, often hear of people's comings and goings; an Englishwoman newly married to a Captain O'Brien might find her way to his church, or he might hear of her through a colleague; it is not at all improbable that I may procure news of her.'

'Can you do that, sir?' Emma's face lit up. 'Oh, I should be so very grateful! Just to know where she is – so that I may write to her – would ease my mind so much.'

'Dear Miss Emma, I fear that you are permitting your sensibility to run away with you and lead you into gothick fancies. Depend upon it, your aunt will be found to be quite happy and comfortable, respectably established in

Dublin. I daresay you will soon hear from her again in a more cheerful vein.'

'I just wish she were *here*,' sighed Emma miserably. 'Here *now*, with me, looking at this beautiful sunset.'

'It is quite particularly magnificent, is it not?' agreed Mr Howard, much relieved at being able to turn to another, more agreeable topic. His eyes rested on Emma's face, he began to speak, but then evidently changed his mind. After a moment, however, he said, 'Dear Miss Emma – you know – we *can* make sunsets for ourselves. The world need never be entirely grey for us.'

At that moment the expression on his face was so eager and pleading that she might have asked him to explain himself more distinctly, when a voice hailed them from the lane.

'Good day!'

'Ha! Here comes Purvis,' Mr Howard said hastily. 'I believe you have not met him yet, Miss Emma? Allow me to introduce you.'

Emma received a strong impression that he felt their interview was most fortunately brought to a conclusion. She picked up her basket and walked composedly into the lane.

Mr Edward Purvis was not at all handsome, but he had a sensible, benevolent face and a kindly, cordial manner, especially when he learned that he was meeting the youngest Miss Watson.

'I see a great look of your father in you, Miss Emma,' he remarked.

Emma, showing the two clergymen up to her father's chamber – after first making sure that he was awake –

thought how unspeakably sad, how unfair it was that this solid, excellent man had been beguiled away from Elizabeth by the stratagems of Penelope. I shall never, never trust Penelope, she thought. I can see that this Purvis would have made just the husband for Elizabeth – good-natured, cheerful, full of energy, spirit, and sound sense. What a waste! What a dreadful waste!

The two gentlemen visitors remained with Mr Watson for three-quarters of an hour. Emma left them alone together. Their purpose was to make a selection of his sermons to offer to a publisher; but Mr Watson would permit them to take only the ones which Emma had recently read to him. The others, he said, must wait until they, too, had been through that process. 'Emma reads so well,' he remarked fondly, 'that I can very readily perceive all their merits and demerits, and so speedily reach an estimate as to which are worth preserving.'

'Miss Emma is a most valuable member of your household,' said Mr Howard.

Mr Purvis said nothing. But he sighed.

Emma, out in the stable-yard, fetching a basket of wood for the fire, discovered her sister, back from the excursion to Dorking, quietly leading the pony to its stall.

'Elizabeth! Back so soon? How did you fare? I want to hear all your story. But first – you will have seen their horses – Mr Howard and Mr Purvis are here, upstairs, with our father, talking about sermons.'

Elizabeth turned perfectly white. She sat down abruptly on the edge of a corn-bin.

'Mr Purvis! Oh, *no*! Then I cannot go indoors. I cannot – *cannot* meet him. Not for anything in the world.'

Emma was smitten to the heart. I never, no, absolutely never felt anything to that degree about Mr Windrush, she thought. It was my vanity that was affected, never my feelings.

'Walk into the orchard,' she suggested gently. 'They will not be here above ten minutes longer, I daresay; Mr Howard said that he did not wish to tire my father. I will come and call you when they are gone.'

Indeed, as Emma made her way into the house by the back door, she heard the gentlemen descending the stair.

Mr Purvis had glanced out of the landing window.

'Do the young ladies have their aunt staying with them?' Emma heard him ask Howard in a tone of surprise. 'I thought I saw her in the stable-yard.'

'No, that must have been the older Miss Watson that you saw – their aunt is in Dublin; indeed Miss Emma is somewhat concerned about her aunt –' Mr Howard was heard to reply, but Purvis did not heed the latter part of his remark.

'*That* was Miss *Elizabeth*? But she is so changed! She looks so much older. I would never have known her –'

Downstairs, the two men said a friendly goodbye to Emma, and Mr Howard patted a fat package wrapped up in brown paper.

'I have some of your father's works safe here, Miss Emma, and shall take the very greatest care of them, I promise you. And shall call for more as you pursue your excellent programme of reading them aloud to him. I am in good hopes that there may be a most successful outcome to this scheme. And,' he added in a lower tone, 'I will not forget my promise about Mrs O'Brien. I will write to my friend Montagu tonight.'

'Thank you, sir. I am obliged to you,' Emma answered him rather shortly.

As she watched the two men ride away down the lane, her heart was full of anger. Against whom this anger might be directed, she would have found it hard to specify. It is all very fine for *them*, she thought rather confusedly, to come here and perform their kind deed; *they* are not going to be turned out of their homes, *they* are not subject to the whims of husbands who spend their money and behave unkindly; *they* are not arbitrarily deprived of their assured place and future.

But then she sighed, remembering Sam had told her that Mr Purvis had an ailing wife and a miserably small income to support her on; that Mr Howard was in some way committed to Lady Osborne, which situation did not seem to put him in very cheerful spirits. He is only happy when he is with his sister and nephews, Emma thought. And it is certainly amiable of the pair to take so much time and trouble over my father's writings, when they cannot really have very high expectations of the outcome.

She walked out to the orchard, and called, 'Elizabeth! Elizabeth! They are gone. You may safely come in! And did you remember to buy the gum tragacanth?'

4

Washed, rinsed with rosemary, and anointed with all the care that Emma's eager affection could achieve, employing a mixture of gum tragacanth, almond essence, olive oil, rosewater, and old rum, Elizabeth's crown of hair began, after some days, to display a most gratifying improvement, especially when the treatment was combined with an application of brandy to the scalp three times a week. The hair began to show a far thicker, more glossy, and luxuriant aspect. This had the effect of making Elizabeth look younger, and the confidence given her by awareness of the change added an extra cheerfulness and glow to her whole manner and appearance.

'If only we had some of my aunt's Milk of Roses, which she declared worked wonders for the complexion,' sighed Emma, studying her sister's undeniably weather-beaten cheeks. 'But for that you need gallons of rose-water, and benzoin, and oil of almonds.'

'The people of Dorking are accustomed to my complexion,' Elizabeth pointed out calmly.

'That is why we want to surprise them.'

Emma had to content herself with rubbing lemon peel twice daily on her sister's face.

'You have a duty to yourself as well as to the other members of the family,' she scolded. 'And I wish never to see you wear that terrible old cap again, which causes you to look like a washer-woman. Give it to old Nanny for a duster.'

The next Dorking Assembly was now little more than two weeks away, and Emma had resolved that her sister should, for once, forget the cares and anxieties of the parsonage, above all forget her heartache over Purvis, and spend a thoroughly enjoyable evening, if possible dancing every dance. Elizabeth was an excellent dancer, graceful and light-footed, and in younger days dancing had been her favourite pastime.

'If only she had a new gown!' lamented Emma to Mrs Blake. With this lady she had, by degrees, struck up a most comfortable friendship. They frequently took their walks together in Osborne Park, with the children, when the weather was favourable, and, when it was adverse, sat together, sewed, and mended the children's clothes in Mrs Blake's parlour.

Though invariably invited, Elizabeth could seldom be persuaded to make one on these occasions: 'She was not so fond of walking as Emma – had too much to occupy her at home – she had not Emma's easy way with the children – she was certain that Emma and Mrs Blake must have a thousand things to talk about together, books, poetry, music, history, painting, on all of which topics she was wholly ignorant – when she did have a little free time, preferred to pass it usefully in her garden – did not like to leave their father too long unattended . . .' In short, she could not be enticed into the park or into Wickstead Cottage.

Whereas, for her part, Emma did not deny to herself

that she preferred, if it was possible, to escape from the parsonage on those days when Mr Howard might be expected to come and sit with Mr Watson. For some reason she was no longer comfortable in Mr Howard's company, indeed felt thoroughly uneasy with him; she could not have explained precisely why, but so it was. The single brief encounter with Lady Osborne had implanted most forcibly the suggestion that Mr Howard was not his own man, but was bound in duty to his benefactress. In consequence of which, Emma had rather be elsewhere when he visited the house.

Frequently, after one of these calls, Mr Watson would remark in his mild voice, 'Howard was asking after you, Emma. He told me he has not seen you these two-and-a-half weeks. He said, I think, that he was sorry to miss you.' And Emma always replied, 'Mr Howard does not come to see me, Papa; it is your company and conversation that bring him here, that and the meritorious wish to introduce your sermons to a wider audience.'

'Well, well! It may be so.'

When Emma lamented her sister's lack of a new gown to her friend Mrs Blake, the latter said at once: 'If your sister would not be offended, I have some dark-blue Persian silk. I bought it for an Assembly in Portsmouth a year ago, but then my husband was ordered off to sea at two days' notice, and I never made use of it. That, with a piece of black gauze, I think, by an afternoon's contrivance, we might very readily convert into an evening cloak for her – I have been so thrown about the world, into so many naval lodgings, that I am at least tolerably handy with my needle at creating an *appearance* of fashion –'

'Oh, Mrs Blake! That would *transform* Elizabeth's old blue muslin!'

The afternoon's contrivance was readily achieved, and the cloak created. Elizabeth, tall and slender, with her crown of shining hair, and the new cloak to veil the deficiencies of her old muslin gown, was pronounced to be both elegant and striking.

'But indeed I do not know why you should be taking all these pains about *me*,' she protested, over and over.

'Because you work so hard for others and your life is so lacking in frolic,' and may become much worse, very soon, Emma thought to herself. 'Compare your situation with all those indulged and petted years I spent in the house of Aunt Maria.'

'Oh, poor Aunt Maria. I wish so much that Mr Howard's friend might send news of her.'

Sadly, so far, Mr Howard's friend had nothing to report.

Four days before the Dorking Assembly, Emma walked down to Wickstead Cottage intending to take an airing in the park with Mrs Blake and the children. The arrangement had been made, in a conditional manner, two days earlier, depending upon the state of the weather and the health of the younger children, who had coughs; and, in fact, when Emma arrived at the appointed time she discovered that Mrs Blake thought it too cold for George, Frank and little Sophie to venture out; there was a sharp white frost, the puddles were iced over, hard as stone, and the farther reaches of Osborne Park were veiled in mist.

'Indeed, to be honest, I hardly expected you, Miss Emma; but you are an intrepid walker, I know. Meanwhile

Charles is already gone out into the park with Miss Osborne; however you may very easily catch them up.'

'Miss Osborne!' Emma felt considerable surprise at hearing that one of the castle ladies had been so obliging.

Mrs Blake explained. 'Miss Carr, the lady who lives with them, is laid up with a badly swollen chilblain. So Miss Osborne, who dislikes to be alone, wanted a companion; and of course Charles was wild to go with her, for he admires her above everything in the world. He looks on her as some kind of fairy queen. But do you step along after them, Miss Emma, for they will not have gone very far or fast; they took the bilbo-cups and ball with them (somewhat against my wishes, I may say, for Miss Osborne is such a scatter-brain that they are sure to lose the ball and then my brother will give me a fine scold; but it is impossible to refuse her).'

'But they will not want me,' objected Emma. 'Little Charles will be entirely happy with his grand companion. And I am very sure that Miss Osborne is not interested in *my* company.'

'Quite the contrary, there you are wrong, my dear; she has several times expressed an interest in making your acquaintance. Ever since she saw you at the last Assembly she considers you look most delightfully interesting. It is her mother who – as you must be aware—' Mrs Blake paused, delicately, 'her mother who has reasons for feelings of – perhaps jealousy, animosity – though *perfectly* unfounded, I am sure.'

Deeply embarrassed, Emma stammered some disjointed reply, in which the name of Mr Howard might be heard among wishes not to cause offence – or presume to imagine – or give rise to any unfounded, ungrounded suppositions –

Mrs Blake smiled, a little sadly.

'My brother is the dearest man in the world,' she said. 'And – and he has a most rigid, unbending sense of honour, the power of which I could not wish to be otherwise than it is. But this means, I know, that he considers himself contracted – he is under an obligation – I am not certain if the lady in question considers herself equally committed, but she makes it plain enough that *he* is to be regarded as engaged. He is not at liberty to allow his fancy to wander or to contract other ties of any kind. And he must at all times be most carefully guarded in his behaviour. In short – well, I need not particularize; I can see that you, with your innate good sense, have perfectly grasped the situation and are taking practical measures to avoid seeing too much of my brother. Men, in these sorts of matters, are often amazingly blind to their own interest. And other people's, too,' she added thoughtfully. 'I will not conceal from you, my dear Miss Emma, that I cannot whole-heartedly rejoice over this state of affairs; Lady Osborne is charming, cultivated, most comfortably situated, and – if events progress as they seem likely to – must provide my brother with a foothold in realms of society which would otherwise remain quite beyond his reach; but – but – but –'

'You are not certain he will be happy with her,' said Emma bluntly.

'My brother Adam is so sweet-tempered that he will be sure to make the very best of any situation,' said Mrs Blake, sighing. 'But, no, I must confess that I would be hugely relieved if some honourable means would present itself through which he could be freed from this connection. But I see none. And he is by far too scrupulous even to consider such a possibility.'

'I perfectly understand you,' said Emma. 'And I only wish I could talk to Lady Osborne and convince her of my wholly harmless intentions.'

'I think that would hardly allay her anxieties,' said Mrs Blake, laughing. 'But now do not let me delay you from your walk any longer, dear Miss Emma; Charles and Miss Osborne took that path over the slope towards the lake.'

Walking briskly along the frozen track, Emma pondered over what had just been said. None of it was news to her; but to have unspoken assumptions, matters that have been permitted to hover in the mind only as half-formed thoughts, suddenly put into plain language, may yet cause considerable shock and distress; it is possible to be ashamed of the almost unexpressed hopes and wishes that, despite all caution, can linger in the heart; one may wish such hopes to remain undefined. Emma made a strong resolve to suppress all such reflections entirely from that moment onwards.

Mr Howard need not suffer any displeasure from Lady Osborne on *my* account, she thought firmly. I shall make it as plain as I possibly can that he means nothing to me. I have no wish to be likened to my sister Penelope, capable of laying claim to any male person, trying to entice away other women's suitors; such odious practices are not for me!

Surmounting the frosty slope, she saw that the pair she sought had not paused beside the lake, but had followed a track which led away to the right, past a miniature grove.

They were walking at a fair speed, and a little dog that accompanied them raced ahead, chasing something that was repeatedly thrown for him.

Emma recalled Charles's often-expressed wish to go to the ice-house, which lay at a distance generally beyond the walking powers of his younger brothers and sister.

I believe that is where they are bound, she thought, and set herself to overtake them, walking forward at a quick pace and looking about her with some disappointment, for this was an area of the park that she had hitherto not visited, but today it was almost entirely veiled from view by the freezing mist.

Miss Osborne, she thought, probably knows the park from childhood, so I daresay there is no danger of their losing their way. Otherwise it might seem only too possible in this thick light.

At last the pair ahead came to a halt, and Emma was able to catch up with them.

'Miss Emma!' cried Charles joyfully. 'Mamma thought that you probably would not take a walk today as it is so cold. So I came out with Miss Osborne. But I am mighty glad to see you! Look, there is the ice-house that I wished you to see.'

Emma smiled at the young lady who stood with Charles, and said, 'Allow me to introduce myself! I am Emma Watson, and you, I believe, are Miss Osborne. Mrs Blake sent me after you with instructions not to let Charles lose the ball.'

'How do you do,' said Miss Osborne. 'I am very happy to make your acquaintance.'

Seen close to, she was a slight girl, of more than average

height but very thin, transparently fair in complexion, like her mother and brother, but without her mother's sparkling eyes and strongly marked brows. Her brilliantly red hair was today concealed under a warm plumed hat. She seemed amiably enough disposed, but rather shy.

'The ball is quite safe, as you see,' she offered after a moment. 'We have been throwing it for Fido. Charles wished to play at bilbo-catch, but my fingers were too cold.'

She had the two wooden bilbo-cups with straight handles in a bag slung over her arm.

'Will you play now, Miss Emma?' said Charles hopefully. 'You are a capital hand at bilbo-catch.'

'In the garden, on a fine day, I thank you, yes!' said Emma, laughing. 'But here, in the mist and frost, I do not think is the right occasion. So this is the famous ice-house that you have told me of so often? I am very glad to see it at last. And it is exactly like a cave out of the Arabian Nights.'

The ice-house was a round-domed building, made of brick, and set into an artificial hill. Trees had been planted around it, which had grown into a grove, so that it presented a mysterious appearance, like a pagan temple or grotto, the more so as thick green moss had spread over the bricks, and dead leaves were plentifully heaped in the low-arched approach passage, which led down a gentle slope to the dark interior.

Fido, Miss Osborne's little terrier dog, seemed roused to great excitement by this tunnel-like passage, and yapped loudly at its mouth, kicking and scratching up the dead leaves, sending them flying in clouds.

'Perhaps badgers have been using it as a house, or rabbits,' suggested Charles.

'Is it not used for ice any longer, then?'

'No, they have dug out another ice-house closer and more convenient to the castle,' said Miss Osborne. 'This place has not been employed since I was a child. Indeed my brothers and I used to call it our bandits' cave.'

'I wish I had been here then!' said Charles with sparkling eyes. 'How deep does it go, Miss Osborne?'

'It is quite round inside, you know, like a brick basin sunk into the ground. I suppose it may be about ten feet deep. In the winter it would be packed full of ice, which they took out in summer for ice puddings.'

'Yes, I know,' said Charles. 'I have seen them taking ice from the new one. I would *dearly* like to go in. Do you think I might?'

He looked with longing at the dark arched passage, which was only three or four feet high.

'No indeed! I am very certain that your mamma would not wish you to,' said Emma, firmly, and Miss Osborne agreed.

'Indeed you must not, Charles. On no account! For one thing, there is no rope now, to pull you out of the cave – and the brick slope inside is sure to be horribly slippery with ice—'

'Rope?' Charles looked perplexed.

'There used to be a young elder tree, it is gone now, growing near the entrance, and my brother Chilton always tied one end of a long rope to it before we went in, so that we had a means of pulling ourselves up out of the bowl. It is quite steep, you see. My brothers used to push

93

me from behind. Sometimes we played that we were miners, going into a gold mine,' Miss Osborne said, and looked suddenly rather wistful.

'I believe that we should turn back,' said Emma. 'Charlie, you are beginning to shiver. It is too cold to stand here talking. Some time when your uncle Adam is with you, and has brought a rope along, you may go into the cave.'

'Oh, please, please, may we not play one game of bilbo? Here is a capital flat place, in front of the cave! Just so as to warm us up!'

'Two catches then, no more,' said Emma firmly; she felt that Charles, disappointed in his evident longing to enter the ice-house, should at least have one of his wishes granted.

Overjoyed, Charles took the bilbo-cups from Miss Osborne and gave one to Emma.

'I shall begin walking back,' announced Miss Osborne hastily. 'It is by far too cold to stand watching. Come, Fido!'

But Fido, seeing the ball tossed back and forth between Charles and Emma, believed their intention was to play with him, and he became wildly excited. He dashed from one to the other, yapping and frisking. He ignored the calls of his mistress, who therefore set off without him.

'We had better stop, Charles,' Emma said panting as she sprang to one side and dexterously caught the ball he had sent her in her wooden cup. 'Fido thinks we are doing this in order to tease him. And Miss Osborne is leaving us behind.'

'Just one more, Miss Emma – oh, botheration!' For Charles, slipping on a patch of frosted grass, accidentally shot the ball off at a tangent, far away from where Emma might possibly have reached it. It fell on the grass, just outside the entrance to the ice-house, and Fido was after it in a flash, hurling himself under the arch and in among the dead leaves.

'Fido! Come back! Come here, sir!'

But Fido did not come back with the ball. And suddenly his yappings became a great deal fainter, as though he had fallen to a considerable distance below the ground.

'Oh, mercy! I am afraid he must have fallen down into the bottom of the ice-house. I had better go in and see what has happened,' said Charles valiantly.

'No, Charles! Wait – wait!'

But Miss Osborne, running back, cried, 'Fido? Where is Fido gone?' so piteously and with such fear in her voice that Emma's protests were overborne, and Charles hastily scrambled under the low brick arch.

'Fido? Where are you? Come here,' they heard him calling, and then there was a thump and a loud wail of surprise.

'Oh help! I had not thought it would be so steep!'

'Oh dear, Charles! Are you down in the bottom?' called Miss Osborne.

'Yes, but I am not at all hurt. There is a whole heap of dead leaves down here. And Fido is quite happy too, Miss Osborne. He thinks it is a great lark.'

'Reach up a hand to me and I will try to pull you out,' said Miss Osborne, and, in her turn, she scrambled under the arch.

'Just a moment, Miss Osborne! Wait!' cried Emma urgently. 'Wait, I beg you – take hold of my hand. Or you may slip in also!' She darted forward and stretched out an arm. Miss Osborne, scrambling down the slope under the arch, did catch at her hand, but then precisely what Emma had feared came to pass. There was a treacherous layer of ice under the dead leaves in the approach tunnel, and Miss Osborne, like Charles and the dog, glissaded down it and so, helplessly, into the deeper brick cavity beyond.

'Oh, no, no!' she shrieked, jerking wildly on Emma's wrist. And then, luckily for Emma but unfortunately for herself, she let go, and fell on top of Charles.

Emma, with a sick sense of dismay, had felt something snap in her wrist when it was jerked so hard; she guessed that damage, perhaps severe, had been done to it.

Doing her best to ignore the pain she knelt by the tunnel entrance and called, 'Miss Osborne! Can you hear me? Are you hurt?'

'No – no,' came back in a moment. 'I am not hurt, and nor is Charles – and Fido is frisking about as if it were all a great joke – but we cannot by any possible means get out of this detestable hole. The brick sides are covered in ice. It is like being inside a glass basin. Do *not you* come any closer, Miss Watson, else you may fall into the trap too. Go for help – run to the castle, it is the closest. Or, if you should see any of the estate men, tell them to come at once with ropes and pull us out.'

'Yes, I will do that,' said Emma. 'I am very sorry not to be able to pull you out myself, but I can see that would be beyond my power. I will go as fast as I can.'

Without mentioning her hurt wrist, she set off in the direction of Osborne Castle, which might be half a mile away. She knew approximately where it lay, across on the other side of the ornamental water, though from here it was invisible in the mist.

'I will make as much haste as I can!' she called again.

Pulling off her glove as she hurried along, she nervously inspected her wrist, which was beginning to swell. The pain it gave her was acute, but she endeavoured to withdraw her mind from that, and to concentrate, instead, on guessing what her reception might be at the castle, and which of the inmates might be at home. Eagerly, she glanced about her in the mist, wishing that some gardener or gamekeeper might make his appearance and prevent her being obliged to enter the great house, but no such person was to be seen. She crossed the arched bridge over the lake (no very simple matter, for it, too, was iced over and slippery) then ascended the long gentle slope which ran up to the castle.

In her wrist the throbbing was now so extreme that it was all she could do not to let out small whimpers of pain while she forced herself to hurry as fast as possible.

The approach to the front of the castle was imposing. An undercroft below a great formal balustrade contained a blocked entrance, doubtless the original main door; now the caller must ascend one of two huge symmetrical sweeping stone stairs which led to an upper level. Seeing no help for it, Emma toiled up the right-hand stair. As she did so she became aware of the scrunch of hoofs from a single horse down below her on the gravel. She paid no heed to the sound, for all her concentration was now focused on her errand, the need to transmit her news to some helpful person, and the really atrocious pain in her left wrist, which throbbed rapidly and began to make her feel queasy and somewhat light-headed.

She traversed a wide stone terrace to the double front doors, beside which there was a bell-pull, but before she could make use of this the door was flung open by a manservant who must, through a flanking window, have seen her approach.

With a gulp of relief she explained her mission.

'Oh, pray – Miss Osborne – and young Master Charles Blake – and the little dog – are all fallen – trapped in the old ice-house – can you quickly send men there with ladders and ropes –'

Behind her now she heard rapid steps on the stone pavement, and Mr Howard's urgent, anxious voice: 'Miss Emma! Whatever is the matter? How comes it that you are here?'

But Emma was beyond speech. The panelled entrance-hall began to sway dizzily in front of her, and with a small pitiful moan she crumpled forward, striking her head a sharp blow, as she fell, on the black-and-white marble tiles of the floor.

When Emma recovered consciousness she stared around her in bewilderment and was, for a moment, under the impression that she must be dreaming. She found herself lying down on a soft couch. This was certainly not, she realized, the low-ceilinged chamber that she shared with Elizabeth at the parsonage. A few feet away she could see the leaping flames of a large fire, and above it a high marble mantel, on which were ranged various objects of sparkling glass and gilded china.

Attempting to raise herself on one elbow, she let out a moan as the movement jarred her wrist.

'A-a-a! Pray do not excite yourself, Miss Watson! Remain quite still for the moment, if you please!'

Perplexed, Emma thought she recognized the tones of Mr Sindell, the apothecary, a helpful, gentlemanlike man, who regularly called at the parsonage whenever Mr Watson required attention.

'Mr Sindell!' she said weakly in relief. 'Where am I? What has happened?'

'Softly, softly, Miss Emma! You dislocated your wrist, but that is no great matter. I have set it, and put a compress on it, and you will be better in two shakes of a lamb's tail. Now that you are awake I will give you a dose to ameliorate the pain. Here, drink this, my child, and then you will soon be as right as rain.'

'Thank you – ugh – it tastes disgusting.'

She drank the nauseous mixture and then leaned back limply against a pile of cushions, beginning slowly to take in the fact that she lay on a sofa in a large and handsome drawing-room. Another fire burned at the far end of the room, where stood, or sat, a small group of persons. One of these now came forward eagerly to demand, 'Is she better, Mr Sindell? Have you made her well again?'

Emma recognized the voice of Miss Osborne. That young lady came and knelt by her, looking into her face.

'Poor, poor Miss Emma! I am so very sorry about your wrist. That must have been my fault – for I remember I gave it a great jerk as I fell – and then, Mr Sindell said, you knocked your head as you fainted away in our hall.'

'So I did,' said Emma, putting up her good hand to

find a large lump on her brow. 'I cannot think how I came to be so stupid. But it is no matter. Pray don't apologize. I shall be quite the thing again directly. But you – did people *soon* arrive to rescue you? And Fido? And Charles?'

'Oh, very soon,' began Miss Osborne, but now the silvery tones of her mother came as an interruption.

'My dear Harriet, you really must not bombard Miss Watson with questions, or she will never be well enough to drive home. Indeed it was a most foolish escapade – most regrettable – but we must be thankful there is no particular harm done; and let it be a lesson to *everybody* concerned never to do it again.' She laughed, a humourless icy tinkle. 'I trust that it will be so!'

'I assure your ladyship, it was the purest accident,' began Emma weakly. 'The little dog ran after the ball, which had rolled down the slope –'

'*Indeed*, Mamma, that was how it came about,' put in Miss Osborne earnestly. 'Then Fido slipped in – for the slope was all icy – and Charles, going after him, slid like-wise –'

'We will say no more about it, Harriet,' said Lady Osborne coldly. 'I do not wish to hear another word on the subject. It was a disgracefully hoydenish escapade. I am surprised at you. As for the boy, he deserves to be sent to bed with no supper.'

'I have no doubt, Lady Osborne, that my sister has already administered some suitable reprimand,' put in Mr Howard's mild voice. Emma could not avoid a slight start at the sound – she had not been aware that he, too, was in the room. But he and the short, light-haired woman whom she knew to be Miss Carr, now joined the group round the sofa.

'How are you now, Miss Emma, are you feeling more the thing?' he asked gently. There was, Emma thought, a certain constraint in his voice.

'Thank you – yes – I am so very sorry to have given everybody this trouble . . .'

Emma had some ado to control her own voice. She began to feel a little ill done by; the accident, after all, had not been her fault, and she had made all speed to fetch help; yet it seemed to her that she was being held to blame for the whole.

'It was a very lucky stroke of fortune that Mr Sindell was in the castle at the time, prescribing for my chilblain,' said Miss Carr consolingly. 'So he was able to examine your wrist at once and take the necessary measures to set it right. And, in a few minutes, as soon as you are feeling a little more gathered together, he has offered to drive you home in his carriage.'

'Oh, yes, thank you!' exclaimed Emma, sitting up rather too quickly, and putting a hand to her brow as the room swung about her. 'I would be so grateful for that. My sister Elizabeth will be most distressed if I am not home by – pray, what time is it?'

'Do not distress yourself, Miss Emma. It is not yet half past three. I am in no hurry,' said Mr Sindell kindly.

But Emma knew that he must be anxious to get on to his other patients. And she herself wished for nothing but to escape from Osborne Castle, where she felt a most unwelcome intruder. It was a piece of good fortune, she thought, that Lord Osborne and his friend Tom Musgrave were not present; their clamour and comments, against the icy atmosphere of Lady Osborne's dislike and disapproval would have made the situation even more uncomfortable.

'I am sure that in a moment I shall be quite well enough to walk to your carriage, Mr Sindell,' she said, attempting to sound firm and matter-of-fact.

'If you were to give the young lady an arm, Sindell,' said Lady Osborne coolly, 'and one of the footmen can assist her on the other side —'

Emma rose rather totteringly to her feet.

Unfortunately just at this juncture Lord Osborne and Tom Musgrave did make their appearance, grumbling loudly to each other about a young dog which had spoiled their shooting by putting up the birds before it ought.

'Hey-day! Here is Miss Watson, I vow and declare!' jovially announced Tom, while Miss Osborne ran to her brother crying, 'Only fancy, Cedric! Such a thing! We have had such an adventure! Little Charles and I fell into the ice-house! And Miss Emma Watson was obliged to go for help! And she has hurt her wrist badly and must ride home in Mr Sindell's carriage.'

'Fell into the *ice-house*?' Lord Osborne repeated wonderingly, scratching his tumbled fair locks. 'Why, how in the world could that be?'

Tom Musgrave, always livelier and quicker to grasp any situation, cried, 'Why, Osborne, we came just in the nick of time. We can be of assistance by carrying the young lady down to the carriage – can we not? I daresay she don't weigh a feather – do you, Miss Emma? Stand aside,

Sindell, we'll whisk her down to the carriage sweep in a brace of shakes.'

A tart old voice from near the other fireplace now recommended that the young lady be allowed to put on her pelisse and hat before going out of doors. 'And try not to be more of a dunderhead than the Almighty created you, grandson! Or you, Tom Musgrave!'

Emma was for the first time made aware that the aged withered lady wrapped in shawls on a sofa by the second fireplace must be the dowager Lady Osborne.

'Let's take a look at you, miss!' snapped the old lady as the two young men bore Emma towards her. 'Yes! You do bear a certain resemblance to your mother. I can see it. She was a woman with a considerable degree of sense. I used to pay heed to what she had to say. But none of the young folk have any sense nowadays. Rattle-pated fools, the lot of them. Doubtless you are the same as the rest.'

'I – I hope not, ma'am,' gasped Emma, as she was borne past. The younger Lady Osborne had remained behind, with an air of cold detachment, beside her daughter, Miss Carr, and Mr Howard. Emma was sorry not to have been given a chance to say goodbye and offer some kind of thanks.

As the two young men – more carefully than she might have expected – lifted her into Mr Sindell's carriage, she said to Lord Osborne, 'Pray, my lord, express my gratitude to your mother and – and say everything that is proper to her for her hospitality.'

Not that it amounted to anything out of the common, she thought privately. All Lady Osborne did was allow me the use of her sofa and permit Mr Sindell to foment my wrist in her drawing-room.

'Oh, to be sure,' said Lord Osborne. 'No matter for that. But I hope you are soon in a better way, Miss Emma! Pity to see you in such poor trig. Come, Musgrave – Sindell wishes us at the devil, I dare say.'

Mr Sindell contented himself with saying, as he drove away, 'I wonder that Lady Osborne did not invite you to pass the night at the castle! If it were not for you, her daughter might have been much longer incarcerated in the ice-house! But she is one of the high ones, Lady Osborne, she takes very little thought for the concerns of those beneath her. I am surprised, though, that Mr Howard did not suggest it to her.'

'I would not have wished to stay overnight in the castle,' said Emma quickly. 'Not for the world! I did not feel at all comfortable there.'

Elizabeth, when her sister was delivered at the parsonage, repeated Mr Sindell's sentiments, but more vigorously.

'My word!' she cried. 'I marvel at Lady Osborne, I do indeed! Why! you saved her daughter from a night in the ice-house – for it might have been hours before anybody went in search of her there, if it were not for you – and all the thanks you receive is to be scolded for hoydenish behaviour. Any other person for fifty miles around would have put you to bed and kept you overnight; anybody else would have given you dinner and nursed you and petted you. And you say that Mr Howard was there? Why did he not speak up and say you was not fit to be moved? I think the worse of him, indeed I do. I have no patience with him!'

'But, Elizabeth, I did not want to stay at the castle. I should have been worried to death about you and my father.'

'The castle folk could have sent a message to us by one of the estate men. Or Mr Sindell.'

'But Lady Osborne is so cold and rebuffing. I am much happier at home. I should have hated above all things to be obliged to pass the night under her roof and have to feel beholden to her.'

'Now,' said Elizabeth sadly, 'we shall never know if they really do have silk sheets on all the beds, and if the gentlemen really eat baked lobster and oyster fritters for breakfast, as Betsey's sister told her.'

5

The following morning brought a visit from Miss Osborne and Miss Carr in the pony-phaeton. It soon became plain to the parsonage sisters that a certain amount of reconsideration and readjustment must have taken place overnight in Osborne Castle; perhaps Mr Howard had delivered a homily on Christian charity to the lady of the manor; or the dowager had intervened; or the intercessions and pleas of Miss Osborne had in the end borne fruit and exerted a mollifying influence; whatever the cause, the visitors delivered a basket of flowers and fruit from the castle succession-houses, and all manner of gracious messages from Lady Osborne herself: 'She hoped that the young lady's wrist was not causing her too much pain or inconvenience, was deeply obliged for the kind service that had been rendered to her daughter, supposed that the injury must prevent Miss Emma Watson from attending the next Assembly at Dorking, therefore regretted the loss of an opportunity of seeing her there, but hoped that on a later occasion this might prove possible, etc. etc.'

Such a signal civility from Lady Osborne must, of course, be reciprocated; the callers were invited into the parsonage and pressed to partake of baked apples and sweet cake, Elizabeth's unvarying provision for morning guests. These refreshments they civilly declined but Miss

Osborne, immediately catching sight of the pianoforte in the parlour, at once inquired which of the parsonage ladies might be the musician?

'It is my sister Emma,' said Elizabeth with eager pride. 'Emma has a voice like a nightingale! Her masters at Shrewsbury could not speak too highly of her talent. She has perfect pitch! And performs on the instrument most beautifully, as well—'

'Only not at present, of course,' Emma said in haste, exhibiting her bandaged wrist. She had no wish to be called on to perform in front of these ladies whose standards of taste and performance, no doubt, far outstripped her own, and felt herself lucky to have so impregnable a defence.

'Oh, Miss Watson! If only you would sing to us!' breathed Miss Osborne with round, admiring eyes. It was plain that she was in the first stages of a hero-worship. 'I should like to hear you above all things! My friend Miss Carr here could play for you – she always accompanies us when we dance – she is never tired of playing – and she could sing duets with you as well. Pray, *pray*, Miss Emma, do give us that pleasure! Do permit us to hear you.'

Emma, cross, and, in truth, fatigued from a bad night and feeling in a low state of health, was obliged to conquer a very strong disinclination to perform; but she could see that Elizabeth was afraid of offending the ladies from the castle. And she herself was anxious to conceal from Elizabeth her own state of slight indisposition lest her sister consider this a reason for not attending the Dorking Assembly. After so many pains had been taken, Emma was determined that Elizabeth should reap the benefit.

Accordingly she made no more difficulties but, ignoring her slight headache and the throbbing in her wrist, complied with Miss Osborne's wish and sang a couple of ballads.

Miss Osborne was in raptures. 'What a miracle of a voice! She had heard nothing better in London – no, not even at Covent Garden. Miss Emma must not hide her light under a bushel. She must come – some evening – very soon – and sing at Osborne Castle – did not Miss Carr agree?'

Emma thanked, and demurred. 'She was very obliged but did not think it would be within her power at present – her father in such an uncertain state of health – not advisable to make evening engagements – later, perhaps, in the spring, and when her sister Penelope had moved into Clissocks—'

This provided a most welcome diversion of interest and topic. News of Dr Harding's purchase of Clissocks had evidently not reached the castle yet – Emma was amused to discover that what had become a common subject of neighbourhood gossip among the village folk apparently took longer to percolate to the upper gentry – and the ladies were all astonishment and eager inquiry.

'So Clissocks was at last to be put into proper repair and occupied by a family? What an excellent thing! Such a handsome, historic old house! Such a pity that it had for so long remained uninhabited. So sad about Sir Meldred and Lady Torridge – the last of an ancient family . . .'

'My grandmother will be particularly interested to hear this news,' Miss Osborne declared, 'for I have heard her many times tell that the Torridges were one of the most respected families of the country. And so your sister and Dr Harding really plan to come and live there?'

'Yes, very soon,' Elizabeth was beginning, when Miss Carr, who had for some time been attempting, by various significant looks, to remind her young companion that the ladies had remained quite long enough for a morning call, at last succeeded in her purpose.

After they had taken their departure, with many friendly professions, Elizabeth gave her younger sister a great scold.

'*Why* did you not wish to sing at Osborne Castle? It would have been such an entry for you among the great ones! Such a fine way of making yourself known.'

'Yes! As a hired performer!' said Emma with curling lip. 'Much obliged, but I prefer to make my entry on the basis of personal friendship, or not at all!'

'Emma! Emma! You have too much pride for your own good.'

'Pride! Yes, I have! I do not choose to be fetched in like a circus animal, as a professional performer. Did you not notice how amazed they were to hear that Penelope and her husband were to occupy Clissocks? And how shocked? They look on us as a lower order of beings. For persons of our degree to aspire to live in such a style is not at all the thing!'

'Oh, fie, what nonsense, Emma! You are imagining far more than is the case. They were surprised, that is all.'

'Very well,' said Emma. 'We shall see, when Penelope and her doctor are moved in, how much recognition they receive from the Osbornes. We shall discover whose estimate lies closer to the truth.'

Elizabeth still found it exceedingly hard to convince

herself that Penelope and Dr Harding would ever really return and move into Clissocks; but the reality of their intentions soon became more apparent when the next day's post brought a letter from Penelope.

'Dr Harding and I decided to extend our wedding journey to Weymouth,' wrote the new Mrs Harding, 'the more reason to do so as, from what we hear of the builders' progress at Clissocks, the workmen are being disgracefully behindhand and dilatory in the business. Pray, my dear Elizabeth, do you step along there and urge them to work faster! We had hoped to be moved in by the time this finds you, but fear there is little chance of that. I certainly cannot consider setting up house without a properly appointed kitchen and a closed stove.'

'Dear me,' remarked Elizabeth, greatly puzzled. 'From where can our sister have acquired such grand notions? We have no closed stove here, nor ever thought of one.'

'Well, let us by all means go and harry the workmen at Clissocks,' said Emma cheerfully. 'I have a great curiosity to see the place again, I must confess. I can recall being taken there once by our mother when I was about five. It seemed to me then like the palace of the Sleeping Beauty.'

Clissocks, the manor house purchased by Penelope and her husband, stood at the foot of a wooded hillside, above a river, about a mile from Stanton Parsonage, in the opposite direction from Osborne Park. It was by far the oldest house in the neighbourhood, very much older than Osborne Castle, parts of it dating back, some historians believed, at least to Saxon times. And the family in occupation, the Torridges, were of comparably ancient lineage, but in the present century had fallen upon hard times, especially the last representative of the line, Sir Meldred Torridge, who, it was said, had gambled away all his inheritance, worth £70,000 a year, at Watier's, and recently threw himself over the cliff at Brighton.

The approach to the house lay along a winding track by the river, with the beech-hung hillside above, and the gleam of water seen through bushes below.

'This is very beautiful,' said Emma, as Elizabeth guided the pony-chair at a pace appropriate to the meanderings of the track, 'but imagine driving along here at night! Or in snowy weather! I wonder that our sister Penelope proposes to establish herself at the far end of such a tortuous approach. Can she really have given it serious thought?'

'I have been asking myself the same question,' said Elizabeth. 'Penelope saw it once, once only, on a fine day in October when the scene was brightened by dead leaves on the ground. But when this hillside is masked by summer foliage, it will be dark – very dark. Our sister is exceedingly apt to make a hasty decision on the basis of a scanty, curtailed judgement – and then, if matters go amiss, as they often do, she refuses to accept the blame, but denounces the nearest person who can be found as scapegoat.'

They drove round a corner and saw before them the house, which was a long, low, rambling structure, most pleasingly situated on a moderate eminence above the water. It was evident that repairs were in hand: sawing and hammering could be heard, workmen trundled wheelbarrows to and fro. Elizabeth, who knew every man, woman, and child in the country for twenty miles around, caught the attention of one such man and asked him if the master builder, Josiah Dawkins, could be located, as she had a message for him.

He nodded and disappeared under an arch, while the mare made her slow way forward into the main entrance-yard of the L-shaped building.

Here they discovered another carriage.

'Hey-day!' said Elizabeth. 'It is the Osborne phaeton! And there, to be sure, is Miss Osborne herself, I do declare, with Mrs Blake.'

As the old mare came to a willing halt, Miss Osborne came to greet them:

'Ha! My dear Miss Watson, I fear you have caught us peeping through the keyhole! I hope that you will forgive us. Grandmamma was *so* curious to know what changes were being made here – even when assured that it was so, she could hardly believe that some intrepid person was really going to restore and live in this ruin of a house.'

Mrs Blake smiled at Emma, and said, 'In addition to which, my brother chances to have visiting him a cousin of ours, Captain Fremantle, a great enthusiast for architectural curiosities, particularly of the Saxon period. Hearing how close we were to Clissocks, he confessed to an overmastering wish to look at the place – especially before many alterations were made, in case, you know, it were to be improved out of all recognition – as sometimes occurs. He has gone round to the back, and is climbing over piles of masonry and inspecting Saxon stonework – in short, dear Miss Watson, you must forgive our outrageous inquisitiveness!'

Elizabeth, a little flustered by this unexpected company,

civilly bade the ladies welcome and invited them to look at whatever they wished; then, seeing the master-builder, she gladly made use of the excuse to walk across the yard and convey Penelope's messages to him. Miss Osborne walked after her, in search of their male companion.

Emma made friendly inquiries of Mrs Blake as to the health of little Charles, expressing the hope that he had suffered no subsequent ill-effects from the adventure in the ice-house.

'No, no, I thank you, my dear Miss Emma, none,' said Mrs Blake. 'Charles remains at home doing extra lessons with my brother as a penance for his rashness; in fact (between you and me) this is just to appease the castle, since we do not see how else he could have conducted himself, and it is no great penalty after all, for he loves his lessons with Adam. He himself suffered no ill-effects; though he is grieved, of course, about little Fido – *very* grieved,' she added in a lower tone, as Miss Osborne moved farther off, to speak to a gentleman who at this moment emerged from under the arch.

'Little Fido?' said Emma, surprised. 'Why? Was he injured? I thought Charles said he was unharmed?'

'That is so, but Lady Osborne was so displeased at the incident that she gave orders for the animal to be done away with.'

Emma was inexpressibly shocked, and could only stare in silence for a moment as she digested this information. Then she asked, in a subdued tone, 'But *why*? I do not understand. The dog was not at fault – the whole thing was an accident – the ball rolled . . .'

'I am afraid,' replied Mrs Blake in the same tone, 'that,

once she has taken this kind of a notion into her head, there can be no reasoning with the lady in question. She is very implacable. But come,' she added in a louder voice, 'Miss Emma, permit me to make Captain Fremantle known to you. Matthew, this is our friend and neighbour, Miss Emma Watson.'

The gentleman stepping forward was not particularly tall, but looked so, because of his extreme thinness. He wore his light brown hair somewhat longer than was customary, and had a long smiling face to match, with a narrow, prominent jaw, a bony nose, and keen hazel-brown eyes under a jutting forehead.

'Miss Emma Watson!' He bowed over her hand. 'Allow me to congratulate you on your sister's acquisition of this most interesting property! I have an idea that Clissocks might have been one of the royal estates of Ceawlin of Wessex, who, as you doubtless know, was Bretwalda of Southern England in the sixth century, conquered the regions as far as the Severn and was one of the first major rulers of this country. *Soke*, you see, from the Old English *sacu* and *socn*, means a right of jurisdiction, so *Clissocks* might well derive from Ceawlin's socage – of course the words *soken* and *sokemanry* came in later under the Danes. Naturally the property might equally have belonged (and very possibly did later) to Caedwalla, who, in the eighth century (as you are probably aware) made himself master of Sussex and the southern Thames basin as far as Kent, and quite eliminated the Jutish element from the Isle of Wight.'

Captain Fremantle's smile at Emma as he delivered this information was so eager and ingenuous that she could not help a similar smile in return.

'Did he indeed do so? That seems a long way for him to have travelled, just to eliminate the Jutes.'

'Upon my word, it was so! Caedwalla in his turn was succeeded by Ine, who issued a number of laws greatly admired by King Alfred; although his influence was, in some degree, curbed by Wihtred of Kent. Unfortunately Ine was followed by Athelbald of Mercia – who was, I am sorry to say, a most discreditable villain.'

'How shocking! I mean, was he so?' said Emma.

Captain Fremantle smiled at her again delightfully, displaying two rows of brilliantly white teeth. His eyes sparkled.

'Athelbald was a most scandalous villain, I assure you! But luckily his sins came home to roost and he was murdered by his own bodyguard, after which his cousin, Offa (of Offa's dyke), soon succeeded in restoring order.'

'I am very glad of that,' observed Emma.

'But the situation of this property here – by the river, you see, very important for transport in those days, when so much of the country was still covered by impenetrable forest – especially the Weald – makes the royal attribution highly probable. There are other possible owners – Cynewulf was another king of the West Saxons, defeated by Offa in 777; or, for that matter, it might be Cwichelm, a previous king who died in 636. Cwichelm defeated the Britons at Beandun, but was himself defeated by Eadwine of Northumbria in 626. (However, he lived to be baptized ten years later.)'

'I am very glad that he did not die in the battle,' said Emma. 'What a great number of kings these West Saxons seem to have had.'

Captain Fremantle gave her another of his delightful smiles.

'And I daresay that you, like most other inhabitants of this land, consider that what took place between 55 BC and 1066 AD is of supremely little importance. But I promise you that, once you turn your attention to that period, you will find it of the most engrossing interest. It has occupied and absorbed my mind during many a long and uneventful sea-voyage. And some that were, if anything, *too* eventful.'

'I think that you should come and make the acquaintance of my father,' said Emma, 'if you are visiting this neighbourhood for an extended period. He, too, has a great respect for King Alfred and dearly likes to read history.'

'I should ask nothing better! I have heard from my cousin of your father's great erudition and keen intelligence; I should esteem it a privilege to meet him. Unfortunately my stay here is likely to be of fairly short duration. But if, during that time —'

Mrs Blake's call interrupted him.

'Come, Miss Osborne; come, Cousin Matthew. I think we have incommoded Miss Watson and Miss Emma for quite long enough; we should be on our way. And Lady Osborne will no doubt be impatient for Miss Osborne's report.'

'Do you think that your sister will really be able to move into the house quite soon, Miss Watson?' eagerly demanded Miss Osborne.

'So Mr Dawkins assures me.'

'But something tells *me* that Lady Osborne will *not* be among those who come to call on Penelope and Dr Harding when they are installed here,' Emma remarked to Elizabeth in a dry undertone, as the Osborne Park phaeton rattled away out of the courtyard.

'What makes you say that?'

'Elizabeth, do you know what Lady Osborne has *done*?'

In a tone of outrage, Emma told her sister of the untimely end of little Fido.

Elizabeth shook her head, equally shocked, but a great deal less startled.

'I have heard other such stories of her behaviour when provoked. Her anger can be quite ruthless. If servants incur her wrath, they are dismissed on the spot; an old coachman who would not drive along a snowy lane was given his marching orders then and there . . . and I believe that, when they were younger, she treated her children very harshly —'

'What *can* Mr Howard see in her?' cried Emma vehemently, as Elizabeth turned the mare and began driving back along the riverside road.

'I fear, Emma, that he sees which side his bread is buttered on.'

'But he is a good man! A man of principle and good sense!'

'Perhaps he hopes to help her mend her ways.'

'Ha! I see small chance of that. After all, she must be nearly fifty years of age. Persons that old are not liable to change; they are much too confirmed in their manners and habits. How can he possibly endure the prospect that lies ahead of him?'

Emma's voice, her whole demeanour were so distressed that Elizabeth, who loved her sister and wished to shield her from needless pain, said briskly, 'Well, there is nothing *we* can do for him. He has made his bed, he must lie on it. And everybody agrees that Lady Osborne dotes on him. I daresay they will settle down together comfortably enough. What did you think of Captain Fremantle? Mrs Blake was giving me his history while you talked together; he lost an arm, poor fellow, at the battle of Occa Bay; he has been home on furlough, for it did not mend as it should and he was consulting a physician in London, but now he is soon to return to his ship—'

Emma was gazing at her sister in horror.

'He lost an *arm*?'

'Yes, did you not observe? He had his sleeve pinned to his waistcoat.'

'I never noticed.' Emma was appalled. 'How could I have been so inattentive – so unobservant? I suppose I was watching his face – listening to what he had to say. His face is so—'

'Oh well, I daresay the captain prefers it that way.' Elizabeth was untroubled. 'Mrs Blake says that he does not like the injury referred to – makes as little of it as he can. Oh, by the bye, I have discovered why Penelope is not too greatly concerned about this winding approach; they are felling the avenue at the back, and cutting a new driveway across the shoulder of the hill . . .'

6

The night of the Dorking Assembly finally arrived, and Emma, whose wrist was now almost entirely recovered, drove her sister into the town; according to long-established custom, Elizabeth would dine and spend the night with the hospitable Edwards family, and she hoped, while there, to acquire more information as to the legacy from the uncle in Plymouth and poor Sam's blighted prospects.

'Though I shall feel decidedly awkward,' she said. 'This legacy seems to create a gulf between myself and Mary Edwards – we used to be such friends – but now I shall not know how to be comfortable with her. And Mrs Edwards always wears such a reserved air, and behaves with such formal civility; if only you were coming too, Emma! You are so much easier in genteel society than I; it is the result of all those years with Aunt Turner.'

'Oh, my poor aunt,' sighed Emma. 'How I wish that word might come from her.' So far, none had arrived. 'But, Elizabeth, you are not to be talking like this! You will look most becomingly, in your new cloak, your hair is a triumph and does us both credit – never mind the reserves or the formalities of Mrs Edwards or Miss Edwards! I wish you to feel completely at ease, to spend a thoroughly enjoyable evening, dance every dance, and, if possible, refuse an application from Lord Osborne because of a prior engagement.'

'Not much chance of that, dear Emma,' said Elizabeth, laughing, as they drew up outside the handsome house of Mr Edwards, its street frontage guarded by white posts and chains. 'But I hope that *your* evening proves equally agreeable in a different way. It is kind of Mrs Blake to come in and sit with you.'

'Yes, we shall have a fine gossip and tear Lady Osborne's character to shreds between us,' Emma said, as a footman in livery with a powdered wig opened the front door. She waved her sister a fond goodbye and turned the mare in the wide street, observing as she did so that Lord Osborne and Tom Musgrave were riding along, not far away, deep in conversation. So engrossed were they with one another, that they did not at all observe Emma, in her humble conveyance, passing them on the other side of the road at a brisk trot – for well the old mare knew that now she was on her way home. But Emma, glancing back, was startled to observe the pair of gentlemen halt and dismount at the door of the Edwards mansion.

Well! she thought. My sister Elizabeth is about to have more society than she reckoned for! And, furthermore, if the gentlemen are calling in order to solicit Miss Edwards's hand for a pair of dances apiece, they can hardly avoid offering the same civility to Elizabeth; which will get her evening off to an excellent start. It certainly looks as if the Edwardses are right in their belief that Lord Osborne is paying attentions to Mary Edwards; *I* think she would be far better off with our dear brother Sam, and, from the way she blushed when she said that I resembled him, I do not believe she is entirely indifferent to Sam, poor girl! But still, she will live in a castle and be called Lady Osborne; I suppose her parents think it a fair bargain, and she is bound to fall in with their wishes.

Arriving home, Emma drove the pony-chair round to the yard, and led the mare into her stable. When she entered the parsonage by the back door, old Nanny told her that Mrs Blake was already come, not five minutes before.

'So I showed her into the parlour, Miss Emma, knowing that was what you would wish. There's a nice fire, and she had the gentleman with her to keep her company.'

'The gentleman?' Emma's heart leapt foolishly. 'Mr Howard, you mean?'

'No, no, miss, the gentleman as is staying with Mr Howard (*he's* gone to the ball with Lady Osborne and the castle folks). I mean the poor gentleman with only one hand.'

'Oh, dear me—'

'So I told the master they were here, Miss Emma, and he says to ask will you be so kind as to help him downstairs. For he'd like to take a dish of tea with the gentleman, Captain Fremantle. Seems he was acquainted with his father many years ago when they was both at Cambridge college.'

Emma made haste into the house and put her head round the parlour door to say: 'Will you both excuse me for five minutes while I assist Papa to come down? I know he will be very happy to see Captain Fremantle.'

Upstairs she found her father already endeavouring to put himself into the thick, monk-like woollen robe in which he was accustomed to entertain guests if they came after the dinner-hour. He had got the cords in a tangle and his slippers on the wrong feet. He submitted patiently to being put right.

'Thank you, my dear. Just imagine, the son of my old friend Gareth Fremantle – *Gaiters* Fremantle, we used to call him, even then, at Cambridge, and that was many years before he became a bishop, as he is now . . . It will be a great pleasure, a great pleasure indeed, to see his son . . . Now I think I am presentable, my dear Emma.'

She escorted him carefully down the stairs and into the parlour, while Nanny came clucking to and fro with trays of tea-things.

'Though I imagine it is likely, my dear Fremantle, that you would prefer a beverage somewhat stronger than tea?' suggested Mr Watson, when the introductions had been completed and they were all sitting comfortably round the fire.

'On the contrary, my dear sir! Tea is just what I like. At sea, you know, we may be obliged to go for long periods without tea – pea-soup is about our nearest approach to it. So to drink a dish of real tea is, to me, nothing less than a treat.'

'Tell me, now, about your family. You are the youngest son?'

'Yes, sir. My brother George followed my father into the church, and no doubt will likewise, in due course, become a bishop.'

'Gaiters Fremantle, yes, yes, indeed. At Cambridge, you know, even then, thirty years ago, we all called your father Gaiters Fremantle.'

The bishop's son, who had already heard this story twice, grinned his infectious, endearing grin at Emma.

'Just so, sir! My next brother, Frank, went into the army, the Guards, under the command of Sir Harry Burrard – no gaiters for him – and, as I was the youngest, that left the navy for me.'

'And doubtless one day you will be an admiral.'

'No, sir, such is not my ambition. If it were not for the national emergency, I had planned to become an historian. That is my real preference.'

'Ah yes! My daughter Emma was telling me that you have a theory as to the Clissocks property having once belonged to the estate of Ceawlin or Caedwalla. Now, my dear sir: I hesitate to contradict a guest in my house on such exceedingly short acquaintance – but it is by *far* more probable that Cynegils, who, as you must know, controlled Wessex—'

Captain Fremantle's eyes sparkled. He beamed disarmingly and said, 'Ah! *Perhaps*, sir – but, just the same – with due deference—'

In no time they were at it, hammer and tongs.

Emma, pouring tea, said softly to Mrs Blake, 'Oh, this is so *good* for my father! He is loving it. I believe he has not enjoyed an argument such as this since my mother's brother, my uncle Francis, used to come and dispute with him about historical matters – see how he waves his hands about . . .'

'I only hope that it does not prove too fatiguing for him. It was taking a great liberty to bring Cousin Matthew to call, but he did not wish to accompany my brother to the Assembly – his dancing days are over, he says; and he was so very anxious to make your father's acquaintance. I can see that he is enjoying their talk quite as much as your father. It takes his mind off his arm . . .' Mrs Blake sipped her tea and added after a moment, 'What a very fortunate circumstance it is, my dear Emma, that your sister Mrs Harding proposes to establish herself in that romantic house. How many pleasant visits we shall have there – what historical discussions, and excursions, and explorations. I have yet to meet your sister Penelope, but if she is like yourself and Miss Watson, I greatly look forward to meeting her.'

Emma tried to imagine Penelope and Dr Harding taking pleasure in an argument such as this; she failed to do so. 'I do not believe that my sister Penelope is very interested in history,' she said doubtfully. 'But perhaps, having come to live in a dwelling of such antiquarian importance, she will acquire the taste.' Privately, Emma thought this unlikely.

'Is your sister fond of Nature? Will she delight in the woods and the river and the hillsides?'

'I – I really am not sure,' Emma was obliged to confess.

In fact the more she thought about it, the more she wondered why in the world Penelope and the doctor had selected such an unsuitable dwelling-place.

'Cousin Matthew,' said Mrs Blake presently, 'I think it is high time that we retired. Mr Watson is an invalid, we must not forget. We must not exhaust him. And remember also that you plan to catch the early mail-coach to Portsmouth tomorrow.'

'I am indeed reluctant to break off this delightful discourse,' sighed Mr Watson. He gazed with genuine regret at Captain Fremantle. 'And I am sorry about your arm, my dear boy, very sorry. But while you were at sea you have been keeping your wits razor-sharp; so long as you do that, and continue adding to your stock of learning, you will do very well. The loss of an arm is not the end of the world.'

'Thank you, sir. You are perfectly right. And I am surpassingly glad to have had this opportunity to meet you – and some of your family.'

'Our guests should have a stirrup cup to speed them on their way,' Mr Watson now suggested to his daughter. 'When your father and I were lads, Captain Fremantle, we were wont to drink a cup of hot chocolate, accompanied by rum, in our college rooms of an evening – a most excellent, heartening beverage it was, both invigorating and sustaining. I think, my dear Emma, that I should fancy a small dram of it now; and I am sure Captain Fremantle will bear me company.'

Captain Fremantle's eyes sought those of Emma in query.

'Are you *sure*, my dear sir?' said Mrs Blake doubtfully.

'Yes, yes! I have enjoyed it many a time. Pray, Emma, ask our good Nanny to prepare it.'

But Nanny had long since gone off to bed, so Emma herself prepared hot chocolate in the kitchen and brought it, with the rum separately, on a tray, to the parlour.

'Excellent, excellent,' said Mr Watson, adding a substantial measure of spirit to his cup of chocolate. 'I do not know when I last took such pleasure in discussion. You have brought back old times, Captain Fremantle. Pray remember me to your good father, when you write to him next. Gaiters Fremantle, we used to call him,' he chuckled reminiscently.

'And I, too, my dear sir, after I have rejoined my ship tomorrow, I shall very, very often find myself thinking of this pleasant hour.' Captain Fremantle's smiling eyes met those of Emma. He added, 'Miss Watson, you make the very best chocolate that I have ever tasted.'

'And I,' she said quietly, 'I also have enjoyed listening to you and Papa. I should like to know more about those Saxon kings.'

'Would you? Then I shall take the first opportunity of sending you a book about them – if you would care to read it?'

'I should like that very much.'

'Then it shall be done.'

After the guests had departed, Emma helped her father up to bed. He sighed, 'If only we could pass an evening like that more often! Howard and Purvis are two excellent fellows, but they always behave as if they were afraid of over-exciting me; they are so very deferential in their behaviour. Now, this young fellow—'

'They mean it for the best, I am sure, Papa.'

'But now I feel as if I shall sleep very well. Thank you, Emma, my dear. Just leave the bedside candle burning. I shall blow it out by and by, when I have said my prayers and regulated my thoughts.'

Emma tiptoed away. She left her own bedroom door open, so that she was able to see the reflected gleam of the candle-light on the landing wall. Once or twice she tiptoed out and peered round the corner, but her father was still reading his prayer-book. When at length she fell asleep, the light still shone. But when, hours later, as dawn began to break, she softly entered her father's room, the candle had guttered to its socket. Her father lay dead, with the bedclothes untidily flung about, as if he had heaved and twisted himself from side to side in his struggle with death; it had not been an easy fight, or a willing surrender. Emma, frightened and distressed at the evidence of this solitary, losing battle, felt an urgent duty to straighten him out, close his mouth and eyes, wipe his face, make all things neat and pull the covers smoothly over him, before she summoned old Nanny.

The winter sun was beginning to rise. Just about now, thought Emma, Captain Fremantle will be climbing aboard the Portsmouth coach. It may be many months before he hears of this. Perhaps he will never hear at all.

A cold, paralysing sadness laid its grip on her. Another part of my life is lost, gone for ever, she thought.

It was going to be a very long day.

In fact the day that followed the death of Mr Watson seemed, to his daughters, to continue for weeks. Messengers must be sent to Robert and Jane in Croydon, to Sam in Guildford. A letter must be despatched to Penelope and Dr Harding in Weymouth. More messages must go off, to young Mr Marshall the curate, and to Mr Tyrwhit, the future incumbent of Stanton parish, who lived, at present, in Hindhead with a large young family, and was known to be most anxious to accomplish the move as soon as it might be arranged. Yet more messages went to Mr Sindell the apothecary, to the Edwards family, to Mrs Blake, and other neighbours.

'Do you think we should send to inform Lady Osborne at the castle?' asked Elizabeth, harassed and ink-stained, at her father's desk.

It was the first direct question she had asked Emma for some hours. She had been so inexpressibly shocked and grieved, on her arrival home, at receiving the unhappy news, that she had hardly spoken to her sister for the rest of the day; among Emma's many miseries lay a fear that her sister held her in some way responsible for the fatality. And this apprehension was confirmed during the visit of Mr Sindell.

'His heart gave out, Miss Watson, that is all,' said the apothecary soothingly. 'It might have occurred, you know, at any time these last nine months. Indeed I wonder that he has been with us so long as he has . . . Yes, well, it is true that an evening of lively conversation *may* have been instrumental in hastening matters – that, certainly, and a rich and stimulating stirrup-cup of hot chocolate with rum in it – imprudent, yes, no doubt a trifle imprudent – but who, after all, is competent to pronounce in these matters? There would be no purpose, no purpose at all, in ascribing blame, or laying responsibility at such a time, my very dear Miss Watson.'

Nonetheless, Emma felt that responsibility *was* laid, and was laid firmly at her door. And this was made plain to her, first by the unaccustomed silence and reserve in Elizabeth's manner to her, then by the behaviour of Robert, Jane, and Margaret, who were the first of the family to arrive at the parsonage.

'Gave him *hot chocolate*? With *rum* in it? What can you have been thinking of? What put such a wholly extravagant and ill-judged notion into your head? And that following a long, tiring, unnecessary argument with this Captain Whoever-he-was—'

'How *can* you have been so *shockingly*, so *wickedly* inconsiderate? So regardless of my poor father's welfare? Let alone the rest of us.'

'But he himself suggested it! He asked for it, he wanted it! He was enjoying such a lively, animated discussion with Captain Fremantle about the Saxons—'

'Saxons, indeed!' said Robert.

Emma felt herself in undeserved disgrace. Mr Watson had had a thoroughly happy evening for his last on earth, had entirely relished the visitors and the refreshment. I must try to hold on to that and remember it, Emma thought. It is of no use to dispute, and would be the height of indecorum; I must just endure this trouble as best I can. I do wish, though, that Mrs Blake would come up to the parsonage. She, I am very sure, would sympathize with me, and bear witness to the fact that Papa was in excellent spirits last night, and had said repeatedly that he was delighted with his company.

But Mrs Blake, perhaps feeling that the Watson family had no need of outsiders at such a sad period, tactfully stayed away.

Robert, as the family attorney, had, several years previously, supervised the framing of his father's Will, which therefore contained in it no surprises, and very little pleasure. The main part of Mr Watson's estate, not a large one, was divided between his two sons; the daughters received one hundred pounds apiece. The parsonage, of course, was not his to bequeathe, and must at once pass into other hands. Emma privately grieved over the loss of the orchard, the duck-pond, the garden, and the copse; and she had an unhappy fear that Elizabeth's heart was well-nigh broken at the prospect of quitting these much-loved refuges; but Elizabeth's heart was at present closed to her.

Emma had never even been given a report on the Dorking Assembly by her sister, and that was a particular sorrow, for she longed to know if all the care and pains lavished on her sister's appearance had been to any purpose. Nor was it possible for her to exchange comments – as she longed to do – with Elizabeth on the ferocious, if unacknowledged and genteelly conducted warfare which now began to rage among the family regarding the disposal of Mr Watson's personal effects, furnishings, and household goods.

During his life, moving from one vicarage to another, Mr Watson had always taken along with him a considerable supply of china, plate, and linen, as well as much excellent, solid, if old-fashioned furniture which he had himself inherited from parents and grandparents. Some of these pieces, previously despised as being out of the mode, were now, by the arbitrary whim of fashion, held once more in high esteem; and various other articles such as towels and table-linen edged with Mechlin lace, and several unblemished sets of Crown Derby china, received long ago as wedding presents, must command respectful attention at any time.

Penelope (who had now arrived, post-haste, from Weymouth, with her husband), Margaret, and Jane were all at daggers drawn over the disposition of these items, many of which were not individually assigned in the Will.

'*You* have your house already furnished, my dear Jane, so what need can you possibly have for any more plates or towels, let alone chairs or tables? You are amply supplied in this regard. But Clissocks is all to furnish, and those rooms are so very big that I shall be at my wits' end to know how to fill them – Papa's desk would go so very well, be just the thing for the room that is to be Dr Harding's study—'

'Papa's desk must *indubitably* go to Robert, as the eldest son,' said Jane, white about the nostrils with rage. 'There is absolutely no question as to the propriety of that. And we should also certainly have the pianoforte, since our little Augusta is the only member of the younger family at present, and the dear little angel shows decided musical talent – or would if she had any instrument to play on. Besides, a handsome Broadwood like that would be wasted at Clissocks. The damp would ruin it in a month.'

'My sister Emma should have the piano,' said Sam, who had hitherto remained silent. 'She plays so beautifully.'

'Emma? Where could *she* put a pianoforte? She has no home of her own. Nor likely to have one.'

'I do not see why the lack of homes should deprive the girls of some valuable possessions,' said Sam sturdily. 'They could be stored.'

'Stored?' shrieked Jane and Penelope, in unison for once. 'With the cost of storage so high? Preposterous! And it is quite disgraceful that Emma is to have all those papers – ridiculous – unsuitable. Where is she to keep them, pray?'

'I am going to look after them. And,' persisted Sam, 'items such as the piano could be allotted to the girls but kept, for the time, in one of your houses, on the under-standing that they are a loan, to be reclaimed should they marry and set up homes of their own.'

'A wholly unpractical plan!' And a most improbable eventuality, declared Penelope's out-thrust lip and chin.

Poor Dr Harding, exposed for the first time to a full conclave of the Watson family, could be seen to find it a decidedly quelling experience, and retired in silence to a corner. If asked his opinion by his wife or brother-in-law, he resorted to one unvarying defence:

'I don't want disagreeables! I never like disagreeables. Why can't we all be pleasant and easy-going with one another?'

Emma, Elizabeth, and Sam, the three genuinely grieving children of Mr Watson, were no match at all in acquisi-tiveness against Robert, Penelope, and Margaret, let alone against Jane, who, before she had been inside the parsonage for half-an-hour, had set aside a large empty trunk, and was piling into it items of crockery, cutlery, tableware, vases, and candlesticks.

Even her husband was a little taken aback at this.

'Should you not wait until after the funeral, my love? Would that not be best?'

'But Sam Hitchens is returning to Croydon tonight, Robert; he may just as well take this load with him. You know that it will save carriers' fees.'

Penelope, for months, if not years to come, would be conducting a furious inquest into all those articles and heirlooms 'which Jane made away with on the day after Papa died'.

The funeral was fixed for three days hence, to allow

a sufficiency of time for bombazine and crape to be purchased and made up into mourning garments. The service was to have been conducted by Mr Howard; but another most untoward and tragical happening now disrupted this plan.

Emma, two days after her father's death, chanced to be in the kitchen, conferring with Betsey from the village and old Nanny about arrangements to satisfy the appetites of the extended household with a large but economical dinner.

Inspection of some jars of preserved blackberries reminded her of the bramble-hedges in Osborne Park, and she remarked, 'I wonder that we have not yet had a call from Mrs Blake. That is passing strange. It is not like Mrs Blake to be tardy in a visit of neighbourly sympathy.'

Betsey gave a great gulp of horror.

'*Oh, Miss Emma!* You've not been told yet – in truth, we didn't like to tell ye – so friendly as you were with the lady –'

'Tell me what?' Emma demanded, wheeling round sharply to look at the two colourless faces and shocked eyes that confronted her.

'Mrs Blake is killed! And so is little Master Charlie!'

'*Killed?* That cannot possibly be true. What can you mean?'

'It's Bible truth, Miss Emma. We hadn't the heart to break it to you, so grieved as you are over poor Master –'

'But what happened?'

'Thrown from the phaeton, they were! Mr Tom Musgrave was driving – and if ever there was a useless, feckless, reckless, worthless young castaway, he's the one –'

'He was a-bringing of them up *here*, to pay a visit of sympathy like you said—'

'Yesterday evening, it was—'

'Poor Mr Howard would a brung them hisself, but Lady Osborne had just sent for him, most urgent—'

Now they were properly embarked on the narrative, the two women could hardly speak fast enough, and kept interrupting each other. Emma brought them to the point.

'But how could it happen? Was Tom Musgrave drunk?'

'Ah! Bosky he was, no doubt of it at all. Three sheets in the wind—

'As he often is these days—'

'Almost always, Mrs Suckling she says—'

'Turning the corner by Cathanger Lane, one wheel went into the ditch—'

'The lady and the little lad was thrown out, clean on to their heads—'

'On the hard road—'

'While, as for Master Musgrave, all *he* suffered was a scraped knee!'

'Of course, *now*, he's properly gravelled. Won't show his head out of doors. Lurks inside, mute as a fish—'

'As one should *hope*, indeed!'

'But this is terrible – terrible!' Emma ran distracted fingers through her hair. 'Does my sister know?'

'Miss Elizabeth?'

It was plain that old Nanny hardly regarded Penelope or Margaret as qualifying any longer for the appellation. 'No, she don't, Miss Emma; leastways I haven't had the heart to tell her. Not after Master Tom distinguished her so particular at the Assembly: *four dances* he took with her, everybody was remarking on it! So I heard from Patty Wilson, the chambermaid at the White Hart.'

'Oh, gracious heavens! I must go and tell Elizabeth at once.'

Emma found Elizabeth in the bedroom they shared, silently and tearfully putting her possessions in order and beginning to pack them up.

'Our future has been decided,' she remarked shortly, without lifting her swollen eyes to look at Emma. 'It has all been planned by the others, without reference to us. I am to live with Penelope at Clissocks, you with Jane and Robert at Croydon. Penelope has apparently come to the conclusion that I may very easily earn my keep at Clissocks by my services as a housekeeper; and Jane has decided that your proficiency in music may compensate for your argumentative nature. (Miss Osborne sang your praises to her, it seems, at the Dorking Assembly.) So you are to teach little Augusta. The pianoforte will not be wasted.'

'*Elizabeth!* Have you heard about Mrs Blake?'

'Yes; I have. Sam – Sam told me.' Now Elizabeth did raise her eyes. They were brimming with tears.

'But what will become of those three children?'

'Sam says that a sister of Mrs Blake's, Mrs Chivers, may have them; she lives in Hampshire.'

'Would you not think that Lady Osborne would have made an offer – ?'

'Would you?' said Elizabeth in her new dry tone.

'Poor, *poor* Mr Howard! He was so very attached to his sister. How can he bear it?'

'We all have to bear what we must,' said Elizabeth.

'Oh, Eliza!' Emma knelt down and put her arms around

her sister. 'I shall miss you so *much*! Pray, pray do not be angry with me! Indeed, truly, I am as unhappy about Papa as you are. But I do not think—'

Elizabeth quietly detached herself from Emma's clasp and stood up.

'There is no use to talk about it,' she said. 'He is gone, and we have to reconcile ourselves to our loss.'

There came a knock at the door. It was old Nanny.

'If you please, Miss Elizabeth, Mr Howard is here. He particularly wishes to see you and Miss Emma, to explain why he feels he can't take Master's funeral.'

'Why can he not talk to my brother Robert?'

'He asked to see you and Miss Emma, special, miss. I have put him in Master's study, as the family are all in the parlour.'

'*You* go and see him, Elizabeth,' urged Emma. 'My presence is not necessary.'

'He asked to see you too, Miss Emma.'

With the greatest reluctance, both sisters went down. Both were in a state, at present, of such acute sensibility that the smallest new occurrence, the briefest or most trifling encounter, would have seemed almost intolerably painful. And the sight of Mr Howard, pale and distracted, moving restlessly and miserably about their father's half-dismantled study, gave evidence that he was in the same condition of extreme mental affliction. With a few broken phrases and half-finished ejaculations, he took their hands in turn; this proved too much for Emma, who, after one brief, strong clasp, one momentary meeting of eyes, almost ran from the room and made her way blindly to the orchard, where a burst of tears relieved her overcharged sensibilities. Then, feeling heartily ashamed of herself, she returned to the house. Here she discovered that Mr Howard had already left, and Elizabeth was once more upstairs, occupied with her packing.

'Mr Howard asked me to give you a message,' she said tonelessly to Emma. 'He had a letter from his friend Montagu in Dublin, who had heard that an English lady was shortly expected to come and take up residence at a lodging house that he knows of; but he had not as yet been furnished with her name. He hoped to have more information within a week or so, and would supply the news as soon as he had it. He did not wish you to think he had forgotten the matter.'

'Oh. That was kind of him. I wish, so *much*, that we had more certain information. After all, there must be many English ladies in Dublin. And, if it were indeed our aunt, where was Captain O'Brien? Can she have left him? We ought to write to her – about my father – but where to send the letter?'

Elizabeth made no response to this, but continued her occupation of folding muslins and sorting ribbons.

'Penelope wishes to leave for Clissocks as soon as the funeral is over,' she said in explanation of this activity. 'And she thinks it best if I accompany them immediately, so that I can make myself useful in helping to set matters straight there.'

'Good heavens! But will the house be ready for occupation, so soon?'

'Penelope thinks so. They spent this morning over there, it seems, giving directions to the builders. And Penelope has come to be of the opinion that it will be best if she and Dr Harding are in residence; then the work will go faster.'

'You will all be exceedingly uncomfortable.'

'Yes,' said Elizabeth without expression.

'But, concerning our father's funeral? What did Mr Howard say about that?'

'Poor man.' For the first time, Elizabeth's chilly tone faltered. She said, 'He is in such anguish over the death of his sister. And that he must break the news to Captain Blake. He told me – he told me how he himself had proposed to drive her up here – but Lady Osborne suddenly summoned him – she wished for his opinion on some parish matter – that was how Tom Musgrave came to offer his services – he does not blame Tom Musgrave – he, he feels no indignation—'

'Tom Musgrave will never be able to show his face again in the neighbourhood—' began Emma, and then stopped short, recalling old Nanny's gossip – 'Master Tom distinguished her so particularly at the Assembly.' Had this proffered service to Mrs Blake been suggested in order that Tom Musgrave might see Elizabeth again? Could he have been serious in his intentions?

'Mr Howard also told me,' Elizabeth went on, speaking with evident difficulty, 'that – that his sister had given him an account of the evening that she and Captain Fremantle spent here . . .'

'Oh?'

'He said – Mrs Blake told him – how very, *very* much our father had appeared to enjoy the company of Captain Fremantle. That she had hardly ever seen him so happy and animated.'

'I am glad,' Emma said, choking on tears, 'I am glad at least to have *some* corroboration that our father's last evening on earth was a happy one. But, as to the funeral, Elizabeth, who is to conduct it?'

'Mr Howard suggested Mr Purvis.' Elizabeth bent over a shawl that she was folding in silver paper. 'But I told him – I said that I would prefer it if some other divine might be found – he seemed rather puzzled but asked for no explanation; and then he told me that in fact the bishop, Dr Richards himself, had offered to officiate if the family were agreeable – he held our father in great esteem. So that is how it is to be.'

'The bishop! I am very glad of that.'

The door flew open abruptly and Penelope walked in.

'Elizabeth! Must you be for *ever* lurking upstairs, fidgeting about with your things? Here are some men come to dispose of the farm tools, and not knowing which belonged to my father and which are the property of the rectory. So do pray come down at once and instruct them. And, Emma, Jane wishes you to go and assist her with the table-linen. It is a great inconvenience, I must say, that there must be this tiresome luncheon tomorrow, after the ceremony, so that all the plates and dishes must be left out. Very tiresome indeed.'

'It is customary, however,' Elizabeth said quietly. 'Especially since the bishop himself is to be with us.'

'The bishop! I see no need for that. Purvis would have done quite as well.'

7

The funeral was past, the bishop had uttered his eulogy, and the mortal remains of Mr Watson had been committed to Stanton churchyard. Most of Mr Watson's parishioners and three of his children had grieved sincerely; the rest had put up a respectable pretence. The funeral cold meats had been eaten, and the carriages had all rolled away.

'I have been talking matters over with Penelope, my love,' said Jane Watson very kindly to Emma. 'We have been laying our heads together, and we have decided that Penelope needs you even more than I do for the next few days. You are, therefore, to go first to Clissocks – you may very easily ride there, you know, in the carriers' cart with all the bed-linen and curtains – and it is quite certain that you will be of *sovereign* assistance to our dear sister during the troublesome period of arranging and settling where the furniture is to go. You and our sweet Elizabeth between you will soon have matters there just as they should be; and *then* it will be time for you to come to us in Croydon and enjoy some city pleasures and well-earned holiday before you begin to instruct our precious little Gussie! We shall, I promise you, show you all the sights of Croydon – the Whitgift Hospital, you know, and the famous cherry orchard . . .'

'I see,' said Emma.

The real reason for this rearrangement of plans had been the flat refusal of Margaret to share a bedroom with Emma in Beech Hanger, Robert's house.

'Why can you not put her up in the south attic, Jane, alongside Kate the scullery-maid? Emma is the youngest of us, the attic is quite good enough for her.'

'But my sweetest Mag, the attic has no furniture in it whatsoever.'

'Well, good heavens, a bed is easily found – and a chair and table from among the parsonage kitchen things – I do not see what there is to make such a piece of work about.'

'I thought that you and dear little Emma would like to be together.'

'Well, I would not! I am accustomed to be on my own. I do not at all care for Emma's airs and affectations.'

'And it is true besides,' added Jane later to Emma with a little air of thoughtful solicitude, 'that the removal to Clissocks will not be so melancholy for you, since it is close by, in the same neighbourhood as Stanton; it will be an easier transition, you know; and then, by the time you come to Croydon, the period of mourning will be somewhat past, you will be in better spirits, and more in a frame to preside over our little angel's lessons and to enlarge her mind.'

For Jane had been seriously dismayed by Emma's air of shocked misery during the days after her father's demise, and had asked herself and her husband several times how they were ever to put up with such a figure of woe creeping about the house.

'Well, well,' he said, 'a few days will surely mend

matters. And Mag, I suppose, does have a right to a room of her own. In any case it is to be hoped that she and Hobhouse will soon bring matters to a conclusion; then she, at least, will be off our hands. The furniture from the maid's room at the parsonage will do very well for the attic at Beech Hanger and Emma may go there in the meantime. There, she will be in nobody's way.'

So matters were decided.

In the event, Emma did not travel to Clissocks in the carrier's cart, but was driven by Miss Osborne and Miss Carr in the Osborne carriage.

'I have been so anxious to do something for you, to be of *some* use during this sad time,' ardently declared Miss Osborne, who had developed, for Emma, all the worshipful admiration that may be felt by a young and rather plain and clumsy girl in her teens for an older, prettier and more talented contemporary. 'I have felt for you so sincerely! Your father was such a kind, good old man! And then I knew you had formed such a great, great friendship with dear Mrs Blake; her dreadful end must have shocked you inexpressibly.'

'It was a hard loss,' said Emma, touched by the young girl's fervent sincerity. 'But for – for Mr Howard, it must have been worst of all. To lose his sister – to whom he was so devoted – in such a sudden and – and *needless* manner . . .'

And, she thought, small comfort, probably, to be had from Lady Osborne.

She was a little disconcerted when Miss Osborne, continuing, seemed to echo this very thought.

'My mother, you see, could not enter into his feelings

– she had seen little of Mrs Blake – and my mother has *never* approved of Tom Musgrave as a friend for my brother – always considered him a shocking rattle. And so – when – when this happened – it made her very angry – she has been so angry, indeed, that – that in regard to the children – her judgement – she and Mr Howard did not –'

'Miss Osborne,' said Miss Carr. 'I do not think you should be entering on this topic. What Lady Osborne does or thinks can be no concern of ours. And Miss Watson can have no interest in the issue.'

'Well, I did wonder about the children,' Emma could not help observing bluntly. 'As anybody might, you know. Having seen how greatly attached their uncle was to them, and how much time he has been accustomed to spend with them, it was not unnatural to expect that – until Captain Blake comes back to claim them – they might have been offered a home at the castle – to wonder why it was not.'

'Her ladyship did give the matter careful thought. *Nothing* she does is undertaken without the most earnest consideration; but the scheme was not thought to be practicable – not feasible – the children too small – the castle not a suitable environment – you must know, however, that her ladyship most kindly offered to defray the cost of their removal from here to Hampshire – *and* to send generous hampers of fruit and vegetables twice a year – besides some toys and books which were once used by Lord Osborne and Mr Chilton and Miss Harriet here – her ladyship has behaved with her usual liberality . . .'

'That was most affable of her, indeed,' said Emma in a dry tone.

Miss Carr, evidently considering this subject best abandoned, now made some appropriately admiring comments on the beauty of the landscape which, even in midwinter, with the tree-shrouded hillside above, the tranquil misty river below, and the narrow, winding track, might be thought to equal, or even rival the more famed glories of the Lakes or the Dales.

'Yes, yes! In the summertime this will be so romantic! What excursions, what explorations, what picnics you will be undertaking,' Miss Osborne exclaimed with enthusiasm. 'Do you not dote on picnics, Miss Emma?'

'Unfortunately,' said Emma, 'I shall not, by the time that summer comes, be in residence here. So soon as my sister Mrs Harding is quite settled into Clissocks, I am to remove and go to stay with my brother and sister-in-law in Croydon. The family have arranged it so. My sister Elizabeth remains here.'

'Oh – I am very sorry indeed for that!' Miss Osborne looked quite stricken at this information. 'You will be so much missed! Mr Howard will greatly regret—' She stopped, blushing. 'That is – I am very sure that he will miss you. And Croydon is such a noisy bustling place, because of the gravel pits and the charcoal manufactory – set by the turnpike and the canal as it is, with business people from London beginning to build their new houses on the hills around. Mamma says—' She stopped again, looking conscious. 'But there is an excellent dentist, Mr Pilsbrow, near the Whitgift Hospital – we sometimes consult him – I do *hope*, Miss Emma, that we shall not lose sight of you entirely. Perhaps – I hope – you will be coming back to pay visits to Mrs Harding at Clissocks? I shall be so eager for a view of the house, now that it is occupied again.'

They came round a corner of the hill and saw that Clissocks did appear occupied, inasmuch as the windows were curtained now, and smoke issued from the chimneys. But the approach to the mansion still zigzagged between stacks of timber and piles of stones; it was plain that structural work was by no means yet completed.

When they drove within sight of the large open court-yard they found that it was in a state of clamour and turmoil from many different conflicting elements: builders' wagons delivering materials; coaches and carriers' carts discharging people and furniture; builders' men and carters' men involved in acrimonious exchanges. Penelope stood on the high doorstep wearing a brow of thunder; Dr Harding was there too, but looking helpless among all these opposed factions; and Elizabeth slipped to and fro, in and out, evidently bearing precious items not suitable to be entrusted to paid labour.

'Oh, good heavens,' said Emma. 'I can see that I am arrived here not a moment too soon. There will be a great deal to do. I wonder who *that* is? One of the builders' overseers, perhaps — ?'

For, evidently directing many of these activities, there stood a square-built youngish man, dressed rather too fine, it seemed, for a builder, and yet there was something about him not entirely the gentleman: the rough, easy, but jocular style in which he gave orders to the underlings – to which they responded in kind; his manner of familiarity, perhaps undue familiarity, yet mixed with a kind of subservience, when addressing himself to Dr Harding and Penelope.

His dress seemed an uneasy compromise between an attempt at fashion and a garb more suited to his present occupation; he kept twitching at his cravat, arranged rather too high for all the rapid movements he was obliged to make. And his striped stockings had been a most injudicious choice for continual passage among dust, mud, straw, and the disorder left everywhere by workmen.

'Oh dear me!' murmured Miss Osborne faintly. Emma observed with surprise that she had turned even paler than her natural colour.

'Are you not well, Miss Osborne?'

'No – no. It is nothing. Nothing at all. But I can see that we are absolutely *de trop* here; we had best say goodbye to you at once, dearest Miss Emma, and take our departure directly. This is no moment to ask for an introduction to your sister. Is that Mrs Harding, on the step?'

'Yes, that is Penelope. And the white-haired gentleman behind her is her husband, Dr Harding. Another time, I hope, you will allow me to make you known to them. I am so very much obliged to you for your great kindness . . .' apologized Emma, rather distractedly.

The carriage was turned, not without difficulty, and Emma and her luggage deposited.

Seizing advantage of the noise made by a cartload of bricks, which came cascading from a tipped bogey, and the shouts of the workmen involved, Miss Carr observed to Emma in a low tone:

'That burly dark-haired man – the one just now berating the carter yonder – his name is Thickstaffe. At one time, he acted as steward and overseer at Osborne Castle. But there were difficulties – he was found in some way unsatisfactory – I am able to tell you no more than that. Indeed I know no more. I should not wish to allege anything in his disfavour. But it makes me a little uneasy, just a little concerned, to see him so very much in command here at Clissocks. I do not know if I ought to have told you this – you will not take what I say amiss?'

'Indeed no. I am obliged to you for the caution,' Emma replied in the same tone.

'Emma!' called out Penelope, setting eyes on her youngest sister at this moment. '*There* you are at last! Here are so many things to be done, I hardly know which way to turn. Heythrop! That pembroke table is to go in the large front room on the left. And the two paintings on tin, and the elephant's tusk, and the battle-piece, are to go in the Master's study. See that the carpet is laid down *before* the desk is taken in. Emma – now you *are* come – you had best see what you can do to make them set all to rights in the kitchen. That woman we brought from Chichester proves a perfect fool, and has no notion at all how to set about matters.'

'But what of my bundles? If I leave them on the ground here, someone is sure to drop a plank or a bag of mortar on them – ?'

'*Oh!*' cried Penelope, as if this were the last straw, and then, her eyes lighting on the brawny Mr Thickstaffe, 'Percy! Mr Thickstaffe! Will you pray order Baggot to take Miss Emma's bags up to the second landing?'

'With all the pleasure in the world, Mrs H.!' cried Thickstaffe, and swept a flourishing bow, ignoring her curt tone and look. 'But rather I will give myself the honour of doing that service. So this is little Miss Emma?

The flower of the flock, I can see! Do they not say that all the best things come in small packets?'

Mr Thickstaffe's survey of Emma, from top to toe, was both rapid and accomplished, and the smile accompanying it contrived to be equally expeditious and lingering. Emma thought that she had never met a man of whom she formed such an instantaneously bad impression. That he could assume an air almost of flirtation towards a person in deep mourning was an outrage in itself, let alone the manner in which he did it.

'Whose was the carriage that just drove away?' demanded Penelope, glancing over Emma's shoulder. 'Oh, the castle ladies – very obliging of them, I am sure, to bring you hither, but a mercy they would not stay – they would have been abominably in the way – *Fielding!* for heaven's sake take care how you handle that sofa, you will tear the fabric.'

'Do you care to step this way with me, Miss Emma, and I will show you where you are lodged, with your sister Miss Elizabeth,' said Thickstaffe, nimbly finding a passage among furniture, building materials, and piles of baggage. 'Ha! Ha! You see us at our very worst, for your sister Mrs H. was so amazingly precipitate in removing here – she would not be swayed by my words of warning, she would come directly – "Otherwise," says she in her forthright way, "that cat of a Mrs Jane will, for a certainty, get her hands on all the best pieces" – oh dear me, now, I see that the front stairs are quite blocked by the four-post bed, just at this present, so let us betake ourselves to the back, along this passage, through the green baize door – but, forgive me, dear Miss Emma, I have not yet introduced myself, since your sister Mrs H. was too pressed to do so just then – Percy Thickstaffe, very much at your service!'

He contrived to bow again, while conveying Emma's quite heavy bags up the back stair with an ease which suggested that he must be extremely strong.

'Thank you, sir,' Emma said faintly, following behind him but quite out of breath from the speed of their progress and the steepness of the stair.

'So Miss Harriet Osborne from the castle fetched you hither, did she?' Thickstaffe continued, embarking on a second, even steeper flight of stairs. 'That was like her affability – she is a charming young lady, is she not? Always so gracious, not a bit of condescension – unlike – but mum! Did Miss Harriet allude to me, I wonder? At one time, in the days when I—'

Emma was opening her mouth for an emphatic negative, when she heard Elizabeth's voice from the landing above.

'Emma? Is that you? Come this way, and I will show you where we are accommodated.'

Emma had had little time to take stock of her surroundings, apart from a sense of chill, damp, and considerable antiquity. The unmistakable smell of ancient stonework, ancient woodwork, was very pervasive in the narrow back stairway. A dim greenish light percolated through high, arched, very dirty windows which appeared to look out into the midst of tall trees. This mansion, she thought, would make a perfect setting for *Udolpho* or *The Necromancer of the Forest*. Ah, poor Aunt Maria, how she did enjoy those novels! Where is she now, what can she be reading?

Elizabeth led the way through a low-lintelled door into

a chamber at least four times the size of that shared by the sisters at Stanton; it was low-ceiled and lit by a row of square, small-paned windows which looked straight out on to a steep wooded hillside. Down the middle of this tumbled a small rivulet between high banks.

'Thank you, Mr Thickstaffe,' and,

'*Thank* you, Mr Thickstaffe, I am very much obliged to you,' came from both sisters simultaneously.

Even a man so self-satisfied and impervious to rebuff as Mr Thickstaffe appeared to be could not ignore this unmistakable conge: 'Only too delighted to be of use, ladies,' said he, and, bowing again, retired.

'What an odious man,' said Emma, when the door was shut.

'He is my brother-in-law's man of business,' said Elizabeth in a colourless tone. 'Look, Emma, that is your bed, this is mine. Our clothes can go behind this curtain for the time, until a wardrobe is found.'

'It is hardly worth the trouble of unpacking mine,' said Emma, quelled by her sister's brusque manner. 'I am not required to remain here more than a night or two.'

'Well – as you wish. Or rather, as *they* wish. Now I must leave you – I am supposed to be supervising the furnishing of Dr Harding's study. Penelope wishes you to take charge of the kitchen. Go down there as soon as you can – it is in chaos. Oh!' For a moment, Elizabeth put her hands over her face, exclaimed, 'It is all so *wretched*!' and hurried from the room.

Emma knew that she, too, should be bustling about, in a show of grateful repayment for the hospitality of a sister whom she could not like or admire; but instead she crossed to the window and knelt down by the sill, which was raised only a foot or so from the floor. How very quiet it was in this room! The stream's murmur was audible, that was all. It is even quieter than Stanton, she thought. There, you could hear the cows on the farm, roosters, and the quack of ducks. Here, nothing at all. Not a single echo comes up from all that commotion going on at the front.

Poor Elizabeth, thought Emma. She feels I have robbed her of her home and her happiness. And I suppose that is true. But it would all soon have come to an end in any case. Papa could not have lasted many more months. Sam said so. And here, living with Penelope, who knows? Elizabeth's life may take some new course, at present undreamed-of. So long as she does not allow herself to be turned into a mere drudge. I have *never been* in so quiet a house! I am sure that it will not suit Penelope. Why, of all the places in the world, did they decide to settle here?

Emma, without any trouble, found her way down the back stair again and to the kitchen regions, from where, as she approached them, a considerable clatter and gabble of voices proceeded. Here three different sets of persons were attempting to pursue their conflicting ends: builders' men were installing shelves and pipes, carters' men were fetching in tables, cupboards, and crates of pots and crockery; bewildered servants, most of them newly hired, were attempting to sort these articles, set them in order, and prepare a meal. Old Nanny, from the parsonage, theoretically in charge of all these proceedings, could do nothing but shake her head helplessly.

'If ever I saw such a discombobulation in all my days!

But, to be sure, it's just like Miss Penny – she always was a helter-skelter child, wanting all finished as soon as the first idea came into her head; lord save us, though, the new master must be as rich as Crusoe, when you consider all the money that's gone into this kitchen alone: just *look* at that brand-new Rumford stove, Miss Emma, and that great steamer, and the fine porcelain sink and that warming cupboard – and the pastry-room – and those shelves in the pantry, solid slate, beautiful they are. 'Tis plain money's no object.'

Emma looked, and was likewise impressed. And she could see, too, the imprint of a practical mind. Dr Harding might look elderly, vague, and bewildered, but his appearance must bely him; the shrewd intelligence that had planned this kitchen and its appurtenances certainly did not belong to Penelope, who was perfectly capable of sewing a sleeve upside down into a bodice. Dr Harding might, in family disputes, retreat to a corner, but he was no dotard. Unless, of course, Mr Thickstaffe had planned the kitchen?

While engaged in these thoughts, Emma had begun organizing the servants, who were only too glad to find themselves under one firm authority; and soon, with the help of old Nanny, order and calm began to prevail; articles were not picked up and put down twenty times by as many people, but were assigned to their correct place, or stored in temporary harbours of safety. Fortunately there seemed an abundance of these. Emma, snatching moments to explore, discovered a maze of unused ancient offices, dairies, still-rooms, game-larders, sculleries, cellars, and other dark dank little rooms whose function remained unknown, unguessable. They seemed so old that she could easily imagine Saxon warriors ensconced in them, with shields and swords and flagons of mead. This notion brought a sudden warm recollection of Captain Fremantle discoursing with ingenuous enthusiasm on Saxon kings, and Emma smiled involuntarily at the thought.

She slipped out of doors, momentarily, and found a brick-paved yard to the side of the house, with a central well, and stables, coach-houses, and tack-rooms; also a series of walled gardens, all in a state of shocking neglect; this shortcoming was now being remedied at breakneck speed by a troop of gardeners digging, scything down brambles, chopping dead branches, and laying turf. Emma was a little sorry to see the wilderness so speedily put straight, and hoped their activities would not be too extensive.

Papa would have enjoyed this place, she thought, peering into an ancient rose-garden where the spreading, straggly boughs interlaced like cobwebs. I am sorry he did not have an opportunity to come here. But perhaps he may have, years ago, when Sir Meldred was still alive.

Conscience-stricken, she hurried back indoors, summoned by cries of 'Miss Emma! Miss Emma!' and gave orders as to the disposition of china, silver, milk-pans, and laundry baskets.

By working without cease during the next five or six hours, a state of rational tidiness was finally achieved; Emma, during that period of time, had not set foot in the rest of the house, but was interested to observe, when she did emerge from the kitchen region, that the areas which had been under the governance of Mr Thickstaffe were now equally orderly; Dr Harding, with the aid of Elizabeth, had arranged for himself a calm sanctuary of study and library; but the saloons, boudoirs, parlours and ballroom, under the ordinance of Penelope, still remained in a state of very considerable confusion. Penelope, it seemed, had not the imaginative eye, she could not conceive how an object would look in a particular spot unless it were actually in position there, and articles of furniture were continually being dragged hither and thither according to her cry: 'Try it the other way again! No, put it back, but turn it around. No, that will not do either!'

At last Dr Harding, assuming a hitherto unsuspected authority, said, 'My dear, I think we have all had enough. Should we not dine? Here is Bertrand, to say that dinner has been ready this last half-hour.'

Bertrand, to the amazement and suspicion of Nanny, was a genuine French chef, and the meal he had produced in such adverse surroundings was a surprisingly excellent one.

'I had no idea that Dr Harding was quite so well-to-do,' Emma murmured to Elizabeth after the meal when they were making up beds and hanging curtains in their own room. ('For it is little use expecting servants to penetrate up so high as this on the first day,' Elizabeth had remarked with her usual common sense.)

Now she said simply, 'Penelope tells me that Mr Thickstaffe has long advised him – advised him about his investments. Advised him how to accumulate a nest-egg.'

'To some purpose, it would seem! But I still consider Thickstaffe an odious creature.'

At the dinner table Mr Thickstaffe, who comported

himself in all ways as a member of the family, had cried out: 'Here's a toast to little Miss Emma, who has a head on her shoulders worthy of Boney himself! And here's to our industrious Miss Elizabeth, who has achieved ten times as much as any other person here, and will not even let me fill her glass with wine, though I have invited her three times!'

He bowed and raised his glass, and Dr Harding remarked, 'Indeed I think myself fortunate to have acquired two such notable sisters,' while Penelope pressed her lips together, looked at her plate, and remained silent.

Very soon after the meal Emma, who felt really exhausted, retired to bed. She had been too fatigued and harassed, all day, to think much of her sorrows, but now they came swooping back: her father, Mrs Blake, and Aunt Maria; oppressed and low-spirited she knelt huddling by the window and stared out. At this time of a winter evening the scene outside was almost pitch black; she could see only the reflection of her own candle on the pane; but, as she looked, that reflection was joined by another point of light, the light of a lantern, carried by somebody climbing the hill outside; and shortly afterwards a second tiny spark approached. They twinkled together, on the dark hillside; two people, apparently, standing, talking by the little cascade.

Who could it be? Who would take the trouble to go out for a private conference in the wintry cold and dark?

Emma felt a little ashamed of even appearing to overlook their meeting; she moved away from the window and began on her toilet. When she returned to the window later, the lights were gone.

Elizabeth had long since retired, and her slow regular breathing showed her to be in deep sleep. Emma's last thought before she, too, slept, was: *who*, what company can Penelope hope to entertain in this house, with all those plate-racks and warming-cupboards?

8

Emma spent five very active days at Clissocks, arranging, rearranging, stowing, sorting, making lists, and listening to the arguments of Elizabeth and Penelope as to the disposition of the furniture.

'Why in the world do you trouble to argue with Penelope?' Emma ventured to ask one day when she and Elizabeth were alone in the still-room, making an inventory of its contents. 'She only asks advice in order to repudiate it and put forward some superior plan of her own. She does not deserve the effort of rational opposition.'

A pause ensued. At first Emma thought her sister did not intend to answer. But at last she replied briefly, 'Penelope loves to argue. And if I engage her, it somewhat lessens the risk of her disputing with Dr Harding. I have noticed that such contentious discussions fatigue him greatly . . . These tools should certainly not be in here. Jem?' She put her head out of the door and called, 'Jem, take all these things to the garden-room.'

Emma looked after her sister with surprised respect. Penelope's curt impatience with Dr Harding had already struck her as unexpected and improper in such a new-married wife; that Elizabeth had not only observed it, but taken her own measures to alleviate the friction, impressed her greatly. Elizabeth has far too low an opinion of herself, thought Emma. Mrs Blake often said so. She rates both her looks and her intelligence far too humbly; that is partly because Penelope, who is younger, has always asserted herself and put down her elder sister; it is a shocking pity; Elizabeth has by far the better nature, her looks are superior, if only she would take pains, and she is quite as shrewd as Penelope. How I wonder what Elizabeth and Tom Musgrave said to each other during those four dances! I shall never dare to ask. Poor Tom. How can he ever lift up his head again, after causing the death of Mrs Blake and little Charles. He will be obliged to leave this neighbourhood and move away.

Mr Thickstaffe also kept an observant and watchful eye, Emma noticed, on the relations between Dr Harding and his bride. Sometimes he would jokingly intervene, or would seize the first opportunity to carry the conversation away into some more innocuous area. While Emma respected him more for this, she did not like him any better – indeed, after five days, her antipathy had grown to a point where she found it a penance even to be in the same room with him, and strenuously avoided being alone in his company.

She wondered if he had noticed this. He was certainly no fool, despite his unpolished and often offensive manners. He could and quite often did converse intelligently on a variety of topics of public interest; he knew a great deal about money, since he had for some time followed the profession of a bill-broker, as had his father before him; he had been born and brought up in rooms above the family office in Lombard Street.

Emma wondered why he had left this lucrative profession. Perhaps there had been some untoward occurrence?

Akin to that at Osborne Park? Whatever the reason, at some point he had become Dr Harding's adviser, and it was through his offices, apparently, that the doctor had gained the opportunity of turning a modest competence, amassed by industrious years of medical practice, into a handsome fortune.

'I'd say it was a lucky stroke for your family, Miss Emma, that brought me into Dr Harding's path and him into that of your sister,' Mr Thickstaffe told Emma while they were making a catalogue, she with great reluctance, of some silver and plate which the doctor had bought at an auction.

'No doubt,' she responded coldly, writing down *6 Queen Anne teaspoons, much tarnished.*

'And I am hoping to put your brother Mr Sam in the way of doing as well for himself as the doctor; Mr Sam Watson is a clever man and a good surgeon and it would be a great pity if his lack of advancement were to be caused simply by straitened means.'

'Perhaps so,' said Emma reluctantly.

Thickstaffe ignored her chilly tone. He chuckled.

'Poor young fellow! He still dangles after Miss Mary Edwards. But he has no hope of her, no hope whatsoever, since she came into that fortune. I have it on firm authority—' (Mr Thickstaffe, it seemed, had many relations in the countryside) – 'that Lord Osborne is to make her an offer any day. Why, Nanny, what is it? Why do you seek me here in the butler's pantry?'

Old Nanny, who had been hovering in the doorway, regarded Mr Thickstaffe with a gimlet eye. She had decided from the start that he was no gentry, but a jumped-up chaw-bacon; and as such she treated him. He was well aware of this and bore her no ill-will; her usage seemed to amuse him.

'It's not you I want, Mr Thickstaffe, but Miss Emma; ~~here's your brother, miss, Master Sam, come a-calling, and~~ who do you suppose he has with him but Lord Osborne? Seems they met a-riding along the river road.'

'Well, well, well!' chuckled Thickstaffe. 'Romeo, and what's the other young feller-me-lad's name, Count Paris, *both* come a-calling at the same time? Now I wonder what brings them hither? Can they know something that we do not know? It falls out handily, for I, too, wished to see Mr Sam Watson.'

Emma walked into the morning-room, which, by one means or another, had been made tolerably fit for the reception of callers. Here she found her sister Elizabeth, somewhat ill-at-ease in the company of Sam and Lord Osborne, who seemed awkward in the company of each other. It was plain immediately to Emma that Elizabeth, though always happy to see Sam, had left some task unfinished which was preoccupying her mind; and that she wished Lord Osborne at the bottom of the sea.

'Dr Harding will be here soon,' she explained rather distractedly. 'I have sent to fetch him – he and Penelope – Mrs Harding – went out with Heythrop to inspect the new approach road they are digging.'

To Emma's annoyance, Mr Thickstaffe had followed her into the morning-room and now saluted the two young men.

'Mr Sam Watson! And Lord Osborne! Pray convey my best respects to Lady Osborne, when you see her, and to

Miss Harriet. How are those new birch plantations doing, sir? Were they badly affected by the cold winter last year? And the new cut and fish hatcheries, did they prosper?'

Emma was indignant that Mr Thickstaffe assumed so much the air of the householder himself; what right had he to do so? And Lord Osborne, she observed, received his greetings with a degree of confusion and with very little pleasure. It was true that Lord Osborne never, at any time, seemed particularly confident or easy in company; he was pale, as usual, mumbled something in which the words 'happy' and 'obliged' could be heard, looked at his feet, and presently was heard to explain stammeringly that Lady Osborne had gone to London for a few days on business related to the new incumbent at Stanton. She had been accompanied by Mr Howard. Lord Osborne evinced very little enthusiasm at this disclosure, but that might be just his natural manner.

Emma had hardly thought that her spirits could be reduced any lower, but these tidings caused her heart, inexplicably, to sink. They will come back from London engaged to be married, she thought sorrowfully. He will find it easier to make the offer in London. That is certain to happen.

Now Penelope appeared, all smiles.

'Lord Osborne! How truly delightful! My husband will be here directly, he is just changing his footwear! *The mud!* I had forgotten how much mud there is in the country. But how is your lady mother? Is she well?'

Lord Osborne lamely repeated his information regarding Lady Osborne's visit to town; as he did so Penelope darted lightning glances at her sisters: why was I not called sooner? they demanded, why have no refreshments been offered, where is Fielding with the sherry?

'And so your dear mother is enjoying the delights of town; but when she returns, and when we are more settled in, I do hope and trust that we shall see her here. We should value her opinion of what has been achieved so far.'

Lord Osborne muttered something that might, or might not, be accepted as a declaration of his mother's intentions in that respect.

'She is – that is she has – or, at least I believe so . . .'

'*Delightful* to have town within such easy reach from here!' exulted Penelope. 'We plan many, many excursions to the metropolis – do we not, my love?'

For at this moment Dr Harding made his appearance, in clean boots, looking moithered, and as if he wished himself elsewhere. However, his face lit up at sight of Sam.

'Of course, from Chichester, a visit to London was *quite* out of the question – but now – quite another matter – and, also, when the builders have at last left us in peace, we shall hope to see a *great deal* of our neighbours – nothing too formal, you know, at first, but to have some young people gathered in for games of lottery tickets and a little dancing – that is the kind of entertainment that Dr Harding *so much* enjoys – and a little hot supper you know – then, by and bye, closer to Easter, when our good Bertrand has made plenty of white soup, perhaps a ball . . .'

Sam had been talking earnestly to Thickstaffe, but the word *ball* caught his ear.

'A ball?' he said with brotherly bluntness. 'Good heavens, Penelope! Flying rather high, ain't you? Have you a sufficiently large room for such a purpose? Or indeed a large enough acquaintance?'

Penelope gave him a quelling look, but Emma thought she caught a brief flash of what looked like relief and partisanship in the eye of Dr Harding.

'Certainly there is room. The two saloons at the side have been thrown into one, and it would be the most shocking waste not to make use —'

But, in truth, whom will she invite? thought Emma. Which of our former neighbours would be prepared to come so far, along a muddy road? And most of those were old – and poor. A ball is not at all the kind of entertainment that would attract them.

She noticed Sam's eyes straying to the window. By now the state of affairs in the front courtyard was more orderly, less chaotic; Emma, following the direction of Sam's glance, saw a carriage come round the sweep and pull up out of sight.

'Gracious! I declare, more visitors!' cried Penelope in high feather. 'Who can it be this time, I wonder?'

Emma was suddenly, piercingly reminded of a morning at Stanton Parsonage, when Mrs Blake had come calling with the children; that was the same day, she thought, on which Penelope turned up to announce that she was married. What a deal of things have happened since then, and all of them sad . . .

She was plucked from these unprofitable thoughts by Fielding's announcement of Mr Edwards, Mrs Edwards, and Miss Edwards.

Emma realized at once, from a swift glance at Sam's conscious countenance, that he had been privy, beforehand, to this intention of the Edwards family, and had planned his own visit accordingly; she wondered if the same was true of Lord Osborne. Sam, of course, in his profession, received intelligence from every door and window in the country; and Lord Osborne, as the accredited suitor of Mary Edwards, might be supposed to be in communication with her; certainly he did not seem at all surprised at her arrival.

Mary Edwards was twenty-one, a year younger than Margaret; she was not pretty, her complexion was too colourless, but she had a very sweet countenance, pale blue eyes, and a quantity of very soft, fair hair, which would not stay tidy but continually tumbled out of its curl; she had delicate manners, was rather shy, and looked anxiously and often for guidance to her parents. She reminds me greatly of somebody, thought Emma, who had seen her only once before, at the first Dorking Assembly; now who can it be? Mr and Mrs Edwards were correct and civil, but somewhat stiff; the lady particularly so, with a reticent air, as if she were reserving judgement on this new, lavish establishment that had been so hastily set up in the neighbourhood; Mr Edwards had a much easier and more communicative manner, and was soon on cordial terms with Dr Harding, chatting about fishing rights, and coppicing, and the excellent properties of the chalybeate waters at Epsom.

Penelope, in vigorous conversation with Lord Osborne, was saying, 'A hunt breakfast! Now *that* is a capital idea! Dr Harding would be delighted to give one, and so meet many of our neighbours in a lively and informal manner. Formality, you must know, is our abhorrence! Consider the thing settled, dear Lord Osborne! When do your hounds next meet in this country? Oh, by *that* time all these great piles of stone will be gone, I promise you, the house and grounds will be quite completed. We shall greatly look forward to seeing you in all your glory. By the bye—' she lowered her voice – 'what has become of poor Tom Musgrave? I hear he is all to nothing, poor fellow, after what happened?'

Lord Osborne looked extremely grave. He muttered, 'I think – I believe – I do not know – not quite certain . . .' Emma could not hear the rest of what he replied.

Mr Thickstaffe had entered the conversation with Mr Edwards and Dr Harding.

'Very good in its way, as far as it goes, the Wey and Arun Ship Canal,' he was saying, 'but what is urgently needed hereabouts is a Grand Imperial Ship Canal from London to Portsmouth – a route from Dorking via Wotton and Abinger to Ockley might be possible – perhaps a canal down the valley of the river Mole – or, possibly, communication by means of the Surrey Iron Railway at Merstham.'

'Mule-pulled trucks are far more efficient than horse-drawn barges,' objected Mr Edwards. 'And speedier, too.'

'But the cost, my good sir, the cost! Think of laying all that track! It would be far better to extend the Croydon Canal to Portsmouth.'

'Ay – by chopping through lord knows how many hill-sides, building tunnels, and viaducts, and re-routing waterways—'

'An Act of Parliament will be needed in either case—'

Good God, said Emma to herself, visited by a sudden shaft of illumination. Can *that* be why Dr Harding has purchased this house? Because of its situation beside the river? Because the property may be of considerable value, should one or other of the schemes they are canvassing ever come into being?

She glanced out of the window. The morning-room, situated on the south-east corner of the house, had a clear view down the wooded slope, and across the road, to the narrow river below, which wound peacefully between its bushy banks, reflecting a sky for once clear and spring-like. Emma tried to imagine it busy with river-traffic, barges filled with coal, charcoal, and lime, tow-ropes flashing through the water, massive horses plodding along the bank, the shouts of carters, perhaps a wharf at the foot of this very hill . . .

'Well, my dear sir, you had best consult Osborne about it. He sits in the House of Lords—'

Lord Osborne, now talking to Mary Edwards, appeared most unwilling to be approached.

'I know little of such matters – I do not – I have not – I cannot undertake . . .'

Mrs Edwards was bidding a gracious goodbye to Penelope. 'Such an *interesting* house. Such a challenge for you to undertake. We shall often be wondering as to your progress. Of course too far to come so often as dear Stanton. Come, Henry, come Mary my love, you must remember that we have *considerably* farther to go, now, to the turn-pike. Goodbye, Miss Watson, goodbye, Miss Emma.'

To Sam she contrived not to say any goodbye at all.

'She was not a bit pleased that I was here,' Sam said to Emma and Elizabeth after the visitors had all departed.

'Well, Sam, I did rather wonder that you were able to

take time off from your work,' replied the literal-minded Elizabeth. 'And, very likely, Mrs Edwards thought the same. And she did not like it at all that you were talking to Mary Edwards, over by the window, for such a long time. Indeed, I wondered at it myself.'

'She is not engaged to Osborne *yet*,' said Sam doughtily.

Old Nanny pottered into the room at this moment, picking up glasses, and caught the last remark.

'Miss Edwards engaged to Lord Osborne!' she squawked. 'The idea! I should hope not, indeed! That would never do! My gracious goodness! The very idea!'

'Why, Nanny?' said Emma, puzzled. 'I know he is above her in rank, but she *has* inherited all that fortune, you know, and the Edwardses are very respectable people. Many would think it a fair bargain. And so might we, if it were not for our poor Sam.'

'But,' said Nanny in a voice of doom, 'like as not Lord Osborne don't know it, but Miss Edwards is not their true daughter. She was adopted.'

'Well, but, Nanny, everybody knows that. She's their niece. The daughter of Mr Edwards's sister who died.'

Emma's thoughts strayed away. The word *niece* carried her to Aunt O'Brien. Now that Mr Howard was in London, doubtless enjoying the pleasures of the Season, there would be even less chance of hearing through him about the possible movements of Aunt O'Brien.

Sighing, Emma returned to the pantry, and her catalogue of spoons and forks.

9

Emma was driven into Croydon by Mr Thickstaffe on a rainy, misty March morning with a chill wind blowing, when, perhaps, in other company, it might have seemed highly agreeable to exchange a damp, cold, silent and remote country residence for a modern abode in a growing city full of activity and bustle.

Emma was not pleased either with her company or her destination, but she had been given no choice in the matter. The convenience of others came first. Mr Thickstaffe was bound on several errands for his employer, Dr Harding: he had to visit the bank, an attorney, an estate office, and make various inquiries regarding taxes and grazing rights; also he was required to pick up and bring back with him Miss Margaret Watson, who now wished to remove herself from her brother Robert's house in Croydon and pass some months with her sisters at Clissocks.

Elizabeth had had a letter from Robert about it:

The truth of the matter is, my dear Eliza, that Hobhouse sheered off like lightning the very moment he knew that Mag was to receive no more than a hundred pounds under my father's Will. I cannot say that I blame him. I would not take her on myself with ten times the money. I was afraid he might shab off;

*and he did. So Mag wishes to quit the scene of such
a humiliation and try her luck elsewhere. Jane would
write to Pen about this, but, as you know, they are at
daggers drawn at present over that stupid business of
my mother's embroideries. Heaven knows why
Penelope should want them; you would think she had
sufficient of Mother's things, including that very
valuable marquetry workbox which she removed from
Stanton without consulting anybody's views but her
own. However I was never one to repine, as you
know, and there is no more to be said on the matter
except that I have never witnessed a more ill-judged,
scrambled affair than that distribution of my father's
effects; if you can persuade Pen to send back the
workbox it would be a good thing. The whole business
was a crying shame and you may think yourself
lucky, my dear Eliza, that you were not very greatly
involved in it. At least nobody can blame you. The
codicil about the sermons, leaving them to Emma, was
quite disgraceful. But that is by the way, and there is
no more to be said. If Jane refuses to write or speak to
P., the duty must devolve on me, though the lord
knows I have work enough of my own. Candidly,
sister, I shall be glad of M.'s departure, for she has
been dismally bad-tempered of late and, as you know,
even at the best of times she can be very tediously
fretful and complaining. Also she eats an amazing
quantity of butter. I hope that country air may
improve her spirits and looks, which have fallen off
shockingly; & that P. may have better fortune in
finding her a husband. All kinds of talk is flying about*

*the countryside as to P.'s lavish style of entertainment
at Clissocks, and her card parties and hot suppers.
Well for Dr Harding's purse, is all I can say.*

Yr affc bro: Robert

*By the bye, Jane says, little Emma may as well
come in by the equipage that removes Margaret, for
she may now have Mag's room & commence
teaching young Gussie, who badly needs a firm
hand.*

*Did you know that Purvis's wife was brought to
bed of a dead infant & it is said she herself is not
expected to survive.*

'I have been hoping for a chance to talk to you privately,'
said Thickstaffe, driving along the turnpike. 'But you are
always so elusive, Miss Emma. Like a little will-o'-the-wisp,
you are!'

'Oh?' said Emma. 'What did you wish to say to me,
Mr Thickstaffe, that could not be spoken out in company?'

'First, I wish very much that you will drop a word in
my favour in the ear of your brother Mr Sam Watson.'

'Why in the world should I do that?' said Emma, very
astonished.

'Because he is very fond of you, and would listen to
what you say.'

'But what is all this about?'

'I have asked him to take a stake in my Grand Imperial
Ship Canal venture.'

'Invest money, you mean?' She was astonished. 'But
my brother Sam has no money to invest.'

'On the contrary, he has now about seven thousand

from your father which, following my counsel, he may readily double – treble – quadruple – without the least risk to himself.'

Emma distrusted the veracity of every word in that statement.

She replied coolly, 'And what was the second thing you wished to ask me, Mr Thickstaffe?'

He said slowly, 'I have noticed that Mrs Harding pays heed to what you say. Oh, she does not *appear* to, but she listens and marks; I have heard her, sometimes, bring out observations made by you, as her own opinion, later on. I think it is because of all the time passed by you with your wealthy aunt Maria in Shrewsbury; Mrs Harding takes account of that and respects what it stands for, though she will not openly acknowledge the fact.'

'Well?'

'Well!' He clucked to the horses. They were now entering the outskirts of Croydon, untidy with gravel-pits and loading sheds; the traffic had become very heavy; the continuous rumble of carts and drays, the bawling of newsmen, muffin-men and milkmen, the clash of pattens, and the hoots and whistles of barges plying along the canal made a very unwelcome accompaniment, so far as Emma was concerned, to their conversation.

'Well!' resumed Mr Thickstaffe, when he had the horses under firm control. 'All I can ask is that it be suggested to Mrs Harding, *ever* so mildly and delicately, that her husband's resources are not bottomless, and that his patience may not be inexhaustible. I know she is but new-married, and had been waiting many years for such a chance; but a word of warning, a *word of warnings*,

Miss Emma, may be very well advised. She is kicking up her heels just a bit too high, Miss Emma, if you follow me?'

He gave Emma a frowning level glance, then quickly turned his attention back to his reins. 'Croydon is a fine town, is it not,' he observed chattily. 'I believe there are above one hundred and sixty houses in it by now; your brother's, perhaps, is the hundred-and-sixty-first. The town possesses a very fine hospital, the Whitgift, and the sales of walnuts, gravel, coal, and charcoal are prodigious. There is also a notable great cherry orchard – you will be able to admire its blossom in a couple of months' time.'

Emma found little else to admire. The High Street, which had once been handsome, was now overlaid with shop fronts and raucous with traffic.

Robert's house, a smart white villa, stood on a hilly slope by the upper Addiscombe Road, on the eastern outskirts of the town. The garden was still bare and rudimentary. Emma thought how bald and unfinished it appeared, in comparison with the tree-girt and hoary antiquity of Clissocks.

'Well, I will think about what you said, Mr Thickstaffe,' she said, as he pulled up. 'But I cannot promise to say anything to my brother.'

Surprisingly, though, she felt a tinge of respect for Mr Thickstaffe; it was the first such feeling she had entertained towards him.

At Beech Hanger they were greeted with the information that Margaret was not ready to leave yet, would not be packed up for at least half an hour.

'Very well,' said Thickstaffe, unperturbed. 'I will drive

down into the town, perform my errands, and return.' And he departed among the raw new houses, the unfinished chalky streets, and the clattering traffic.

Despite the fact that Robert's house was called Beech Hanger, there was not a beech tree in sight. Emma's first impression was how cramped the house felt, and how crowded with furniture, compared with the large dim spaces of Clissocks. Penelope's taste in colour, to be sure, was rather strident, but her glaring hues were diminished in the distance of the great empty rooms; whereas Jane's neat, crammed quarters continually distracted the eye with clashing colours and variegated patterns.

It was no new experience for Emma to discover that by travelling a few miles, and moving to a different circle of society, a person could feel they inhabited a completely different world. She and Elizabeth had been happy at Stanton, in the gentle ecclesiastical orbit of their father and his pastoral duties. And, she thought, in time to come Elizabeth might recover some sort of happiness at Clissocks; true, Penelope was selfish, dictatorial, and erratic, but the peace and quiet of the house itself, and the mild vagueness of Dr Harding were elements that promised, for the future, a certain degree of harmony and stability (if Mr Thickstaffe's precepts were attended to).

But this new house of Robert's produced a painful effect, a jarring effect, upon each one of the five senses.

Being so new, it was noisy and draughty; doors slammed, feet clattered upon stairs, voices echoed against hard, raw surfaces; it smelt strongly of fresh paintwork and opulent new fabrics; lights glared and windows, opening on to vacant spaces, dazzled too brightly; corners were sharp, the whole atmosphere harsh and unrestful. This was due, too, in some degree to the personality of Jane Watson, a restless indefatigable housewife, who spent her days in pursuit of her servants, harrying and exhorting them, and her nights in complaint about them.

'You may as well help me to finish packing my things, since you are come,' said Margaret to Emma, and set her to work folding shifts and cambrics and rolling stockings into balls.

Margaret's room, which was over the front door, seemed small and cramped compared with Emma's previous quarters, and she was very glad she had not to share it with Margaret, who at once launched into a long and bitter catalogue of angry objurgations against the faithless Mr Hobhouse, against Jane and Robert for not taking her part more vigorously and fetching him back, against all the other people in the world who had better luck than she.

'Why should Penelope, so ill-natured as she is, have plucked such a plum? It is entirely unfair!'

'Oh, come, Margaret,' said Emma, eventually tiring of all this self-pity. 'We have all had our troubles, you know. And no doubt Penelope did lay herself out to be pleasant to Dr Harding, instead of grumbling all the time.'

'Well! *You* have not done so badly, sister,' retorted Margaret, turning on her venomously, '*you* as good as killed our father, everybody says so, you are as good as a murderer, and what is your reward? You are invited to Clissocks, fed on dainties there, meet a whole procession of guests continually calling – so we hear—'

Emma could feel herself turning white with shock.

'Who says such a thing about me?'

'Oh – everybody. It is common talk in Croydon. Ah – there is Mr Thickstaffe come back at last. He took his time! I must say I shall be glad to part from Robert and Jane. He is so purse-proud! And she nags continually. And I certainly wish you joy *of her—*' she snapped, as a valedictory, pointing to a fat pale little girl who just then sidled into the room and stood with her finger in her mouth staring first at the luggage, then at Emma.

'Who that?' she demanded, stickily, round the wet finger.

'*That* is your aunt Emma, come to make you into a good girl. An impossible task,' said Margaret, gathered up her shawl, and left the room.

Emma soon found that what Margaret had said was no more than the truth. Teaching little Augusta Watson *was* an almost impossible task, and a penitential one, as the child was by nature rather stupid, and by upbringing and usage wholly disinclined to apply herself. She would sit quiet for a moment or two, no longer, while a simple air was played to her on the pianoforte or the harp (which Jane had rather ambitiously acquired), but the notion of attempting to learn how to play these instruments herself threw her into transports of disgust; the only form of playing she enjoyed was to draw her thumb along the keys, or across the strings, or to crash her fists down on a clump of notes.

'Dear little soul! She has such high spirits!' said her fond mother. 'But I am sure she has a really strong aptitude for music. You saw how she listened when you played "Barbara Allen"?'

'Yes, but that was only because you had given her a tart, and she was busy munching it,' said Emma flatly.

'The angel!'

Emma soon discovered that almost the entire care of little Gussie now devolved on herself, and this was no sinecure. Jemima, the servant-girl who hitherto had charge of the child, was transferred to other duties and went with visible relief. Jane Watson had in fact acquired an unpaid servant. The promised treats and excursions about the city of Croydon did not materialize; they were in perpetual abeyance. Emma began to consider her own prospects somewhat ruefully, and to wonder how she might ever acquire one or two lighter gowns, now that spring was approaching. She had no money, apart from the hundred pounds left her by her father, and she did not wish to make inroads on that, feeling it should be kept for emergencies.

Once, fatigued after a whole morning spent in the attempt to instil some faint conception of the ABC into the recalcitrant little Gussie, she said to Jane:

'I wonder, Jane, do you think it might be possible for me to give music lessons to a few children or young ladies in the neighbourhood here? Then I need not be a charge on you, but could pay you for my keep. I should be very glad to contribute to the household. And I might save up a little nest-egg for my old age, even!' she added hopefully.

But Jane, entirely scandalized at the suggestion, flew into a passion.

'What! Advertise to all the neighbours that we was too mean and poor to support you? So offer yourself in the public market? A fine notion, upon my word! I wonder at you, Emma, I do indeed!' And to Robert, when he came home that evening, she said, 'I suppose that sister of yours, that Penelope, has been putting ideas into Emma's head, that we are stingy and cheeseparing and necessitous. A fine thing! And she, queening herself out there at Clissocks, giving evening parties for half the county, while half the furniture under that roof properly belongs to us!'

Robert, who came home late and tired every day from his law office, where, to do him justice, he worked long hours and exceedingly hard, listened to the familiar tirade against Penelope and said, 'Well, well, perhaps we should give it some thought. I do not see why Emma should not give music lessons to a few persons of quality. It could do no harm. And then, it is true, she could pay for her keep.'

'But who, then, would look after little Gussie?'

This seemed unanswerable. Robert said, 'Well, well, we shall see. This scheme of Thickstaffe and his friend Mainbrace for a Grand Imperial Ship Canal seems to be attracting a deal of notice. There is to be a Bill in Parliament about it, I understand. The main problem is to pay off the landowners who are raising objections along the route. One can see that no farmer wishes to have a canal dug across his best grazing land. Upon my soul, though, if it was to be accomplished, it would be a fine thing, one cannot deny, for the city of Croydon; the lime, coal, and feed trade would be tripled in a year. So would my practice. Old Harding has an eye to the main chance, I see; aye, he was not such a fool as we all thought when he bought Clissocks. The property might be worth a gold mine. That Thickstaffe (though for my part I would never deal with him as I have heard some exceedingly doubtful tales about him) has put his employer in the way of what may be a very good thing.'

'Thickstaffe!' cried Jane spitefully. 'Why, he is not much better than a gipsy! He has a whole troop of indigent relatives living out at Mickleham. It would not surprise me if, by and bye, they was all found to be removed to Clissocks. They are a beggarly, forward, scheming clan – I wish Penelope joy of them! I daresay she will find them just such a group as she delights in – the manner in which she got hold of that workbox of Mamma Watson was no more than a sly, underhand trick. And winding her way in among the nobility of the neighbourhood – thinking herself so very great! Lord Osborne coming to call! A fine thing! He does not come to call *here*!'

'It was to press his suit – Miss Edwards was there at the time, you remember, Emma told us.'

'Miss Edwards! *She* did not spare much time for him at the last Assembly.'

'She is a very well-brought-up young lady.'

'So she may be! But who were her parents, pray tell me?'

'If the Osbornes do not trouble about it, why should we?' said Robert reasonably.

Emma came in, looking utterly fatigued and discouraged, with little Gussie, who declared, 'I *hate* Cousin Emma! Why cannot 'Mima look after me as she did before?'

*

'Good gracious,' observed Jane Watson some weeks later. 'Here are *two* letters for Emma. And a parcel as well, from Portsmouth. Who in the world can be writing to her?'

'And one of the letters is from overseas,' commented Robert, equally interested. 'Can it be tidings of Aunt O'Brien at last?'

When Emma came to the breakfast table with little Gussie, tidy for the only extended period of her day, Jane said archly, 'Well! What a lucky young lady! It seems that you are much in demand!'

Emma, taking no notice of the letters, said, 'Jane, I think you should dismiss Jemima. She is still filling Gussie's head with the most shocking tales of devils and vampires and snake ladies – it is no wonder that the child has nightmares and screams so in her sleep.'

Jane was up in arms at once.

'Thank you, my dear Emma! I am perfectly capable of choosing and dismissing my own servants. I need no advice from you.'

Emma shrugged, and was silent. As soon as she had breakfasted she carried away the letters and package to her own chamber, and left them there, to be read after lesson-time was over.

Jane fumed to her husband: 'Miss Emma is growing altogether too high-up and presuming. Jemima is an excellent servant, perfectly steady and trustworthy. And she is developing a real talent for doing my hair. I wish you will say a word to Emma, Robert.'

Robert said, 'I wonder who those letters were from?'

*

The parcel, which seemed to contain a book, Emma laid on one side.

The first letter she opened was from Mr Howard:

Dear Miss Watson,

I have been long seeking to convey to you my deep sense of grief and sympathy at the loss of your father. At the funeral, and among your family, no private conference could be attempted. And I myself, at that time, was hardly in a fit state for rational intercourse, with the loss of my dear sister Anna such a new and pressing woe. At that moment, indeed, it struck me most forcibly that I had not entered sufficiently into your feelings at the time of our earlier conversation when you divulged to me your anxieties about your poor aunt. One's own troubles often bring greater comprehension and insight into those of one's friends. And I can share now more fully your sense of deprivation – trebled after the death of Mr Watson and my sister, with whom, I know, you had become very close. She often spoke of you warmly. Our mutual sorrow brings us nearer together.

Let me take this opportunity of saying to you as I did to your sister Elizabeth that I do not pay the smallest heed to the malicious gossip and tittle-tattle which asserts that you were responsible for Mr Watson's death; my sister had described that evening to me fully, related the whole tale of what passed, and I can assign no shade of blame. I know that Mr Watson's end might have come at any time during the past year.

The publication of his selected sermons goes on

prosperously, I am glad to tell you. I travelled to London recently for the purpose of visiting the publishers and inspecting the printed text. It is hoped that the volume will be given to the public in the course of the summer, and it has already attracted much favourable notice. It is to be entitled Discourses of a Rural Divine. *Your father's excellent sense, plain, clear language, and strong, candid devotion cannot fail to impress any reader.*

I am sorry, dear Miss Emma, that I have had nothing to report from my friend Montagu in Dublin. The Mrs O'Brien of whom he had heard rumours proved to be a different person entirely (O'Brien unfortunately being a name often encountered in Ireland). But now he tells me that he is on the track of another possibility, and hopes to have news for me by and bye. I shall, of course, allow not a moment to pass before putting before you any information that comes my way.

This letter discharges a heavy burden from my heart. You have been much in my thoughts, dear Miss Emma.

> *Sincerely, Adam T. Howard*

Emma held this letter in her hand for some time, reading and re-reading, meditating on its contents.

He has not yet made his proposal to Lady Osborne, was her conclusion. If he had, he would have felt it his duty to tell me. Why is he so slow in the business? But his sister always did say that he was slow – even dilatory – in all his actions . . .

Next Emma thought: There is sure to be trouble from Robert about the volume of Papa's sermons, when they are published. I have not heard the last of it, by a long way. But there is no sense in anticipating that. Papa would say, sufficient unto the day is the trouble thereof.

The codicil in Mr Watson's testament had come as a shock to several of his children. It had been drawn up in the office, and witnessed by several of Robert's clerks, on a day when he himself chanced to be out in the country dealing with the affairs of a bed-ridden farmer. Mr Watson, visiting Croydon on clerical business, had dropped into the office and dictated the clause which assigned all the rights in his discourses 'to my daughter Emma, who has diligently read aloud these texts to me and given me valuable assistance in collating them'. Robert had been extremely put out, returning to the office, but, as he said at the time, 'There's precious little chance of publication, and, if they should come out, it's odds that they won't set the world on fire.'

'But why should *Emma*, of all the family, have those rights?' demanded Jane, justly indignant.

'Oh well,' said Robert, 'Emma has not much else.'

I think Mr Howard has a feeling for me, was Emma's final deduction, putting down his letter. He would like to say more, but he knows he cannot.

Small comfort!

Now she opened the second letter, which was somewhat stained, apparently by salt water, and written in a firm, graceful, and totally unknown hand. It was superscribed 'H.M.S. *Laconia*, Sea of Marmara':

My dear Miss Watson,

It is with the greatest enthusiasm that I take this chance to retire to my cabin and thank you for one of the most delightful evenings I have ever spent. It will be embedded in my recollection for the remainder of my days. I find it strange to sit here, under the hot Turkish sky, within sight of the minarets of Constantinople, and remember the charm and peace of an English vicarage. But I can remember it most vividly. My cousin Anna – your father – you, Miss Emma – are three of the most congenial companions I ever hope to pass an evening with. And I wish I may not tempt Providence by expressing the hope that when I return to dry land, I may spend many, many more such evenings. (Forgive me. I know that your father is in a delicate state of health. But oh, may his wide knowledge, benevolence, and wit be preserved to delight his friends for years yet to come.)

At this point Emma put down the paper and stared out of the window, over the empty garden. For a moment her fancy played with the notion of blue Turkish waters and slender white minarets.

How strange, she mused. How very strange. Captain Fremantle does not know – did not, when he wrote these words – that, out of the three companions with whom he shared that evening, two are gone. Only one is left.

Then, with an icy shiver, she looked at the date of the letter. Two months had passed since it was written. Who knows? Life at sea was hazardous. By now, Captain Fremantle himself might be no more. And it might be months later before Emma was apprised of his fate. If at all. Of the four, she might now be the only survivor . . . She went on reading:

Is it not queer, Miss Emma, how, just rarely in life, it is possible to meet a person and know about them, instantaneously and without the shadow of a doubt, This is the one!

That was how I felt about you, while standing outside that Gothic mansion (I hope that by now your sister has moved into it?) exchanging nonsense about Caedwalla and Cwichelm (about whom I am now in a position to give you a great deal more information, the next time we meet). And I sincerely hope that we do *meet again – indeed I cannot really tolerate the prospect of enduring the rest of my life without such a meeting.*

You may, of course, not share my feelings at all. I have no right to hope that you do. And yet, and yet – something about the way in which you smiled at me, something about the way in which our mental processes appeared to dove-tail – something about that happy evening – gives me, I cannot precisely say why, cause to hope. I shall continue to hope, dear Miss Emma! as long as I am above ground, and you are still Miss Emma.

And, as soon as I set foot again on English soil, I shall return to continue our conversation about Caedwalla.

This comes with my friendship and devotion,
Matthew Fremantle

P.S. I entrusted an acquaintance of mine in Portsmouth, a bookseller, with the task of finding and transmitting to you a work on the history of the Saxon kings. I trust that by this time he has fulfilled this commission. When reading the work, pray spare a thought for him who thinks about you a great deal.

For some ten minutes after reading this letter, Emma sat motionless, spellbound, amazed. Then she began to smile. The letter brought Captain Fremantle before her so completely – his long, narrow, expressive face, his bright hazel eyes, his nutcracker grin. *This is the one.* Why did I not understand? But I did, yes, I did, right from the first moment.

If only I could write back to him!

10

'Here's a fine thing!' said Jane indignantly to Robert when he came home one evening. 'Mrs Tomlinson was here with her daughters – what do you think the tale is, that is going around?'

'About the meeting at the White Hart at Guildford? It was held. They have formed a committee of nine to prepare a petition for Parliament. Now they have to choose an engineer to select the best route for the canal; Harding will be on tenterhooks, no doubt.'

'No, *no*, not that precious canal. I am sure I never wish to hear the word canal or navigation again,' said Jane pettishly. 'No, this, this disgraceful gossip about your sister Penelope and Percy Thickstaffe.'

'Why, what about them?' asked Robert uneasily.

'They are saying – oh, dreadful things! Far worse than about your sister Emma seizing the chance to hasten your father's death.'

'I *never* believed that,' said he. 'Why should she do such a thing? Turning herself out of doors? She stood to gain nothing from such a deed – quite the reverse.'

'Well – that's by the way. But now,' Jane told him, on a note of strong condemnation, not unmixed with satisfaction, 'they are saying that Penelope and Thickstaffe formed a plan together that she should marry

Dr Harding so that she might gain control of his fortune!'

'I do not believe it,' said Robert instantly. 'Why should Harding submit to be made use of in such a way? He is not a fool.'

'No, but, Robert, there may be something in it. I have had *such* letters from Margaret since she moved out to Clissocks. She says that Penelope and Thickstaffe are for ever in each other's pockets, meeting all over the grounds, conferring privily with each other, and that Penelope behaves disgracefully to Dr Harding, snubs and snaps at him, never for a moment minds what he says, or pays heed to his wishes, or attends to his welfare – and they have hardly been married six months!'

'Well, Penelope was always a shrewd, contriving creature with an eye to the main chance. How she managed to ensnare Harding in the first place, I shall always wonder. And now he has got her he has only himself to thank. But she will be a fool – more of a fool than I think her – if she tosses her bonnet over the windmill with such a one as Thickstaffe. I daresay he may have insinuating ways – so you women say, though I never saw it myself, I think him a pestilential fellow – but Harding is now a man of solid property with a house that *anyone* might envy; whereas, what has Thickstaffe got? Nothing but a plausible tongue and a scheme for joining several waterways together which will probably never get past its first reading in Parliament.'

'Oh, you are so like a man!'

'I am one.'

'And supposing your precious brother Sam invests his

legacy in the canal and loses it all? *Then* who is going to support him?'

'Not I,' said Robert. 'But I do not think Sam is such a thickhead as to do that.'

The doorbell rang.

'Good heavens,' said Robert, looking out of the bow window. 'That is Musgrave's bay hack. He always has a very tidy piece of horseflesh. But what can he be doing in Croydon?'

'Tom Musgrave?' almost shrieked Jane. 'You are not going to see *him*, surely? After he caused the death of that poor unfortunate woman?'

'There is no pleasing you, Jane,' said Robert. 'First you grumble because Lord Osborne never comes to call. Then you raise objections to his friend Tom Musgrave. But we may as well find out what he wants.'

What Tom Musgrave wanted, it seemed, was an interview with Miss Emma Watson. Very coldly and unwillingly did Mrs Robert Watson permit the young lady (who, in a back room, had been endeavouring to give little Gussie instruction on the harp) to be sent for. She would have remained herself, overseeing the visit, but Tom Musgrave, who looked thin, haggard, and hag-ridden, unexpectedly mustered up the courage to demand that the interview be a private one.

Robert, with a curt jerk of the head, ushered his wife out of the room.

'Perhaps he means to propose, after all! Though I never knew that he showed any interest in Emma. Mag was the one he was partial to – or Elizabeth.'

'But he has disgraced himself! I am surprised that

he dares to show his face in a respectable neighbourhood!'

'After all, though, Jane, he does have six thousand a
year.'

Tom Musgrave had not come to propose to Emma. His
prime intention was to grovel in shame, regret, and useless
repentance. How could he have been such a cow-handed,
reckless, clumsy, cursed fool as to have overturned that
poor unfortunate woman and so made an end of her? And
little Charles too – the best little fellow that ever handled
a bat-and-ball, ready for any lark; it broke his heart to
think of the poor father, Captain Blake, over there in the
West Indies, probably to this very day ignorant of his loss.
And Mrs Blake such a great, great friend of yours, Miss
Emma –

All this was poured out, chokingly, almost into Emma's
lap.

'Please, please, Mr Musgrave, stop!' she besought him.
'You are only upsetting yourself to no purpose. I do not
blame you – indeed I don't. In fact, you and I are somewhat in the same position – it is said of me that I caused
my father's death – perhaps even *on purpose* – and I have
to bear that, knowing that I did no such thing, had *no*
such intention. So I can enter very fully into your feelings.
And I *assure* you that I am not angry with you –'

'You do not blame me? You forgive me?'

'Really it is not for me to forgive – I am not the injured
party,' said Emma. 'But I am sure that – that Mr Howard
forgives you. It is his *duty* to do so as a Christian clergyman,' she could not help adding rather drily.

'Oh, you do me so much good, Miss Emma.' Tom

Musgrave mopped his eyes unaffectedly. 'I am so very much obliged to you!'

She could not help feeling rather kindly towards him – he looked so much like a great overgrown schoolboy.

'I think we are distantly related, are we not? My aunt Maria's first husband, Mr Turner – was he not your great-uncle or second cousin or something of that sort?' she added, in a kindly effort to encourage him.

'It may be so – I am not sure – yes, perhaps . . . But, Miss Emma, what I am also come to ask,' he went on, gathering urgency, 'is, will you put in a good word for me with your sister Elizabeth? She will listen to *you*, I am certain – but *I* can't get near her. She will not see me! I have been out to Clissocks half a dozen times, but to no avail. And I do so, I do so *much* want to see her. To tell truth, Miss Emma, your sister Miss Elizabeth is the one for me. I do not know why I have hummed and ha'ed for so long. I have been the veriest fool. When I saw her at that last Assembly – looking somehow so changed – so smiling and sweet-tempered and *good* – I do not know why it had taken me so long to notice – to understand . . .'

It was the effect of the bandoline, thought Emma. And Mrs Blake's Persian silk cloak.

'Then,' he rushed on, 'your father died, and I did that dreadful thing, and I thought I must have lost her for ever. And everybody in the neighbourhood hates and despises me. I despise myself. I do nothing but stay at home and train my horses. (I have got a rattling fine pair, by the bye, Miss Emma!) I do not wish to see people, not at all. Even Osborne has cut me off. He is courting Miss Edwards – though, between you and I, his heart ain't in the business. If Lady Osborne did not hang over him like one of those Valkyries, obliging him to marry money, he'd be off like a scalded cat – what was I saying?'

'You were talking about your feeling for my sister Elizabeth.'

'Well! She's the one for me. But, you see, I can't get near her to tell her so.'

'Even if you could,' said Emma sadly, 'you might not be able to make any impression on her. My sister Elizabeth is gentle, Mr Musgrave, but she is wholly inflexible and obdurate once she has formed a resolution. Or so I have found. She is angry with me over our father's death, so I do not believe that my good offices with her will be of much help to you, Mr Musgrave. But still, I will do for you what I can. I will write her a letter, and ask her to see you. That is all I can offer. Then it is up to you.'

'Oh, thank you, thank you, Miss Emma. You are a true friend indeed.'

He glanced about the cheerless, crowded room in which they were talking, and said, seriously, 'And if, Miss Emma, by any chance I am successful in my suit – if I should have the happiness of setting up house with your sister – I can assure you that you would be our first and most welcome guest!'

'That is very kind of you,' she said smiling faintly. 'I will remember.'

Two minutes after he had bowed and gone, Jane was back in the room, feverish with curiosity.

'Well? Well? What was all *that* about? Well?'

'He wants to marry Elizabeth,' said Emma.

'*Elizabeth?* And he asks *your* permission? *Why?* And

why in the world should he take a notion to marry *Elizabeth*?'

'He did not ask my permission,' said Emma. 'Merely my good offices in persuading her to see him.'

'How very extraordinary! I must say, I do not see why Elizabeth should be so nice in deciding whom she will and will not see; but why should he want to marry her? Is it because he has disgraced himself and no one else will have him?'

'He did not inform me,' said Emma, and escaped to her room.

A man, she thought, when she was alone, must always have some worth in society even when he has disgraced himself. But a woman has not. Why is that? It is because a man can earn money. Even in disgrace he has command of that. But a woman has no financial value. How unfair that is!

For the rest of the evening Jane was huffing, sparking, and fuming, like a fire that has been laid with damp wood, over the equally provoking mysteries of why Tom Musgrave should want Elizabeth, and why *she* should not want *him*.

Emma wrote to Elizabeth: wrote an earnest, heartfelt letter in which, first, she begged that the relations between them might be restored to what they had been before the death of Mr Watson: 'You and Sam are my best friends in all the family; without your affectionate, sisterly recognition I feel lost indeed;' secondly, she asked for a hearing for Tom Musgrave: 'Poor fellow, I know he has not shown himself, hitherto, a very estimable character, but I truly believe that he has undergone a change of heart since what happened, and I consider that, if anybody can influence him to good purpose, it is yourself. At all events, he has his heart fixed on you, and I think you should at least do him the justice of granting him a hearing.'

She had no reply to this letter. But Elizabeth had never been a good correspondent. At the time when Emma was first exiled from home, as she felt it, to the house of Aunt Turner in Shropshire, and longing for letters from the family, Elizabeth had very seldom found the time for correspondence, and when she did, her letters were scanty, plain, and matter-of-fact: 'The black sow has littered, the fruit blossom is very late, Papa has a cold.' It was from Sam, always, that news came depicting thoughts and feelings and actions, news that made up a recognizable vision of the longed-for life at home. So Emma did not expect a reply from Elizabeth. She knew she must wait for news from some other source.

The source, when it arrived, was not particularly agreeable: Margaret rode in with Dr Harding, who had business in Croydon. Margaret, it seemed, suffered from a troublesome tooth and had need to visit the dentist, Mr Pilsbrow. But the prime reason for her visit was to pay a call at Beech Hanger and give voice to a whole flood of complaints about her house-mates at Clissocks.

'The way that Penelope and Thickstaffe go on is nothing less than outrageous! If I were Dr Harding I would pack them both out of doors. They are for ever colloguing together in corners or out at the far ends of the garden, walking along paths together, whispering under trees.'

'Then he has no need to pack them out of doors,' Emma could not help interjecting.

Robert was at his office, and Margaret's jeremiad was being addressed to herself and Jane. Jane listened, all agog, but Emma, who had heard the same kind of thing before, several times, could not help feeling that even the attempt to educate little Gussie, hopeless though it seemed, would be a more useful way of passing the time.

Margaret turned away irritably from Emma to Jane, who was demanding, 'But what do they talk *about*? Are they making love?'

'Oh, la! I never got close enough to hear. But I think partly he is urging her to persuade the old doctor to sink some more of his cash in the canal venture, and I think she ain't willing. "For," says she, "he is close-fisted enough as it is, he begrudges me the fountain and the hermit's grotto I asked for, and, try as I will, I cannot get him to fix a date for a ball. Ball? says the doctor, why, whom should we invite? We do not know above fifteen couple in the neighbourhood." And Thickstaffe partly agrees with the doctor there. And so they all go at it, hammer and tongs.'

'A ball?' said Jane thoughtfully. 'Does she really intend a ball?'

It gave Emma some amusement to see how the possibility of being invited to a ball at Clissocks weighed with Jane against the day-to-day interest of maintaining her quarrel with Penelope. And did the advantage of being able to display herself as a member of the family in this parvenu mansion outstrip the annoyance of being obliged to watch Penelope queening it as mistress of the occasion?

But Margaret's main object of grievance had yet to be disclosed.

'I do not know why you thought it your business to stand advocate for Tom Musgrave with Elizabeth!' she burst out resentfully to Emma. '*You* was never his best friend. *I* was the one he chiefly addressed himself to in the family, and indeed I could have had him for myself if so inclined, but – a worthless puppy! I would not touch him with a bargepole. Especially now! But why *you* should feel entitled to stand his advocate, Emma, passes comprehension.'

'Oh, did Elizabeth show you my letter, then?' asked Emma, somewhat surprised.

'Of course not, but I read it, as anyone might, for she leaves her things out on her dresser for anybody to see that might chance to pass through her bedroom.'

'Did Tom Musgrave come to see her? Did she agree to that?'

'Ay, he came, but I do not think he can have popped the question, for though they was above an hour talking out in the grape arbour, out of earshot, at the end of it all he left, looking mighty serious, and, as for Elizabeth, she's mum as a mole, an oyster's a tattle-box compared to her. Not a word has she let drop since, as to what passed. But, if she was going to have him, you'd expect she'd be a bit more frisky, not so quiet and meagre as mostly she goes about.'

'Perhaps she is thinking it over. Six thousand a year. She would be a great simpleton to pass that up,' said Jane, sighing at the thought of so much money passing into the hands of somebody else. 'What a shame he did not offer it to you,' she could not resist adding spitefully to Emma.

Emma rose and said that she would take little Gussie for a walk. This was an act of almost pure altruism, for the walks about the outskirts of Croydon were very dull, up littered chalk tracks through vegetable allotments and over grimy, spoiled downland. Apart from its great cherry-orchard, Croydon was fast being eaten up by fugitives from London; there were new houses thrown up every week. And if Mr Thickstaffe succeeds in persuading Parliament to cut his Grand Canal through to Portsmouth, thought Emma, it will soon become a part of London itself.

On a walk, little Gussie was a reluctant, mulish companion. She grumbled, she whined, she trailed her feet in the dust, she complained of being stung by wasps, nettles, and adders.

'Nonsense, Gussie, there are no wasps and adders at this time of year. And if you walk through nettles, you have only yourself to blame.'

Meanwhile, Emma was certain, back at Beech Hanger, Margaret and Jane would be enjoyably pulling her character to pieces.

Never mind. Let them do so. She had Captain Fremantle's letter with her like a talisman; not since she first received it had she been parted from it by more than a hand's breadth. It lay under her pillow by night, and was tucked in her reticule by day. And each night she read a chapter of the book about Saxon kings. I shall be able to discuss Caedwalla on equal terms when he comes back, she thought hopefully.

'Why don't you pick a nice bunch of dandelions?' she suggested to little Gussie.

'Shan't! Don't like dandelions!'

'Well, then, listen, and I will tell you the tale of the fox and the crane.'

But Gussie was not interested in foxes and cranes. She had a blister on her heel big as a penny-piece, she asserted, and she limped and wailed all the way home, ceasing her complaints only as the gates of Beech Hanger came in sight, when she broke into a run.

Inside, all the way up the front path, Robert's gardener had set clumps of blooming pansies in the newly dug flower-beds.

Gussie pranced past these, methodically tweaking up all the pansies on the right-hand side, and tossing them behind her on to the gravel path.

'*Don't* do that, you odious child!' exclaimed Emma, bereft of all patience, and she gave Gussie a slap on the wrist. Roaring with fury, Gussie darted indoors and sought the succour and furtherance of her mother.

'She hit me! Emma beat me! Send her away! I hate her! I hate her!'

'*What is* this I hear?'

Jane, fierce as a dragon in defence of her young, came into the hall.

'Yes, I gave her a slap,' said Emma. 'Which she richly deserved, for pulling up all the pansies. Look!' She pointed through the open front door.

'Didn't do it! Emma pulled them up! Emma did it!' wailed Gussie, clinging on to her mother's hand.

'Oh! You little liar!'

'Don't you dare to call my child a liar, miss!' exploded Jane. 'How could you? Poor little precious, then!'

'Look, look, Mamma, I got a bad foot. I'm poorly, I'm very poorly!'

'There, there, Mamma will make it all better. How about a nice spoonful of apricot jam?'

'I suppose you think McGregor had pulled up all the pansies he had just planted?' Emma suggested, going off to her room.

'Robert shall hear of this directly he comes home!' Jane flung after her. Margaret, emerging from the parlour, helped Jane comfort and cosset the child, who, pleased with this new audience, redoubled her cries and wails.

To her surprise, Emma found a note on her dressing-table.

'Delivered by hand, it was, miss, not twenty minutes since,' said the maid Jemima, bringing in a handful of clean bedroom crockery. 'By the lad who takes round the milk.'

'Who can it be from?' Emma prised open the small, rather dusty cover.

'Dear Mam,' said the note in uneducated handwriting. 'I should be Oblig'd if you could come, as here is a Lady what knows you is not at all Well. She dont know I rite, but I make so bold. Brigit Riley.'

The address was in Epsom.

Good heavens, thought Emma. Brigit Riley? An Irish name? Can it be – it *must* be – Aunt Maria! But – in Epsom? But why does she not write herself? Oh my gracious me! I must go to her at once. But how?

Then she recollected that, at this very moment, Margaret was in the house, about to be picked up by Dr Harding and taken back to Clissocks. The road they would take passed through Epsom, a small pleasant town. On the way hither Mr Thickstaffe had given Emma much more information than she wanted about Epsom's decline as a spa and watering-place in favour of the new seaside resorts such as Weymouth and Brightelmstone.

Having crammed a few needments into a bag, Emma ran downstairs, just as Dr Harding's carriage drew up outside the front gate.

Dr Harding would not come into the house. He would never come in. He disliked Jane Watson and, though he would not be embroiled in the feud between her and his wife, yet while the feud continued, he did not choose to enter into social relations here.

Emma ran to the carriage.

'Dr Harding! I am so glad to see you! Can you carry me as far as Epsom? Can you be so kind? I have an errand there.'

'Epsom? Ay, and farther if you wish, young lady. But what is your business in Epsom?'

'Well, I am not quite sure. I have had a request for help. I think it may relate to my aunt O'Brien. But I will be so greatly obliged if you can carry me there so that I may find out.'

'That's of course,' said he. 'Now, just hurry up your sister Margaret, will you? I don't like to keep the nags waiting on this dismal gusty hillside.'

Emma went indoors and informed a pale, furious Jane that she was off to Epsom.

'Very well!' said Jane icily. 'And, so far as I am concerned, you may just stay there! You are not at all welcome under *this* roof, from now on, let me tell you. Just wait until your brother hears what has occurred!'

Emma nodded, and returned to the carriage, from which she watched with a detached eye the affectionate and clinging embrace of Jane and Margaret as they bade one another farewell.

'Well!' said Margaret entering the carriage and shaking herself. 'What an imbroglio! I should think you was well out of that household, Emma! What a little toad, what a viper that child is! I wonder, I really do, you ever stood her for so long.'

She seemed highly satisfied with the turn events had taken.

'What is all this about?' inquired Dr Harding.

'Oh, that odious little Gussie pulled up some plants, and Emma reprimanded her, so now Emma has been turned out of the house.'

'It did not happen precisely like that,' began Emma, but then she fell silent. Her thoughts were too much occupied with what she might find at the end of the journey to be concerned with self-justification.

'You really think it may be Aunt O'Brien in Epsom?' demanded Margaret, when the contents of the message had been made known to her. 'But what shall you do if it is? Or if it is not?'

'How can I tell?'

Dr Harding looked moithered, as he did more and more often these days.

'We should certainly wait in Epsom – we must undoubtedly do that – at least until you discover precisely who has wrote this note. But then – I do not know – I do not like to keep the horses standing. Perhaps you should plan to come back to Clissocks with us?'

'Oh, no, I am sure Emma should not do that!' said Margaret hastily.

Emma glanced at her in slight surprise, but said to Dr Harding, 'No, my dear sir, you must go on your way home, or Penelope will be wondering what has happened to you.'

Dr Harding seemed relieved at having the decision taken from him, but said they would at least remain outside the house while Emma made inquiries.

'Ay, ay, Epsom is not a bad little place,' he observed, as they drew up. 'If Thickstaffe has his way it will also be on the Grand Canal – give a new lease of life to the place, that would, by gum! Here you are, Miss Emma, here's the address you seek – just by the High Street, close to the Parade, couldn't be handier. Now, I will walk my nags while you discover what's toward – pray do not be longer than you can help . . .'

Emma consulted the paper in her hand and looked for Number 2, Church Street. She found a doorway beside an apothecary's shop.

With fast-beating heart, she rang the bell.

11

'Are you Miss Emma Watson? Oh, I am so happy to see you!'

The shabby, shaggy woman who answered the door spoke with a strong Irish accent, which removed Emma's last doubt.

'Is Mrs O'Brien here?'

'Yes! And she's in such a bad way, miss! Indeed, indeed, I'm at my wits' end! For there's that strength of spirit about her, she won't have any one of ye fetched – and yet, by my soul, there's not an inch of ground between her and the grave – not unless action is taken, immejit! But step upstairs and see for yourself, miss, do –'

'Well, I will, but – just a moment, I had better tell my brother-in-law that I am come to the right place.'

Emma returned to the street and said to Dr Harding, 'It is indeed my aunt O'Brien, sir – I have not seen her yet, but the servant tells me that she is in very poor case, so I cannot be sufficiently grateful to you for having brought me to her. I must certainly remain here and tend her. I thank you again, and I shall be obliged if you will convey this news to my sisters Penelope and Elizabeth. And Sam, when you see him.'

'That I will,' said he. 'And – see here – if the poor woman's in straits, you may find yourself in want of the ready.' He had been struggling in his breeches pocket, and now put a folded banknote into her hand. He looked a trifle shamefaced, as if he knew he ought to be of more active help, but simply lacked the will, or perhaps the energy. Margaret looked merely eager to get away from what might be a potentially awkward situation. So Emma made no demur about accepting the note. She said, 'Thank you, sir, you are very kind. I will write and let you know how I go on. Thank you again – goodbye, goodbye!'

Retrieving her bundle, she fled up the narrow stair. Here at the top she was faced by two doors. One room, a small cramped parlour, looked out on to the street; the maid beckoned her into the other, a dark and equally cramped bedroom which contained little beyond a narrow bed, a table, and a chair.

'Aunt Maria?' breathed Emma.

On the bed, resting against pillows, lay an emaciated figure.

'Aunt Maria? Is that you?'

The figure opened its eyes.

And then a cry of such pain and rapture broke the silence that Emma was obliged to clench her hands and strain her eyes to prevent the tears spurting out.

'Emma! My little Emma! Is it really true? Can it be so?'

'Oh – Aunt Maria!'

Emma hardly dared touch her aunt, so worn, so frail, so spectre-thin with suffering was she; a gentle kiss on the cheek and butterfly contact with the skeletal fingers must suffice; and, for the same reason, it seemed wrong to try her strength by any questioning as to what had brought her to this pass.

'I am so happy to find you,' said Emma. 'But I must not tire you by too much talk. Would you drink a little wine, if I brought it? Or some beef tea?'

A couple of tears ran down Mrs O'Brien's cheeks.

'Beef tea!' she whispered. 'Oh, yes! Brigit is a good, good girl – only she does not know – none of the Irish do – how to make beef tea.'

Emma went into the other room, where she wrote down a list of purchases and gave some money to Brigit. 'And can you find a doctor?'

'Yes, miss, I'll be glad to. Missus would not allow it, for she was feared she'd not enough for the fee – but 'tis plain she needs one, desprit bad.'

'What is wrong with her, do you know?'

''Twas the rheumatic fever, miss, she picked up in Knocka. And then in Dublin it grew worse. And then – the master –'

'Well, tell me all that when you come back. And bring the things. But first, a doctor. I daresay the people in the apothecary's shop downstairs will tell you where to find one.'

When the doctor came, he confirmed the diagnosis of rheumatic fever and prescribed salicylate of sodium, with iodide of potassium, given every three hours; also port wine, beef tea, and beaten eggs. Since there was much risk of the heart being affected, he recommended the services of a professional nurse to help Emma look after the poor lady, and said that he would send one.

Now began a queer, quiet, and at first a terribly anxious time for Emma. For at least a week it remained uncertain whether the patient would live or die. Emma found herself a room close by, and shared the care of her aunt equally with Brigit, the servant-girl, and Nurse Fletcher, a kindly, sensible woman provided by the doctor.

Fortunately Emma was well supplied with money: the folded note proffered by Dr Harding proved to be a bill for fifty pounds, and without it she hardly knew how they would have managed, for poor Mrs O'Brien was found to be completely at the end of her resources. Her passage from Ireland to England, and by coach as far as Epsom, had taken the last of what she had.

Little by little Emma received the story, partly from Brigit, partly from Aunt Maria, as she began to improve in strength.

'Never marry a gambler, my love! They are the worst of all. Indeed it is worse than a vice – it is an addiction, like some terrible drug. And, I must say, poor Captain O'Brien had *shocking* luck – unbelievable! He had only to put money on a horse for it to break its legs. Time after time I have said to him, "My love, what you should do is to pick a horse and then *not* bet on it – that way it is sure to win." But – he would never heed what I said. He always thought he knew best.'

Listening over a period of several weeks to her aunt's narrative, Emma came, in the end, to the surprised conclusion that, though he had used her without the least consideration, and frittered away her entire fortune, Aunt Maria did not feel the least rancour against Captain O'Brien; in fact she still loved him.

'Ah, he was such a charmer! Such a dear man,' she sighed. 'And he meant well, always, God rest him. There was no harm in him, not a whit. Only the dreadful propensity for gambling. "This time," he'd say, "*this* time I'll make your fortune, Maria." Only he never did, bless his heart.'

'What has become of him?' Emma finally dared to ask.

'Ah, he put a bullet through his head, the poor fellow. "Maria," he said to me, "I'm no good to ye at all, at all," and then he did it.'

Evidently through habitude, Mrs O'Brien had acquired a touch of her husband's brogue.

'And I felt so dreadfully low about him, poor man, and in myself, that I was sure I was bound to die also. But I'd a very strong wish to die in my own land, *not* in Ireland, which, I must say, my love, though it has some kindly people in it, is the most untidy, neglected, forlorn little island it has ever been my misfortune to visit.'

'But why did you choose Epsom?' asked Emma, when her aunt was a little stronger.

'Ah, you'll think it a foolish, fond reason, my love, but Captain O'Brien always had a very strong wish to visit Epsom; because of the Derby race, you know; so, thinks I, I'll just leave my bones where he would have liked to come one day.'

'But why did you not send a message to me?'

'Ah, no! I could not be putting such a weight upon you, poor child! And you set up in such comfort, snug among your brothers and sisters.'

Emma had not yet chosen to enlighten her aunt as to the complete lack of comfort and snug family feeling among the said brothers and sisters. Hitherto, the only one to show sympathy and offer practical advice or help had been Sam. Emma had written notes to Robert, Penelope, and

Elizabeth, but had no answers. Sam, though, rode over from Guildford, discussed Aunt Maria's case with Henfold, the doctor, ratified his treatment, and cheered the patient with friendly conversation. He also supplied Emma with a little money.

'I wish I could do more, Emma,' he said, 'but I have sunk most of my legacy in Thickstaffe's canal scheme. He says, and I hope he's right, that my money will be trebled in a year. I daresay Harding will help you, however, if you need more. He is a kindly fellow and feels a trifle guilty that he did not do more. I would not place any dependence on Robert; Jane has him too tightly by the purse-strings. But perhaps he can do something in the legal way – bring a suit against Captain O'Brien's family about all the money he had off her.'

'I would not place any dependence on *that*,' said Emma.

Sam looked thin, and tired, and anxious; she sighed over him as he rode away. No announcement had yet been made as to the engagement of Miss Edwards and Lord Osborne, but it was spoken about and expected daily.

From her sisters at Clissocks Emma finally received answers that disappointed, but did not surprise. Penelope was adamant in her refusal to do anything at all for Aunt O'Brien.

'She never raised a finger for me. *You* were the one she chose to adopt, and if you choose to succour her now, that is entirely your affair. And Dr Harding says he has done what he can – more than she deserves, I daresay, if the truth be known. So she must just manage as best she can from now on.'

Elizabeth wrote regretting that she had only the hundred

pounds from her father's legacy and felt she must preserve that against future contingencies. So she has turned Tom down, thought Emma. 'But as soon as I can I will bring over some Preserves and some Cowslip Wine made last year at Stanton, and some Cloths,' she wrote.

Robert sent Emma a great scold. 'I will not particularize as to your monstrous behaviour against your kind sister Jane,' he wrote, 'though that is shocking enough in all conscience. But to be setting up, *in lodgings*, with your disgraced Aunt in this indigent way must cast a slur on the whole family and lower us most dreadfully in public esteem. How could you stoop to live over an apothecary's shop (for such, I am told, is your situation)? It is enough to blacken the name of Watson. And offering music lessons on a card in a baker's window! I am wholly disgusted at you, Emma, and fear that I am now obliged to cut the connection completely. Yrs etc.'

'Well, he does sound a proud, stiff-rumped fellow,' sighed Aunt Maria, when, in the end, Emma could find no way to avoid telling her about this response to her application for help. 'I must say I cannot feel that *his* friendship is any loss. But how fortunate it is, dear Emma, that you are having such success with your piano lessons. And now the harp too, you tell me?'

For the card in the baker's shop window had rapidly attracted a number of inquiries as to lessons; it seemed that young ladies in Epsom were crying out for instruction on the harp and piano. Emma, to her own surprise, had been able to hire a piano and was now provided with a small, but steady and growing income, so that a large portion of Dr Harding's fifty pounds was still unspent, and this despite the fact that Aunt Maria was now recovered enough to be able to go into the warm bath three times a week, with most beneficial effects on her swelled and aching joints.

One day Emma had been surprised and pleased to receive a call from Miss Osborne, who, shy and blushing, asked if she might contribute to the hire of the harp.

'Mamma does not know that I am come here,' she confessed. 'And I am not sure that she would quite approve! But I think you are such a hero, Miss Emma! And so does Mr Howard, I am sure.'

Emma found, to her own satisfaction, that she was now able to inquire after Mr Howard's health without the acceleration of heartbeat that would once have accompanied such a question.

'Well – we have not seen very much of him lately. Mamma's cousin has come home from Antigua – Lord Rufus Bungay, you know – and he is a great original and very entertaining, and has brought so many curiosities back with him that Mamma's attention has been quite occupied. Mamma had lost money over the abolition of the slave trade,' Miss Osborne added naively, 'so she is glad to ask Cousin Rufus for advice on such topics . . .'

By this time Mrs O'Brien was well enough to sit up in the parlour for some portion of each day, and she was interested in meeting Miss Osborne.

'I was used to know your father, my dear, many years ago, when I was a vain sportive young girl at the Dorking Assemblies, and he was a handsome young lord, quite the beau of the ballrooms – oh, and with such a reputation! Tell me, when did he die?'

'Oh, fifteen years back, ma'am, I can scarcely remember him.'

'And your brother, does he resemble his father?'

'I think he is quite like Papa in appearance, judging from Papa's portraits,' said Miss Osborne hesitantly, 'but not so much in his nature. My brother is shy and retiring in his manners.'

'And is Lord Osborne really going to marry Miss Mary Edwards? Is it announced yet?' inquired Emma, thinking of her poor brother Sam.

Mrs O'Brien gave a great start, and dropped the glass of port wine which she had been about to convey to her lips.

'Oh, mercy! How shockingly clumsy of me. I am still rather weak, I fear. But what a spillage I have caused. I am so very sorry—'

'Pray don't regard it, dear aunt; I will have it all tidied up in a trice—'

Miss Osborne rose to leave, with apologies and fears that she had overtired the invalid. When she was gone, 'My dear!' said Mrs O'Brien, 'a marriage between young Lord Osborne and Mary Edwards certainly must *not* take place. Why, they are brother and sister!'

'What? No, no, I cannot believe that!'

'True, nonetheless. Clara, Mary's mother, was my great, great friend, in those far-off days when we were young. She was the sister of the Mr Edwards that you know. And Osborne was her lover. Oh, he was a wild young sprig in those days! Of course, when the child was born it was all passed off – hushed up – and she went out of the country, and then she died, poor dear, and the Edwardses, most benevolently, took and brought the child up as their own. But who would have thought it would come to this? Such a marriage must not be, it certainly must never be. I had best write a letter to Henry Edwards, he would die of horror if he knew the risk they run – I suppose poor Clara never told him – I was her only confidante . . .'

'Great heavens,' murmured Emma, half to herself. 'Now I come to think of it, there is quite a strong resemblance between Lord Osborne and Mary Edwards – they both have the same fair colouring and fresh complexions and blue eyes . . .'

Mrs O'Brien called for pen and paper and set to work on the composition of her extremely difficult letter. Meanwhile Emma was thinking, what a strange, what a shocking revelation! How differently people must have behaved then from the way they do now, when all is so orderly, so smooth, so proper, so well-regulated. But, my dear brother Sam, this piece of news does seem to improve your prospects immensely!

So soon as Mrs O'Brien found herself able to move unassisted, and walk about, and then venture on her own two feet into the street, Emma suggested that they should find more comfortable lodgings, and a pleasant set of rooms was discovered over a bakery in Burgh Heath Road. Here Emma could have her own parlour, with piano and harp, for music lessons, while Mrs O'Brien need not be disturbed.

'Though indeed, to hear you play the piano, Emma dear,' she said, 'takes me most happily back to old times.'

Now that Mrs O'Brien was on the road to recovery, she and her niece were re-establishing, with the greatest delight and amity, that excellent relationship which had been the basis of their comfort all through Emma's childhood. The only impediment to complete happiness was the aunt's remorse and regret over the loss of her fortune, so pitifully squandered.

'If only I could contribute something to the household,' she sighed, over and over.

'I beg you, Aunt Maria, do not be troubling your head over such a minor matter. Think of all the love and care you spent on me, and the expensive musical education which is now bearing useful fruit.'

They moved into the superior lodgings and found that more friends came to call – old friends, some of these, acquaintances from long ago in Mrs O'Brien's girlhood, the Hunters, the Nortons, the Frenshams, the Deverells.

'It is lucky for us, I believe,' said Emma, 'that my brother Robert will think rooms over a baker's shop even more disgraceful than rooms over an apothecary. We are not likely to be entertaining *him*.'

'Stupid man! I have no patience with him,' said Mrs O'Brien. 'He is not half the man his dear father was.'

But Emma was sorry not to see her sister Elizabeth – or Penelope, or Dr Harding. That part of the family, she feared, must also have cast her off. Nor was there a second visit from Miss Osborne. She did, however, receive news of the Osborne family for, one day, when she was executing some household commissions in the High Street, she encountered Mr Howard.

He seemed a little embarrassed at the meeting and explained that his horse had cast a shoe and he was waiting for it to be shod.

'Will you not come and meet my aunt?' Emma suggested.

He hemmed and hawed – hesitated – but finally accepted the invitation. By now Mrs O'Brien was in spirits quite her old self – lively, alert, and keenly interested in people and public affairs. Only the lines of her worn countenance betrayed the troubles that she had been through.

'Mr Howard! I hear that you were a great friend to my poor brother. I am very glad indeed to meet you.'

Mr Howard had been looking rather pale and dejected, but he brightened at this cordial greeting.

'And I am happy to meet you, Mrs O'Brien,' he said. 'Especially as I was witness to the deep anxiety suffered by your niece during the months when she had no news of you. It is an excellent thing that you are reunited at last. And indeed I can bring you and Miss Emma some cheering news. The publication of your brother's sermons has been attended with a remarkable success; the first edition is already all subscribed, and a second edition is reprinting. I shall have a draft for you, Miss Emma, very shortly, for over two hundred pounds!'

'Two hundred pounds! Why, that is riches! My aunt and I may subsist very comfortably on that for an untold period of time.'

'Not only that, my dear Miss Emma, but the publishers are eager for a second volume – having heard from me that the set of sermons already published is only a very partial selection.'

'Oh, good heavens,' said Emma, 'is that really so? This is wonderful indeed – but all my father's papers and books are at present with my brother Sam in Guildford – we thought it best, after Papa's death – since, though it was true the rights were left to me, my place of residence at that time appeared so uncertain . . .'

'Quite so, quite so,' said Mr Howard, a little embarrassed.

'I will write to Sam and ask him to have the papers conveyed to me here. That will provide a pleasant evening occupation for me and my aunt – sorting and selecting a second series.'

'Indeed it will!' said Mrs O'Brien.

Mr Howard looked a little crestfallen, as if he had hoped to be offered the task.

'Well, I shall look forward to hearing from you,' he said after a moment or two, 'when you have made your choice.'

'Yes, yes,' said Emma. 'And now I am going to send you on your way, Mr Howard, for I am sure your horse is shod, and it is past time for my aunt's egg-nog.'

Reluctant but acquiescent, he took his leave.

'Oh, by the bye,' he said awkwardly on the stair, 'there is a piece of news which you may not have heard – Lady Osborne is to marry her cousin, Lord Rufus Bungay. He has returned from abroad, not long since. They were old childhood playmates.'

'*Indeed?*' said Emma, very much startled. 'But –' However, she choked down the rest of her rejoinder and watched him walk away, slowly and with head bent, along the street.

When she returned upstairs with the egg-nog Mrs O'Brien said at once:

'That man has the intention to return and make you an offer, my dear.'

'Do you think so?' Emma said doubtfully. 'Despite our inferior social standing?'

'He has all the look of it.' Mrs O'Brien spoke with the authority of one who has, in her time, conducted a multitude of flirtations resulting in two marriages.

'But it must be decidedly awkward for him, situated as he is, known to have been, to all intents and purposes, the property of Lady Osborne for so long . . .'

'Ah, my dear, a man will soon forget an inconvenient trifle like that. But the important question is, do you mean to have him?'

Emma thought of the letter in her reticule, the book about Saxon kings at her bedside. She had not yet mentioned these matters to her aunt. Nor would she. She felt like a bird with one precious, fragile egg. She would run no risk, would not tempt Providence.

How foolish I was, though, she thought. I could quite properly have asked Mr Howard if he had any news of his cousin.

'No,' she said slowly. 'No, I do not.'

'But he seems an excellent person, my dear, a clergyman, of good family, comfortably situated—'

Emma said stubbornly, 'He does not have the resolution that I like to see in a man. He was for too long at the beck and call of Lady Osborne, who is a detestable female. I like a man who is deedy, and makes up his own mind.'

'Ah, but, my dear, *you* could supply all the resolution,' said her fond aunt.

The following Saturday brought Sam, in response to Emma's letter, with a large bundle of papers and notebooks.

But he was not the cheerful, affectionate Sam of the previous visit; he looked white and shocked.

'I see you have not heard the news?' were his opening words.

Aunt and niece stared at him in alarm, then at each other in surmise.

'No, Sam, what is it?'

'The canal bill failed to get through Parliament – the petition was dismissed – and, much worse, the Canal Company has declared bankruptcy, for Thickstaffe's partner has absconded with the funds. Harding is a ruined man!'

'Oh, Sam! But what about yourself?'

'Well, I have lost what I put in,' he sighed. 'I am not so much worse off than I was this time last year – but I have lost my hope, for ever, of Mary Edwards. I had thought I might have enough to offer if this scheme prospered – since, for some reason, her engagement to Osborne has never come off—'

'But, good heavens! Dr Harding ruined! Will he have to sell Clissocks?'

'I imagine so,' said Sam gloomily. 'That is not the end of it. Margaret and Thickstaffe have eloped.'

'*What?*'

'Impossible!' burst simultaneously from Emma and Mrs O'Brien.

'No, no, Sam, you must be mistaken! It was always Penelope and Thickstaffe who were supposed to be conspiring together – at least, according to Margaret.'

'Well, it is true enough. I have just come from Clissocks. Penelope is in a fine rage, I can tell you – blames the whole on Margaret and her insinuating ways. For my part, I think Harding is well rid of Thickstaffe – I never cared for the fellow; of course I would like to see him laid by the heels, I've no doubt he feathered his own nest out of the business; but the tale is, they are gone abroad, he has a cousin in Philadelphia. Poor Harding is like a man stunned.'

Sam left soon after, saying that he must pursue his practice with extra vigour, now the chance of making a fortune from investments was lost to him.

As Emma escorted Sam down to the street, Tom Musgrave came riding to the door, and, on Emma's nod, proceeded up the stairs. Sam stared after him with considerable disapproval.

'How does that fellow come to be calling here? He is not at all the thing!'

'Well,' said Emma reasonably, 'he is hoping to win the regard of Elizabeth, and I am encouraging him. After all, he is comfortably off, and *very* attached to her. If the Hardings are ruined, Elizabeth could do much worse! And Tom and Aunt Maria get on excellently well – don't forget, he is a connection of her first husband, Uncle Turner. And he makes her laugh and tells her about his horses, which keeps her entertained, as Captain O'Brien was such a racing man –'

But Sam shook his head, still declaring that Tom Musgrave was not at all the thing.

'Oh, Sam, you are growing as bad as Robert. Heavens! There will be no bearing Robert now! He will be saying to everybody that he told them so, all along.'

12

Spring, which had, that year, been slow in its arrival, now gathered momentum. Bare branches began to be softly outlined in light and brilliant foliage. Gypsies sold bunches of primroses at street corners in the little town. Fruit trees in gardens put forth cascades of blossom, first the pear and cherry, then apple and quince. Emma sighed in secret for the orchards and meadows of Stanton; she felt constricted among houses and streets. Her aunt Maria observed with concern that she grew a little thin and pale. Pupils, however, she had in plenty, and the two ladies were not lacking in society: the Hunters, the Tomlinsons, Mrs Norton, and Miss Styles all recalled their old connection with Mrs O'Brien and came to drink tea and discuss past times. Tom Musgrave paid faithful, if less frequent visits.

Mrs O'Brien still went twice weekly to the warm bath for the relief of her rheumatic joints. At first she had been carried there on a litter by two stout boys, at a fee of sixpence. The enclosure of the Wells was located in a pavilion in a dingle on Epsom Common, about fifteen minutes' walk from their lodgings. Latterly Aunt Maria had ridden thither in a chair, with Emma walking beside. Close to the Wells themselves, with their enclosures, their hot and cold springs, private cabinets for male and female

immersion, and the fountain, where cups of mineral water
might be obtained, had grown up a small parade of
tea-shops and circulating libraries where trinkets, ornamental combs, handkerchiefs, and other such temptations
were offered for sale. Beside the glassed-in building, inside
which palm fronds and tropical foliage luxuriated in the
steamy atmosphere, was an outdoor terrace containing
small tables and chairs where, on mild spring mornings,
tea, coffee, and other beverages might be purchased and
drunk.

Here it was Aunt Maria's one indulgence to sit for a
while, when the weather was propitious, and watch the
customers and the foot-passengers coming and going.

'I do so like,' she said, 'to look at the new hats and the
modes and the various ways they have now of dressing
hair; in Ireland there was nothing of the kind; young girls
in that land wear their locks quite long and plain, hanging
down their backs; they would stare to see all these ringlets
and braids, and the coronets and Grecian knots.'

One morning, as they sat sipping lemonade, Aunt Maria
listening sympathetically while Emma gave a description
of her successful campaign to improve Elizabeth's hair,
and the sad anti-climax that had followed, Aunt Maria,
looking over Emma's shoulder, said in a low tone:

'My love, some lady of consequence is approaching us;
she seems to know you. But she looks very severe. Who
can it be?'

Emma glanced round and saw Lady Osborne walking
towards them between the tables. To call her expression
severe had been no exaggeration; she looked positively
incandescent with wrath.

Coming to a halt by their table she said: 'Miss Emma Watson; I had been informed that you are sometimes to be seen at this place. The lady with you I assume to be your aunt?'

Emma assented.

'I should be obliged for a few minutes' private conversation with you.' She glanced around. 'Shall we take a turn along the paved walk at the side here? It appears to be quite unfrequented.'

Startled, apprehensive, half guessing what might follow, Emma helped her aunt to stand up, and they followed Lady Osborne to the paved path, which ran between clipped box hedges.

Lady Osborne at once said, 'Mrs O'Brien? Do I have your name correctly? I understand you to be the source of a malicious falsehood which has been circulating in this vicinity, regarding a member of my family.'

Aunt Maria calmly replied, 'Does your ladyship refer to my letter regarding the parentage of the young lady known as Miss Edwards?'

Lady Osborne bowed her head, frowning, with tightly compressed lips.

She looked to be, for a moment, almost too angry for speech; the brilliancy and grace, the look of youthful buoyancy which could animate and, at times, make her appear twenty years younger than her actual age, had quite deserted her; she seemed like some vengeful Valkyrie.

Then, in a low, grating voice, she exclaimed:

'How *dare* you? How dare you so traduce the family name of Osborne? With such a barefaced lie?'

'Your ladyship must excuse me,' Mrs O'Brien answered

without heat. 'The statement was no lie. I myself was well acquainted, at one time, with the mother of the young lady in question – poor Miss Clara Edwards was my dearest friend – and I am able to assure any inquirer as to the absolute verity of my statement. I would stand up in a court of law and repeat it without the least hesitation. Nay, I even have a letter in Miss Clara's own handwriting attesting to it . . .'

'By this malicious fabrication you have created a most unfortunate impediment to a thoroughly eligible and desirable alliance!' continued Lady Osborne, ignoring Aunt Maria's previous statement entirely.

'There, I can hardly agree with your ladyship. No alliance can be considered eligible or desirable which involves its participants in behaviour that is expressly forbidden by Holy Writ.'

Lady Osborne seemed momentarily silenced by this decisive pronouncement. But then she went on, 'Moreover your fabrication – for such I still declare it to be – casts a most undeserved slur upon the name of a gallant Christian gentleman, who is, alas, not alive to speak up in his own defence – my husband, the former Lord Osborne. How *could* you have the audacity to slander him so? And who in the wide world would believe such a disgraceful tale?'

'As to that,' said Mrs O'Brien, smiling faintly, 'I know several people still living who can confirm my story. Old Mrs Ranmore, for instance, now living with Mrs Harding at Clissocks.'

'Old Nanny?' said Emma, surprised. And then she remembered and added, 'Why, yes, I recall, she did seem very shocked at hearing that Lord Osborne and Miss Edwards were likely to be married.'

Lady Osborne seemed momentarily silenced. Mrs O'Brien went on:

'Doubtless, by the end of his life, your husband was a pattern of all the virtues and might then truly be described as a gallant Christian gentleman. But at a younger age, when I knew him, though *gallant* might well pass muster as a description of him, I fear the other terms would not; his reputation was sufficiently wild, when I was in my twenties, for him to be known by the sobriquet of *Rakehell Ralph* (and another name which I will not venture to repeat). Others besides myself must certainly remember these facts.'

Lady Osborne was seen to flinch. Evidently these appellations were not unknown to her.

By now they had reached the end of the paved walk. Lady Osborne swung round and declared with great emphasis: 'Unless you instantly take pains to have this story contradicted, and completely denied, I shall make sure that no reputable persons will have anything to do with you and your niece. You will then find that you are quite cast out from good society – ruined, disgraced, as I understand that your connections at Clissocks have been. You will be the contempt of the neighbourhood. I shall further make it my business to see that you are unable to earn a livelihood in this part of the country. Nobody will wish to have any dealings with you.'

'If your ladyship is able to do *that,*' said Mrs O'Brien simply, 'then I suppose we shall be obliged to move elsewhere. I have good friends in Shropshire, where your ladyship's writ, perhaps, does not run. But I fear I am quite unable to contradict the story about Miss Edwards, for it is true.'

Lady Osborne swept back along the path. She did not precisely shake her fist, but the movement of her fan suggested it. Then she vanished from view.

'Oh, bless me!' sighed Mrs O'Brien. 'I can see that it must be very vexatious for the poor woman to have this discreditable old story about her husband come to light just now. But what was I to do?'

'You could do no other than what you did,' Emma assured her. 'And, as to her threats, I do not much regard them. I cannot imagine that she will be able to entice away all my pupils, or even very many of them!'

'But I feel badly about the Edwards family. Henry Edwards has never replied to my letter. I am afraid he must wish that I had never come back to this neighbourhood to cut up his peace and disrupt his plans.'

'Aunt Maria, you did what your conscience told you to do. Nobody can do more.'

'I feel very tired, my dear,' said Mrs O'Brien dejectedly, after a moment. 'I think perhaps you had better find a chair and take me home.'

Emma did so, deeply concerned lest this acrimonious interview should have caused a relapse in her aunt's physical condition; for the doctor had said that, because of his patient's previous extreme debility, the slightest deterioration in her circumstances might result in a severe setback.

Happily, when they returned home, they found two letters waiting, which the post-boy had delivered to Brigit the maid. One of them, addressed to Mrs O'Brien with a

Dorking postmark, proved to be from Mr Edwards. The letter was like the man himself, dignified, courteous, and, to Aunt Maria's immense relief, not at all angry at the revelation which she had felt obliged to make. On the contrary, he expressed himself as deeply obliged to her for preventing a most dreadful, if inadvertent transgression, and for doing a most disagreeable duty and providing the answer to a long-buried mystery.

'My poor sister had always promised that, one day, later on, she would divulge to me the name of her seducer; but death took her before she was able to do so; and our ignorance in this respect has made it doubly hard for us to be certain that we were acting in Mary's best interests during the time of her upbringing. The information you have given us – which is confirmed by many details of Mary's appearance and character, and by some recollections of my own – will give us a firm basis on which to make any future decisions, and we are proportionately grateful to you.'

'Well, *that* is excellent news,' said Mrs O'Brien, greatly relieved. 'Henry Edwards sounds like a sensible man. I think, Emma, that we might feel entitled to nourish a small grain of hope for our dear Sam – why child, what *is* it?'

For Emma was staring at her aunt, quite pale with shock, an open letter in her shaking hand.

'It is from a gentleman – the Reverend James Clarke – he writes from Carlton House – he is the Librarian to the Prince of Wales—'

'Dear me!' Mrs O'Brien dropped Mr Edwards's letter in her amazement. 'The Prince's Librarian? What can he have to say?'

'He writes to inform me of the very considerable interest and moral edification which his royal master has derived from his perusal of my father's sermons; and to express the hope that another collection of them is in preparation. And he tells me, if another such volume *is* in preparation, that I may feel free to dedicate it to His Royal Highness.'

'Good gracious!' exclaimed Mrs O'Brien, picking up Mr Edwards's letter again and fanning herself with it. 'My goodness gracious me!'

13

The following day brought Sam, brilliant with joy. A message had taken him, post-haste, to the Edwards house in Dorking where he had been informed that, owing to new discoveries which had been made as to Miss Edwards's origins, he was now free to press his suit, even invited to do so. And an interview with Mary herself had crowned his happiness. He was the accepted suitor, recognized, permitted, and encouraged.

'I am the happiest man in Surrey,' he told his sister and aunt. 'And, do you know what? Mary has suggested – oh, she is an angel, no other word will describe her, she is just no more and no less than an angel—'

'Marriage to an angel will be quite a responsibility,' murmured Aunt Maria.

'No, but her huge fortune will be no impediment to our happiness – neither of us will allow it to be so. And she has suggested that we buy Clissocks from Dr Harding – since he, poor man, is obliged to sell up to meet his obligations – and then we can offer a home to any members of my family – such as yourselves – do you not think that an admirable scheme?'

'It might not be so easy for me to find music pupils, out there on the hillside,' pointed out Emma.

'My dearest sister, you would not be required to give

music lessons! All that toil could be a thing of the past.'

'But I enjoy giving music lessons – on the whole,' said Emma. She marshalled her thoughts. 'And I am very sure that wealth will not make you give up your surgical practice? Living at home, for a woman – for anybody – is too quiet; too confined; at home there is no company but one's feelings, and they prey upon one. My music lessons are a means, for me, of keeping open a window to the world. Sometimes the lessons are arduous, troublesome; the prospect through the window is not a pleasant one; but it *is* a prospect, and I am enlarged by it. I learn some new thing.'

'Well, well,' said Sam. 'We will not quarrel. But the offer is there. You may alter your views. (I find them a little priggish.) Keep the suggestion and think it over.'

'We will, and with gratitude. Have you seen or heard from Mr Howard lately?' Emma asked with seeming irrelevance.

'No, I have not,' replied Sam. 'Poor fellow, I suppose *his* hopes are quite cut up, just when mine are opening out. He has lost his chance with Lady Osborne. I understand she is to marry her cousin in two weeks' time. Lord Rufus made a great fortune in sugar, it is told. Her son, Lord Osborne, will give her away . . . Perhaps Mr Howard will marry Miss Osborne. That would be a far more suitable match than for him to be marrying her mother. They are more of an age. I was used to think, Emma, that he had an eye for you, but perhaps I was mistaken. He is a queer man to fathom.'

Emma was silent. She longed for news of Captain Fremantle's ship the *Laconia*, but there seemed no one to whom she could apply.

Sam rose to go and Emma, as was her habit, accompanied him down to the street and warmly kissed him goodbye. 'I am so *very* happy for you, dearest Sam. Mary Edwards is a kind, good girl, and you thoroughly deserve your good fortune. I believe you will be very happy together.'

Tears stood in her eyes as she made this prophecy; Sam saw them and was touched.

'Dear little Emma! And I hope that you, too, will some day find equal happiness.'

Tom Musgrave alighted from his horse, bowed cheerfully to Emma, and having entrusted the animal to a lad, prepared to climb the stairs. Sam looked after him with decided disapproval.

'That fellow again! I cannot understand why you permit him to call here so often.'

'Aunt Maria is advising him about the care of his horses. She tells me that is one solid benefit from her time spent in Ireland – she has become a mine of useful information about horse-training. And Tom's pair are to run, you know, at Epsom summer race meeting next month.'

'Pshaw!' said Sam. 'You would think our aunt O'Brien had had enough of horses to give her a dislike of the whole equine kingdom. But listen, Emma: how would it be if I drove you and Aunt Maria out to Clissocks, one of these days? I wish to look at the house and discuss a purchase price with Dr Harding. And Aunt Maria has never been there – she would enjoy that, would she not? I could hire an equipage.'

'Oh, Sam, yes! That would be a most delightful treat!

We would both enjoy it of all things. And I daresay Penelope and Elizabeth, when they actually see our faces, may not be too standoffish.'

Sam nodded and rode off. Emma turned withindoors again and climbed the stairs; as she did so, she heard her aunt Maria's voice:

'A little good ale, or wine, Tom, *never* comes amiss for a valuable horse; gutta-percha should always be used for tender hoofs; soften with hot water, then mix with sal-ammoniac; of course, if you want to *stop* the feet, it should be done with a mix of clay and cow-dung, and you can add moss or tow; for *cracked* hoofs, equal parts of soap and tar; but I trust, Tom, that none of your string have cracked hoofs? Friar's Balsam is sovereign for any wounds. And my dear husband Captain O'Brien always used a mixture of his own invention: olive oil, spirits of turpentine, tincture of camphor, tincture of opium, and the yolk of a fresh egg. But the egg must be really fresh.'

'I will mix that up, Aunt Maria, and I thank you—' somehow Tom Musgrave had fallen into the habit of addressing Mrs O'Brien in this manner – 'none of my string have wounds, I am glad to say, just at this present, but they *are* for ever scraping themselves on briars or cutting themselves on hedgerow stakes; a mixture like that will be invaluable. But, what I really wish to know, is about my pair in training – Lost Hope and Forlorn Hope – I don't wish to train 'em too fine—'

'No, *indeed*, Tom!' said Aunt Maria emphatically. 'Captain O'Brien used to slack off training a little when it came towards the day of the race – he said that would make the horses keen – of course it must be remembered that his example is of doubtful efficacy, since none of his horses ever *did* win . . .'

'But perhaps,' said Emma, entering the room with her aunt's egg-nog, 'none of his horses were really first-class?'

'That is probably true,' agreed her aunt, sighing. 'Poor Patrick was a shocking bad judge of horse-flesh. Now, Tom, as I was telling you—'

'Aunt Maria,' said Emma, 'Sam offers to take us out to Clissocks one of these fine mornings.'

'Oh yes!' cried her aunt with enthusiasm. 'I would like that above everything!'

Tom's face lit up. 'Would you have any objections,' he asked with diffidence, 'if I were to accompany you? It is so hard for me to gain a glimpse of Miss Elizabeth – Mrs Harding and the doctor are not very welcoming . . .'

'And Elizabeth herself?'

He sighed.

'I cannot say that she has given me any cause to hope. But hope is immortal, I think!'

He smiled a little. Emma was suddenly visited by a memory of the time when he had come to call, slightly drunk, at Stanton Parsonage, with his friend Lord Osborne. How very greatly altered he is, she thought, since those days!

'Yes, of course you may come with us, Tom,' she said gently, thinking, Sam will not be pleased, but Sam must be persuaded.

The day chosen for their visit to Clissocks was a warm, grey afternoon in late May. The bluebells lining the steep hillside under the beech trees seemed positively to glow with luminous colour, and the leaves shone a more brilliant green because of the lack of light from the sky. Sam drove a curricle he had hired for the occasion, and Tom Musgrave rode alongside.

Sam, as Emma had feared, was not best pleased to be thus accompanied, but had accepted the situation after some strong pleading from Emma.

'Dear Sam! Being so happy yourself, you should not raise impediments in the way of those seeking similar happiness.'

'Well I do not think Musgrave will find it with our sister Elizabeth,' he said. 'She has more sense than to be taking on such a flibbertigibbet.'

When they made the turn around the hill that brought Clissocks within sight, Emma found herself a little dismayed. She had expected that, by now, some months after the Hardings moved in, the house would present a settled, occupied appearance, despite the reverses that had since overtaken the owners.

But, somehow, this was not the case. Untidy piles of building materials were still to be seen. And, as they drew near, and passed the entrances to gardens, there were signs of incomplete projects and half-finished activities on every hand.

Aunt Maria sighed and shook her head.

'Poor Penelope,' she said. 'As a child she was incapable of ever fully carrying out any undertaking. Never satisfied, never in full control, plans always in a muddle. And I see she has not changed.'

'Well, events here were against her,' Emma pointed out. 'It must have been very hard to run out of cash just when she had so many fine schemes planned. I do pity her very much.'

'But what a beautiful place, despite the confusion! A home for the Sleeping Beauty, with those beech hangers above, and the river below. I hope that Sam succeeds in his offer to buy it from the Hardings; it would be a shocking pity if it passed out of the family. And I daresay Mary Edwards would look after it very well. I should like to see my great-nephews and -nieces frolicking about these woods and falling into the river.'

Emma thought of little Charles Blake's untimely end, and was silent. She did not wish to spoil a pleasant occasion with melancholy allusions. And, from poor Tom Musgrave's thoughts, she felt very certain, the tragedy was never absent for long.

They drew to a halt in the big yard, and Penelope came out to greet them, looking vexed, although both Emma and Sam had taken pains to apprise her of the time and duration of their visit.

'So *very* inconvenient!' she said, almost before they had alighted from the carriage. 'Purvis has chosen this time to come a-calling, without any previous intimation of his intention – and I with all the packing to plan and organize, it is really too bad to be deprived of Elizabeth's aid, just at this juncture –'

'Packing?' cried Emma. 'You are about to move, then?'

'Why yes, it is all decided, we – that is, I – have found a little house in Dorking. It is small, but smart, and very convenient for the shops and circulating libraries. And *perfectly* stylish – we shall be able to maintain a sufficiently elegant manner of living there at comparatively low expense –'

Penelope was running on in her usual manner without much regard for her interlocutors, but here Emma gently interrupted:

'Penelope, here is my aunt O'Brien. I think it is many years since you two last met—'

'Oh, yes, very true – how are you, Aunt, are you quite recovered? Will you walk in and take some refreshment? Unfortunately Elizabeth usually sees to those matters and I do not know where she has wandered off to – It is exceedingly tiresome of her . . .'

Now Dr Harding came out of doors and with more true hostly politeness greeted Mrs O'Brien and made her welcome. Emma was sorry to observe, though, how greatly changed he was even in the few short months since she had seen him last, how stooped and aged, how slowed down in all his movements. She feared that the defection of Thickstaffe, of whom he had seemed extremely fond, had proved a severe blow to him, even worse, perhaps, than the loss of his fortune. But he greeted Emma, who had always been a favourite, very kindly, had cordial, brotherly words for Sam, and was perfectly civil to Tom Musgrave, at whom, however, he shook his head.

'Nay, young fellow, 'tis of no use at all your coming a-wooing round here; I greatly fear your hopes are dished, once and for all—'

'Nay, sir, what can you mean?' cried Tom, greatly discomposed.

'Why, I fancy Purvis has already popped the question – yes, look, there they come, shining like the rainbow—' and the kind-hearted old gentleman beamed with un-affected pleasure. 'Ay, ay, my sister Elizabeth is an excellent good creature, and she deserves the very best – that she surely does!'

In fact Elizabeth and Purvis had strolled round the corner of the garden wall, hand in hand, so immersed in conversation that at first they did not notice the company ahead of them. But when they did so, their faces broke into identical smiles of complete and beatific delight. There was no need for words to be spoken; their situation was plain for all to see.

Mrs O'Brien whispered to Emma, 'but what was all that nonsense you were telling me, Emma, about your sister thinking herself so very plain? Why, she is beautiful!'

Penelope said angrily, '*There* you are, Eliza, at last. Well, well, let us all go in and have some refreshment. I do not know, I am sure, why we are all standing about here in the yard!'

But poor Tom Musgrave, with an inarticulate exclamation of despair, strode away, flung himself on to his horse, and kicked it into a gallop. Its hoofs could be heard, clattering off down the drive, after he was out of sight.

'Ah, the poor young sprig,' sighed Mrs O'Brien sympathetically. 'Let us hope he don't take some foolish, precipitate action while his mind is afflicted.'

'Oh, I cannot see why we should trouble our heads about *Tom Musgrave*,' cried Penelope. 'He has made his bed, he must lie on it.'

But the thoughtful, benevolent face of Purvis showed deep concern, and he said to Elizabeth, 'My love, do you think I should go after him? And try to offer some consolation? Or do you think that would be an impertinence?'

'Yes, go,' she said, adding softly, 'After all, you and I have all the rest of our lives before us . . .'

The rest of the party walked indoors, and Sam drew apart with Dr Harding for a discussion about the sale of the house. The four ladies, meanwhile, sat drinking thimble-sized glasses of ratafia, while Penelope discoursed on the advantage of the new small house in Dorking and the terrible inconveniences and dampnesses of Clissocks. 'A house like a tomb! I cannot think why Dr Harding ever insisted on settling here. So like a man! But there was no dissuading him – he would come here! I am sure I wish Sam and Mary joy of the dismal place.'

Emma told Penelope and Elizabeth about the signal honour offered posthumously to their father by the Prince of Wales. Elizabeth was struck with pleasure at the news, but Penelope simply stared.

'How very strange! What use is *that* to our father, now that he is dead? It would have been more to the purpose to give him some honour, or a pension, while he was still alive. I have no patience with such futile, superfluous gestures.'

On the walk back to the curricle, Elizabeth contrived to fall behind with Emma, who congratulated her on her well-deserved happiness with unaffected joy.

'Oh, Emma, it is so wonderful! I could not ever have believed that I could feel as I do. Even if the bliss were to cease now – this instant – it would have been worth while, even if I lived to the age of a hundred and never felt the like again!'

Emma laughed at her. 'I hope you do live to the age of a hundred, my dear sister, and feel it all the time. As you have a perfect right to do!'

'Dear Emma, I was so unkind to you. I am so very sorry for it now. I felt, just then, as if all the source of joy in the world was gone for ever.' Elizabeth caught Emma's hand. 'Pray forgive me! Oh Emma, I hope that some day you will come to feel as I do now! Perhaps with Mr Howard—?'

But Emma shook her head.

'No, no, if I were married to Mr Howard I might well live to the age of a hundred and *never* feel as you do now. I must wait for my chance and hope for the best.'

14

Aunt Maria felt it was hard that, while two members of the Watson family, Sam and Elizabeth, should be enjoying radiant prospects and unalloyed happiness, Emma, her own protegee, should be obliged to work so hard and have no beckoning future to encourage her, but merely more hard work and the animosity of Lady Osborne.

Mrs O'Brien decided to take counsel with Tom Musgrave, thereby, she hoped, killing two birds with one stone. Accordingly she wrote him a letter. (Tom Musgrave, his friends were relieved to learn, had not blown his brains out in despair at the loss of Elizabeth Watson, but was entirely occupied, and concentrating all his powers, on the training of the two horses that were entered for the Epsom races.)

The letter brought Tom to visit Mrs O'Brien at a time when Emma was busy with a pupil.

'It is not right, it is not just, not at all,' declared Aunt Maria, 'that my poor girl should be growing so thin and pale and down-pin while the rest of the family are as happy as hummingbirds. (Apart from Miss Margaret, that is, we don't know whether she is happy or not with that Thick man.) But why can't you make an offer for Emma, Tom, dear boy? Indeed, she's as good a little creature as ever stepped.'

'It would be of no use, ma'am. She'd not have me. And, you know, we would not suit,' Tom added fairly. 'I'm not bookish enough for Emma. And she'd soon grow tired of my horses.'

'Speaking of the horses,' said Aunt Maria, 'listen, Tom, *whatever* you do, do not let Lost Hope get the colic. That horse has a very colicky disposition. Laudanum – turpentine – linseed oil – hot fomentations – Barbados aloes, croton bean, *calomel*! But, in the first place, do *not* let it happen! It is a thousand pities we are so far, here, from the sea – the very best thing for those horses would be to gallop them a few days up to their hocks in salt water – but, a forty-mile journey – no, I fear it is not to be thought of. So, Tom, you do not think Emma will marry Mr Howard?'

'No, I certainly do not, Aunt Maria. I think she has already rebuffed him – made it plain that his attentions would not be welcome. And I think *he* is now making overtures to Miss Osborne.'

'And Emma would not marry Osborne?'

'Ah, she'd never have *him*, ma'am. He is neither active nor resolute enough for Miss Emma. I'm fond of the fellow, he's good-hearted enough – and has a sensible way with horses – but no. No. No, that would not do.'

'Then what shall we do with her?' lamented Mrs O'Brien. '*Mouldy hay*, Tom! You are taking the very *greatest* care, are you not, Tom, to see that those horses get only the very *best* quality hay? The slightest tinge of mould, and you will have broken wind to contend with. And *then* you will be requiring linseed meal, hog's lard, and tar; but let us hope that you *never* need have recourse to those medicaments.'

'No, indeed, ma'am. Though I thank you heartily for thinking of it.'

'Oh, dear me! What are we to do about my poor Emma? To give her thoughts a more cheerful turn?'

Tom scratched his head.

'Well,' he offered, after a longish pause, 'we *could* take her to see the Derby race. Do you think she would enjoy that? After all, 'tis no more than a step up the hill from here. And I'd like for you to see my horses run, Aunt Maria, after you have had so much say in their management. 'Twould be only fair. They are almost as much yours as mine.'

'Well,' Aunt Maria considered, 'that could do no harm.'

So the outing was arranged.

The day of the Derby dawned grey, windy, and icy cold. National spirits, throughout England, were desperately low at the time, for Napoleon had just dealt a crushing defeat to the Russians, who were in full retreat, with the loss of half their force, and were about to sign a peace treaty with their conquerors. Britain seemed, at that moment, to stand entirely alone against the huge French menace.

All the more reason, then, for celebrating the Epsom races with flags, bands, and festivities. The streets of the little town were gay with bunting, and from early dawn Londoners had been pouring southwards in carriages, phaetons, curricles and farm carts. The Downs up above the town were black with thousands of spectators, who had brought their own entertainments with them – fortune-tellers, stilt-walkers, Punch-and-Judy shows, marionettes,

Morris dancers. Despite the cold, almost wintry weather, people were enjoying the coconut shies, roundabouts, and swings. Gypsies with baskets sold nosegays and told fortunes. Family parties in carriages had encamped themselves all around above the huge oval dip in the Downs where the race-track ran, and were busy opening bottles of champagne and unpacking picnic baskets. Hams were carved and pies were broached. Ladies wore their warmest pelisses and gentlemen had fur collars fastened below their top hats. Hot bricks were on hire from enterprising vendors.

The stables near the starting gate were the scene of frenzied activity. Tom Musgrave was nowhere to be seen when Emma, Mrs O'Brien, Sam, and Mary Edwards drove up Burgh Heath Road and on to the open Downs.

'Let us pick a spot near Tattenham Corner,' said Sam. 'Then we shall be able to see the run-in for the finish.'

It was lucky that they had arrived quite early, for soon there was not a space to be had on this favoured area. Sam was able to point out several prominent members of society – Mr Canning, the Duke of York, Lady D— and the Duchess of B—; then he sighted a friend of his, a clever young London apothecary, a Mr Haden, and brought him over to be introduced. Mr Haden and Emma soon discovered a natural affinity in their fondness for music, and fell into animated conversation; then it somehow emerged that the father of Sam and Emma had written *Discourses of a Rural Divine*.

'Why!' said Mr Haden. 'I have a friend, the Reverend James Clarke, who considers that the most wonderful book in the world—'

'Not the Mr Clarke, the Librarian to the Prince?'

'He wrote my sister a letter!' said Sam, bursting with pride.

'Mr Clarke will be here today; will you permit me to introduce him to you, Miss Watson?'

'Of course,' said Emma. 'I shall be most honoured.'

'So you are playing truant from your patients today, hey, Haden?' said Sam.

'Indeed I am not! One of my patients – the very foremost – is coming here. In fact – excuse me –' He darted away.

In the distance a band could be heard playing 'Rule Britannia'.

Tom Musgrave presently appeared with a broad smile, his cravat half undone, and straw clinging to his jacket.

'Well!' he said proudly to Sam, 'have you placed a bet on Lost Hope? At a hundred to one you can hardly go wrong.'

'What does that mean?' asked Emma. 'A hundred to one?'

'It means, you ignorant girl, that if you place a bet of £1 on the horse and it wins, you get a hundred pounds back,' Sam kindly told her.

'Gracious! We must all go and bet. We shall make our fortunes.'

'Only if the horse should win. The odds are an indication that the public do not think highly of its chances.'

'Which horse is the favourite?'

'The Prince's horse Panjandrum. Odds at three to one.'

There were a number of bookmakers down by the fence that railed off the racecourse, shouting their odds and flourishing them on slates which they waved above their heads.

Several minor races must take place before the main one of the day in which Lost Hope was to run. While these were going forward, Emma strolled about with Mrs O'Brien and Mary Edwards, thoroughly enjoying the scene. In the course of their rambles they encountered Lord Osborne, with his sister wearing a delicious pink bonnet, lined with what appeared to be thistledown, and Mr Howard. Miss Osborne gave a cry of delight at seeing Emma, and ran up to greet her affectionately.

'Oh, I am so happy to see you, Miss Emma! For Mamma says I am not to speak to you, or call on you, that you are beneath the notice of good society, so this is a most lucky chance to disobey her. She is here, but fortunately far off at the other end of the course; she keeps as close as she can scrape to the Prince's carriage, you know, in the hope that he may wish to speak to Rufus Bungay, our cousin, who once performed some small task for the Prince and never lets us forget it. Oh, I am so *glad* to see you, dear Miss Emma, and so angry with Mamma about this stupid breach. For what fault is it of yours, if our Papa sowed his wild oats? And let me tell you' (in a whisper in Emma's ear), 'Brother Osborne is amazingly grateful to you, since he had no wish at all to marry Miss Edwards and was happy to be able to cry off with a good conscience. Were you not, Brother?'

Lord Osborne gave Emma an awkward bow and smile. 'Very happy – greatly obliged,' he mumbled.

'We are going to move out of Osborne Castle, my brothers and I. We shall let it – had you heard that?' Miss

Osborne went on. 'So soon as Mamma is married to Rufus we shall do that, move to the dower house and live much more comfortably on the castle rent. Or, possibly, Osborne plans to move into the dower house with Tom Musgrave and they will run a stable together; that is also under consideration. But the rental of the castle is all arranged – to an exceedingly wealthy admiral, Admiral Crawford and his nephew. Admirals are always the best tenants, you know, for they are naturally so neat and orderly. And I' (breathing even lower into Emma's ear), 'he does not know it yet, but I am going to marry Mr Howard. Is not that an excellent plan?'

Emma nodded, smiling up into the speedwell-blue eyes that were sparkling down into her own.

'An *excellent* plan!' she concurred. 'Miss Osborne, do you by any chance know whether Mr Howard's cousin Captain Fremantle has —'

A huge blast of sound almost deafened them. Men were shouting the results of the first race.

Miss Osborne nodded vigorously. Her lips framed something which appeared to end in 'ound'. Found? Drowned? Homeward bound? Ten thousand pound?

'Hetty – er – ahem – I think we should be returning to our carriage,' enunciated Lord Osborne above the noise. His sister bent and kissed Emma's cheek. The two men bowed and led her away.

'Come, my love,' said Mrs O'Brien, returning from some errand of her own, 'I think we should follow their example.'

But before they could proceed to their own vehicle, young Mr Haden intercepted them, running eagerly across the trampled grass.

'Miss Watson!' he panted out. 'May I trouble you just for one moment? Mr Clarke here so much wishes to speak to you.'

Mr Clarke, a tall, spoon-faced man wearing dark clothes and a consequential air, said, 'Do I have the honour to address Miss Emma Watson? Daughter of the Reverend Henry Watson, late of Stanton Parsonage in the county of Surrey? My royal master, His Highness the Prince of Wales, greatly wishes to make your acquaintance – if you do not object to do so in this informal setting it would much facilitate – make a pleasant occasion even more so—'

'Of course I have not the least objection in the world,' said Emma, immensely startled.

'Follow me then, if you please.'

They followed, and had much ado to keep up with him; in spite of his bulky frame he moved nimbly among the parked gigs, phaetons, and landaulettes. At last they arrived close to an exceedingly grand carriage, stationed where it would obtain the best view of all. In it sat an exceedingly fat personage in a tight blue jacket; Emma, confused, curtseying as low as she could, received a fleeting impression of a large red face, many chins over a tight stock, and a huge diamond glittering among the snowy folds of linen. Above were two surprisingly intelligent grey eyes.

A voice said, 'Ma'am, your father's sermons have been my preferred bedside reading this last month. Ask Clarke if it is not so! Their clarity, their dignity, their luminosity – in short, words fail me to express how delighted I am to meet the daughter of the remarkable and saintly man who penned them. I am only sorry that I never had the opportunity to meet himself . . .'

Good gracious, thought Emma, he really *means* it!

She said, 'Sir, I am inexpressibly touched that you should feel so – and I know how happy my father would have been—'

Mr Clarke's hand plucked hers, the audience was ended. She curtseyed low again, and withdrew to the side of Mrs O'Brien, who was waiting a few paces away. As she rose from her curtsey Emma was startled to meet the glaring, outraged eyes of Lady Osborne, who sat in a carriage near at hand beside a man with a tremendous growth of red bushy beard and whiskers. Lord Rufus Bungay, no doubt.

Emma inclined her head to them politely, and then withdrew, clasping Aunt Maria's arm.

'*Well!*' said Aunt Maria. 'Let her put *that* in her pipe and smoke it!'

Emma burst out laughing.

'Aunt Maria! I am surprised at you!'

'Come quickly, we had best get back to our curricle, the big race is about to begin.'

From where they sat, they were unable to see the start, but had a glimpse of the whole field – a great tangled mass of men and horses – as they surged round Tattenham Corner.

'It is twice around the course,' said Mrs O'Brien, who had imbibed a great deal of information from Tom. 'The first circuit sorts out the sheep from the goats. Next time around, we should be able to see if Tom's horse has any kind of chance.'

'What colour is it?'

'Emma! I am surprised at you! It is a grey horse. Black

and yellow colours. Greys, on the whole, are supposed not to be so speedy as bay or dun – Now: let us see –'

The struggling mass of horses approached again, but now many had fallen behind. And two or three were out in front.

'Good heavens!' said Aunt Maria, who had very keen eyesight. 'I do believe – yes, yes, it is – Lost Hope is one of the three in the lead. Black and yellow colours!'

The crowd was yelling its head off. An outsider at the head of a race cannot fail to win the popular esteem. They were shouting:

'*Lost Hope!* Go it, go it, go it, boy! Hope, Hope, *Hope*!'

And Lost Hope fulfilled their demands by rocketing ahead of the rest and winning the race by a clear five lengths from the second horse, which was the Prince's Panjandrum.

'Good heavens!' said Mrs O'Brien again in a weak voice. 'I had a hundred pounds on that horse.'

'Aunt! You are not to faint! Where in the *world* did you get the money from?' demanded Emma, outraged.

'I borrowed it from Tom!'

'Hope wins!' yelled the crowd.

'Aunt!' called Sam. 'Tom asks if you will come and lead in the winner!'

'And it is certainly right that you should,' said Emma, 'considering all the advice that you gave Tom about colic and how to stuff hoofs with cow-dung.'

So Aunt Maria led in the winner, laughing and crying.

Afterwards she said to Emma, 'Oh, if *only* Captain O'Brien could have been there! But perhaps he was watching?'

'I daresay he and Papa have better things to do, up in heaven?' suggested Emma. But Aunt Maria looked as if she would have liked to dispute this statement.

She said, 'Emma, my dear, Tom Musgrave has asked me if I would consider going to preside over his establishment: he and Lord Osborne plan to set up a racing stable together. I think this is certainly an idea worth taking into consideration. He says it is all thanks to my advice that he has won this race – but what do you think?'

'Dear Aunt Maria, I think that is an excellent plan,' said Emma, hugging her aunt. 'You and Tom may be able to keep each other in order.'

Sam came up to them, his fists full of banknotes.

'Sam! What have you been up to? You have not been betting and gambling?'

'Half of these are yours, Aunt Maria, and the other half for me.'

'Sam! What would Papa say?'

'I will never never do it again,' Sam confessed. 'It was too terrifying. The last of my father's legacy . . . But at least it means that I can contribute five thousand to Mary's housekeeping.'

Emma was indignant.

'You might have put on a few pounds for me!'

'Don't forget,' Sam said, 'that Tom has another horse running in the Oaks tomorrow.'

Aunt Maria said, 'But Emma, my dear. Listen. If I should go to housekeep for Tom and Osborne – what would you wish to do? You could, of course, go to Clissocks – live with Sam and Mary, or, I am sure, Elizabeth and Purvis would be happy to have you at Leith Hill . . .'

Lord Osborne now came up to congratulate Tom Musgrave, who was the centre of a group of laughing, applauding friends. Encountering Emma, Osborne said to her, 'By the bye, Miss Watson, our tenant, Admiral Crawford, has a friend, who was looking for you – or, rather, the friend is not *his* friend, but the friend of a friend of the admiral's nephew – Mr Henry Crawford – do I make myself plain?'

Not very, thought Emma, but she looked attentive and waited.

'He said that he knew you – a Captain – Captain Freeborn – recently returned from the Dardanelles – or was it the Seychelles – Captain Free-something – In fact I think – I fancy – I understand—'

'Aunt Maria?' said Emma. 'I do not believe you need concern yourself about where I am to live.'

She looked over Aunt Maria's shoulder at the thin figure in naval uniform which had now detached itself from a large group of other officers and was coming towards her with long strides over the grass . . .

Postscript

Tom Musgrave's other horse, Forlorn Hope, won the Oaks race, but the odds on it were much shortened after the success of its stable-mate. However, some of our friends contrived to make a little money on the event. Elizabeth married Purvis and lived happily with him at Leith Hill, where she was a kind stepmother to his orphan child. Later, he became a Rural Dean. Lady Osborne married Lord Rufus Bungay and removed with him to Antigua. Miss Osborne married Mr Howard, and cared lovingly for his orphaned nephews and niece, Captain Blake having died of a bullet wound in an engagement off the coast of Portugal. Penelope and Dr Harding settled in Dorking, but he died nine months later of a syncope and she inherited his greatly reduced fortune. She did not marry again, but contrived to live agreeably enough, with card parties, and morning calls, and a number of friends widowed like herself. Nothing was ever heard of Margaret and Thickstaffe, but a man named Percy Crutchley was, three years later, reported in the *Philadelphia Inquirer* as having been imprisoned for passing false bills. Robert Watson unsuccessfully sued his sister Emma for possession of the Rev. Watson's papers, contending that a female was not entitled to inherit such documents in preference to her elder brothers; but he lost his case and a great deal of money. Tom Musgrave, Lord Osborne, and Aunt Maria had remarkable success with their racing stable and contrived, at one time or another, to win all the classic races. Tom and his friend found they had their work cut out attempting to curb Aunt Maria's propensity to gamble, but it was finally arranged that, with Sam Watson, they made her a joint allowance which she knew she might not exceed in her bets. From time to time she did so, but only, as she always explained, 'on a sure thing'. They were indulgent to her, since it was principally due to her shrewd advice and excellent eye for horseflesh that the stable did so well. Sam Watson and his wife Mary lived happily for many years at Clissocks and had nine children.

Emma spent many happy years sailing the high seas with her husband Captain Fremantle, who soon became an admiral. She bore him three children, Ned, Hugh, and Cecilia, who were sent home to grow up with their cousins at Clissocks.

The Youngest
Miss Ward

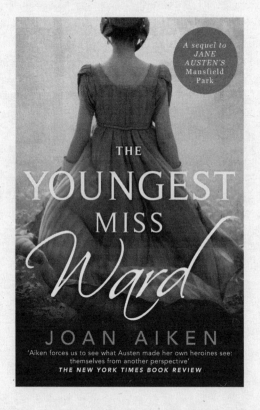

Read on for an extract from another of Joan
Aiken's regency romances . . .

1

TO MR HENRY WARD, a gentleman of very moderate means residing at Bythorn Lodge in the county of Huntingdon, it was a matter of some mortification that he had only seven thousand pounds to give his daughter Maria when she was so fortunate as to capture the affections of a baronet, Sir Thomas Bertram, possessor of a handsome estate not far off in the neighbouring county of Northamptonshire. Mr Ward's other daughters were, subsequently, to fare even worse: due to a diminution of her father's fortune, the eldest Miss Ward, Agnes, could take only two thousand with her when, six years after her sister's wedding, she was able to contract a respectable, if undistinguished, alliance with Mr Norris, a middle-aged clerical protégé of her brother-in-law. More grievous still, at a time when the family was in some distraction, the third sister, Miss Frances, made a runaway match with a lieutenant of marines in Portsmouth. For the rest of her life this daughter would therefore be referred to as 'poor Fanny' with a mixture of distaste and condemnation by her elder sisters – particularly by Mrs Norris. And, to cap it all, the youngest Miss Ward, Harriet, allowed her life to take such an un-looked-for and outrageous turn that she, among the family, was never referred to at any time (except of course by Mrs Norris).

It is an account of her history and misfortunes, with a rebuttal of all false assertions and calumnies that the present narrative sets out to provide.

The youngest Miss Ward, Harriet, or Hatty as she was most frequently referred to did not, at the age of twelve when this journal commences, seem destined for a career of infamy.

From the first, she had been her mother's favourite, and spent much time in Mrs Ward's boudoir with that lady (who became bed-ridden three years after Hatty's birth) reading her lessons, books, and poetry or singing in a soft but true little voice with a small compass.

Good looks had been very unevenly distributed by Providence among the Ward sisters. Two of them, Maria and Frances, resembled their handsome father: they were the fortunate possessors of dazzlingly fair complexions, large blue eyes, and fine, tall, well-formed figures; they were generally acknowledged to be among the finest young women in the county.

The other two sisters, Agnes and Hatty, took after their mother, who had brought breeding to the family, but neither money nor beauty; she had been a Miss Isabel Wisbech, a distant connection of the Duke of Dungeness, and although clever, kind-hearted and elegant, she was unimposing, short and slight in stature, dark-eyed and pale-skinned, with very little countenance; this, as well as her gentle manner and complete lack of animation, caused neighbourhood gossip to assert that she had not been happy in her marriage.

Agnes and Hatty had both inherited their mother's small stature and dark colouring, but not her lack of animation;

Hatty in particular had inherited her mother's elegance, and a sweetness in her countenance that would always recommend her to the notice of discerning strangers. For Agnes, the eldest Miss Ward, had a sharp, bustling and overbearing nature, while Hatty, quick-witted, playful and original in her cast of mind, had always been obliged to provide her own amusements, since two of her elder sisters were too phlegmatic to comprehend her jokes and imaginings, while the third was too short-tempered.

Mr Ward, amid this household of women, had become a disappointed man. His chief and lifelong ambition was to be appointed Master of Foxhounds, for he was greatly addicted to the chase, and would have hunted every day of his life had such a pursuit been possible, and had dissipated the larger part of his fortune on high-bred hunters. At the time of his marriage he had hoped that a connection with Colonel Frederick Wisbech, his wife's second cousin, who was the younger son of the Duke of Dungeness, and reputed, furthermore, to be a very shrewd investor in the City, would bring him both social and pecuniary advantage. But neither of these blessings had come about. Colonel Wisbech thought Mr Ward a dead bore, and kept his distance, while the foxhounds remained under the negligent care of the Duke's brother-in-law.

But Mr Ward's worst and grinding disappointment lay in regard to his estate, which was entailed in the male line and would, in default of an heir, pass to one of his brother Philip's sons. Mr Philip Ward was an attorney in Portsmouth, of no social consequence whatsoever in his brother's estimate; the two brothers rarely communicated and had met but once in the course of eighteen years. It was a continual vexation to Mr Ward that this unimportant family should have the right to inherit his property simply on account of some piece of legal barratry. And life for a man of small fortune, such as himself, who lived on the fringe, but never in the company of titled connections, could never be easy.

Four daughters had the unfortunate Mrs Ward brought into the world by the age of thirty-one, and after the fourth her medical attendant pronounced without the slightest hesitation that a fifth child would indubitably kill her. Mr Ward was outraged at this news. He had taken little notice of the first three daughters; the fourth one he utterly ignored. From the delivery of Hatty, after which she was stricken by a severe birth fever, Mrs Ward's health steadily declined, and by the time of Miss Maria's wedding she had been bed-ridden for eight or nine years.

Preparations for a sufficiently handsome nuptial celebration due to the future Lady Bertram were plainly going to be beyond her power to set in train.

'Why should we not invite my cousin Ursula Fowldes to help us?' she therefore hesitantly suggested to her husband. 'Ursula might, I believe, be prepared to come and stay here, for a few days before the wedding, and take care of all the details; I fancy there is no one so knowledgeable, so capable as she, when it comes to matters of that kind. She has had ample experience, as you may recall, with the weddings of two of her sisters. And, for the marriage of our dear Maria to Sir Thomas Bertram, we would not wish anything to be done improperly or negligently.'

Mr Ward thought very well of this suggestion. Lady Ursula Fowldes, eldest daughter of the Duke's brother-in-law, the fox-hunting Earl of Elstow, had seen two of her younger sisters, the Lady Mary and the Lady Anne, suitably married off; she must by now be thoroughly acquainted with all the correct minutiae of etiquette and procedure. (Why Lady Ursula had never married was a subject of conjecture and rumour in the neighbourhood; there had been talk of a broken romance some years before.) At this time she was twenty-seven years of age, and, by now, hopes of her contracting a matrimonial alliance had, for numerous reasons, long been relinquished.

'I believe Cousin Ursula might be willing to come and advise us,' repeated Mrs Ward, 'although it is a long time since I have seen her. She and I had a great kindness for one another, when we were younger. If you will supply me with pen and paper, Hatty dear, I will write to her directly.'

Hatty obeyed, but she did so with a sigh as she brought the writing materials. Among the Ward girls, Cousin Ursula was by no means a favourite, for she cherished very high notions as to her own position in society and (perhaps as a legacy of that legendary romantic attachment) bore herself in a stiff, acidic, superior manner and maintained a ramrod-straight deportment which tended to cast a gloom over any social gathering in which she took part. Her nose, her chin, her eyebrows were perpetually elevated in astonished condemnation; no one was ever so speedy to depress vulgar pretensions or to snub upstart impertinence as Lady Ursula.

'Ay, ay, your cousin Lady Ursula will certainly be the properest person to oversea Maria's affair,' agreed Mr Ward, quite satisfied for once.

At this period of the family's fortunes, since Maria had been able to contract such a gratifyingly eligible alliance with Sir Thomas Bertram, Mr Ward's frame of mind concerning his future prospects still remained reasonably sanguine. It was to be supposed that Maria's future connections might well achieve satisfactory matches for the younger girls as well. And he was entirely pleased with the notion of persuading Lady Ursula to visit his modest residence, Bythorn Lodge. For up to now, despite the family connection, there had been but few dealings between the Ward family and that of Lord Elstow at Underwood Priors. 'Our cousins, the Fowldes', 'Our cousin, Lady Ursula' echoed pleasantly through the mind of Mr Ward; during the forthcoming wedding festivities, this, he felt, would make a most satisfactory counterbalance to the titled connections of the bridegroom, Sir Thomas.

Abandoning his customary disparaging, not to say surly, manner towards the generality of the female sex, Mr Ward, for the duration of the nuptial celebrations, was prepared to treat Lady Ursula with distinction, cordiality and even with an approach to gallantry which would amaze his daughters.

There were, however, various domestic problems to be overcome before the arrival of the wedding guests. An elderly aunt of Mr Ward, Mrs Winchilsea from Somerset, had been invited for the occasion, and Bythorn Lodge possessed only a single guest chamber. One of the four girls must, therefore, move out of her bedroom to accommodate Lady Ursula. Plainly Maria, the bride, could not be thus displaced; the obvious choice would be one of the two younger girls, Hatty or Frances; but their quarters were inferior.

'Agnes must give up her room,' decreed Mr Ward, when the matter came to his adjudication. 'Agnes has the largest room of the three, with a view over the meadow; it is by far the most suitable, the only chamber proper for Lady Ursula who is, after all, devoting time and solicitude to our affairs; we should neglect no attention that can contribute to her comfort. Agnes must move in with Frances.'

Agnes was by no means pleased with this decision. Further to inflame her sense of injury, Maria had selected her younger, not her elder sister as an escort on the forthcoming bridal tour to Bath and Wells. Frances, not Agnes, had been preferred for a travelling companion. This choice was not particularly surprising to anyone in the family, for Frances and Maria, resembling one another in nature as in looks, had always been each other's best friend, leaving Agnes, the eldest, and Hatty, the youngest – separated in age by thirteen years and in disposition by every possible incompatibility – to get along as best they could during the lack of any other companionship.

But Agnes now felt this exclusion most severely. It was in her nature to resent *all* such slights, whether real or fancied, and the present instance was in no way mitigated by Maria – soon to be Lady Bertram – remarking in her usual calm, languid tone, 'After all, sister, it is your plain duty to remain in the house and look after Mama, when Frances and I are gone off on my wedding journey with Sir Thomas. I have heard you say, I do not know how many times, that you are the only person in the family who is fit to take proper care of our mother, that Fanny is by far too feather-pated to be entrusted with the housekeeping, and Hatty, of course, too young. So everybody will be suited; and I think you had best move yourself into Hatty's bedroom, for there will be a great deal of confusion in Fanny's chamber while she packs up her things to come away with me. Fanny is so scatter-brained. When we are gone off, you know, you may take your pick between my room and Fanny's – if Lady Ursula remains – since I daresay Fanny may stop with me and Sir Thomas for a number of months, once we are settled at his house in Mansfield Park.'

All this was bitter as gall to the irritable spirit of Agnes, the more so since it was based on completely reasonable arguments and thoroughly incontrovertible facts. In the end Agnes did choose to move in with Hatty (much to the latter's dismay) for two reasons: first, because the room was closer to her own; and second, because Hatty, being the youngest, was most subject to her elder's jurisdiction and could be ordered to carry armfuls of garments and other articles from one chamber to the other.

From this minor household displacement followed a mishap which would have repercussions that continued for many years to come.

Maria's wedding was to take place in the month of June. That year the early weeks of summer had been peculiarly close and oppressive, with heavy grey skies and a continual threat of thunder. The invalid Mrs Ward had found the warm and airless atmosphere especially trying, and had begged for as many doors and windows as possible to be kept open at all times. It so happened, therefore, that the front door of Bythorn Lodge was standing wide open when the chaise-and-four arrived that brought Lady Ursula from Underwood Priors. This was several hours earlier than expected. Lady Ursula had never been known to consult the convenience of others in her comings and goings, and since she considered that she was conferring a signal favour by this visit, she felt not the least scruple in advancing the suggested arrival time by half a day.

The household was already in some confusion, with preparations for the other visitor and the nuptial festivities, and no footman chanced to be stationed in the hall at the moment when Lady Ursula, tall, grim and disapproving, stepped through the open front doorway. She rapped smartly with her cane on the flagged floor, looked around her, and called out loudly in her high, commanding voice: 'Hollo, there! Where is everybody? Let me be attended to, if you please!'

Fanny Ward, running down the steep stair with a bundle of household linen in her arms was almost petrified with alarm at the sight of this daunting apparition.

'Oh, my gracious! Cousin Ursula! I – I h-had no notion that you was expected quite so soon! I – I am afraid Papa is down at the s-stables—'

Down at the stables was where Mr Ward invariably spent the hours of daylight when there was no hunting to occupy him.

'That is not of the least consequence,' said Lady Ursula coldly. 'You will escort me to your mother, if you please. Frances, is it not?'

'Yes – yes, of course—' Desperately, Fanny tugged at a bell rope, and when the flustered housekeeper appeared, gave equally flustered directions. 'Direct Jenny and my sister Harriet to prepare Lady Ursula's room immediately!'

'Escort me, pray, to your mother,' repeated Lady Ursula,

a lifting note in her voice suggesting that she was not in the habit of being obliged to repeat her requests.

'Of course, certainly, Cousin Ursula – if you will step this way – I am just not sure that Mama is – but if you will follow me – and if you will just –'

Lady Ursula's expression conveyed that she was not used to being left waiting in passage-ways. A small upstairs hall had an armchair beside a french window leading on to a balcony, but Fanny's hopeful gesture towards the armchair failed to have any effect on the visitor, who continued to follow close behind her nervous guide.

Mrs Ward's bedroom door, like the front entrance, stood wide and thus revealed the scene within, which, to most observers, would have been a pleasing and touching one.

To afford her as much relief as possible from the sultry and oppressive closeness of the atmosphere, the invalid lady was half-lying, half-seated in bed, reclined against a mass of pillows and swathed in layers of the lightest possible gauze and cambric. Slight and thin even in the best of health, Mrs Ward now looked frail as a cobweb. Her dark hair was piled on top of her head, for ease in the heat, and covered with a wisp of lace. To the startled eyes of Lady Ursula her face, small and pointed, and at this moment somewhat smoothed from its habitual lines of pain, looked exactly as it had twelve years before. And the face of the child, holding a book, curled beside the bed in a slipper-chair, was its precise replica. But the expressions of each were at wide variance. That of the child held nothing but dismay; that of the sick woman brightened into joy and recognition.

'Ursie! My dear, dear Ursie! This is such a pleasure! We had not expected you until dinner-time!'

'So I had apprehended from the lack of preparation,' glacially replied the visitor, but mitigated her reproof by approaching and momentarily resting her cheek alongside that of the sick woman. The child, meanwhile, had nervously, like some small wild creature, started away from the bedside.

Lady Ursula hardly glanced at her, but Mrs Ward said softly, stretching out an attenuated hand, 'Dearie, we will continue with our Shakespeare reading at a later time. Soon, I promise. For we had reached such an exciting point! Mind you do not cheat and read on by yourself – I put you on your honour! I trust you! Now, as you may guess, Cousin Ursula and I have many years of conversation to catch up – and you, I know, will help Fanny prepare Ursula and Aunt Winchilsea's chambers – and pick each of them a sweet-scented posy from the garden. Hatty's posies are always the best,' Mrs Ward told her visitor, indicating the lavender, Southernwood and geranium nosegay on her bed-table with a quick, hopeful smile as the child came closer and brushed her cheek against the outstretched hand.

But Lady Ursula, with hardly a glance at her young cousin, gave brusque orders: 'Run along, child, do; you are not wanted here. Your mother and I have private matters to discuss – run away, make haste, go along with you. And shut the door behind you as you go.'

Mrs Ward opened her mouth to protest against this, but then closed it again. She said gently, 'Sit down, my dear Ursie. Find yourself a comfortable chair. It is so *good* to see you, after all this time. You must tell me all about your sisters' weddings. And your Mama. And your Papa – Uncle Owen – how is he?'

'Very ill,' replied Lady Ursula shortly. 'He is drunk more often than sober, when at home. And when in London – which is where he spends the greater part of his time – my mother prefers not to inquire too closely into his doings. And she – she is hardly in this world at all. We will not waste time talking about *them,* if you please.'

With an air of disgust she pushed away the slipper-chair from the bedside and, looking around, chose an upright one more suited to her habitual posture. Seating herself upon it, she glanced frowningly at her hostess and said, 'You should not allow that child to tire you so. One of her sisters could surely oversee her studies.'

'Oh, but my dear Ursie, we enjoy such happy hours together. She is now my only – one of my chief pleasures. Pray do not scold me, Ursie! I hope you have not come here to do that! I have hoped to see you for so long! Why did you stay away?'

Mrs Ward stretched out a caressing hand and took that of her visitor.

'Come! Let us pretend that we are back in the school-room at Underwood. How are Barbara and Drusilla? How is my cousin Fred Wisbech? And my uncle the Duke, is he well? And – and my cousin Harry?'

'I have not the least idea,' replied Lady Ursula in a cold, remote tone. 'Our paths do not cross. Nor is it at all desirable that they should.'

'Oh, *Ursie!*' Mrs Ward's tone was hardly above a sigh, but it held all the sorrow and sympathy in the world. Now she held the visitor's hand in both of hers and softly, condolingly, stroked it. 'Oh, my dear, dear Ursie! Why, why have you never come to see me before this?'

'What occasion was there to do so?'

Lady Ursula's tone was cold, and her expression forbidding, but she let her hand remain where it lay. She sat immobile, like a large armoured vessel, held at the dockside only by the very slightest of mooring cables.